Thurkill's Battle

PAUL BERNARDI

CONTENTS

Chapters 1 – 31
Epilogue
Historical Note

THURKILL'S BATTLE

ONE

Thurkill rushed through the gaping door of the king's hall in Lundenburh. All around him, confusion reigned as men pushed and shoved each other in their eagerness to join the fight, funnelling towards the narrow wooden bridge that spanned the great river that separated the city from the smaller settlement of Suthweca. A steady drizzle had begun to fall from the leaden-dark sky which - whipped up by a stiff easterly breeze - stung his up-turned face like a thousand tiny pin pricks.

As he ran, he looked left and right for his companions. Not only did he crave the safety of their familiar faces, but they had his war garb, including his axe – the same axe that King Harold had presented to him after the battle at the bridge by Stamford.

Not for the first time, he wished his father, Scalpi, were there. He missed his calm, steadying voice by his side. In truth, he'd not yet accepted that he would never hear his voice or see his face again.

"Lord. Lord. Over here."

Eahlmund, thank God. The lanky former farm-hand who'd saved his life after the battle at Senlac was standing to the side of the main thoroughfare along with the rest of his warband: the brothers Leofric and Leofgar and the three other lads, Copsig, Eopric and Eardwulf. Though not warriors by right, they were brave lads; the sort who could be relied upon not to run from a fight.

Thurkill clapped his hand on his friend's shoulder, greeting the others by name. "Best ready yourselves for a fight, boys. It seems the Normans are eager to make our acquaintance once again, and I for one would not deny them that pleasure. Are you with me?"

"Aye, Lord," they answered in unison. If they were scared, it did not show in their expressions. Taking his helmet from Eahlmund, Thurkill then slid his arm through the leather straps of his shield, taking comfort from its familiar feel. As he hefted it into place, he felt a sharp stab of pain lancing up his arm, a reminder of where a Norman sword had opened his flesh back on Senlac Ridge. It would not fail him, though, of that he was sure. Lastly, he took the war-axe, its blade so keen that it would

1

have no trouble taking a man's leg, arm or even head with a single blow.

They joined the throng of warriors heading east, following the bend of the river towards the bridge. They passed through the city's narrow streets, lined with shops and houses all shuttered and locked against the impending danger. Thurkill grew ever more tense with every step, his gut twisting with the all too familiar feeling of dread.

"Where are the bastards?" Eahlmund's question echoed his own thoughts.

"They approach from the south, friend, bound for the bridge as it's the only way across the river for miles around."

One final turn to the right brought them in sight of the river. Thurkill had half expected to see the enemy already on the northern bank, or at least on the bridge, but it seemed secure for now. The scouts had done their work well, bringing word of the Norman attack long enough in advance for them to marshal a defence.

"Come on, lads. Push on to the bridge. We must cross if we are to defend the city."

All around them, warriors surged towards the tall wooden posts that marked the beginning of the bridge. But ahead of them, a great press of men blocked the entrance, preventing them from crossing. With no great lord to lead them, the scene was chaos. Thurkill knew that, were this not to be resolved soon, the Normans would slaughter them where they stood.

Just then, a small group of horsemen burst into the throng, their iron-shod hooves sending sparks from the cobbled streets as the riders pulled back hard on their reins, scattering warriors in every direction.

"Who commands here?" demanded a fierce looking hulk of a man. What was visible of his face behind a shaggy grey beard, bore witness to a long life of many battles.

"No one, Lord."

"Then follow me, Aelfric, Lord of Huntendune. I stood with King Harold in the shieldwall at Senlac, alongside many of you, I'll wager. We've faced these Norman whoresons before and we can do so again. With a few score stout shield-warriors at my back, we will carry the day."

Galvanised, men everywhere thrust their swords into the air and howled, eager to plunge their blades into enemy flesh. As Aelfric dismounted, Thurkill pushed his way over to be as close to him as possible. He didn't recognise him from the battle, but saw that he was a man worth following. A man to be close to when the fighting was at its fiercest.

Thurkill's shield, much patched and repaired, still bore the red wyvern showing him to be a man of Wessex, a warrior from Harold's household. As he drew close, Aelfric spotted the device, nodding in respectful appreciation. "Welcome, lad. You were with the king at Senlac?"

"Aye, Lord. In the front rank, with my father, Scalpi, near the king's banner. We were there to the end."

Aelfric laughed, his eyes sparkling with joy. "You're Scalpi's boy? I know the old goat-shagger well. How is he? Is he not here with you?"

"No, Lord. He lost his life in defence of his king. I am Thurkill; the last of his line." There was no grief in his words, though, just pride.

Aelfric clamped a huge paw of a hand on Thurkill's shoulder, fixing a steely gaze on the young Saxon. "It grieves me to hear that, lad. Would that we had more of his kind here today." As if sensing a misstep, Aelfric's face broke into a rueful grin, "though from what I can see, this particular acorn did not fall far from the old oak.

"But enough talk, Thurkill. We shall we have our revenge for his death today, eh? Stand by me and help me gut as many of these bastards as dare to stand in front of us."

With that, Aelfric, Lord of Huntendune, strode onto the bridge. Thurkill kept pace with him while his warband followed just behind, walking alongside Aelfric's men. Still there was no sign of the enemy and Thurkill began to wonder if it had been a false alarm. Surely the scouts had not been mistaken? Perhaps they had decided to abort the attack, deeming the city too strongly defended?

But before they had even reached the half way point, he knew he was wrong as the far end of the bridge was suddenly filled with a teeming mass of humanity.

"Shields!" Aelfric roared, hefting his own round, linden board into position. Thurkill and his men quickly followed suit, lifting their shields until they overlapped with each other. But it soon became clear this was not the enemy.

The bridge was filled with rank upon rank of townspeople, scurrying for the safety of the city walls, weighed down by whatever belongings they had been able to rescue. As the refugees drew close, the warriors were forced to squeeze over to one side of the narrow span to allow room for the panicked masses to pass.

Eventually, the flood thinned to a trickle, and they were able to complete the crossing. They spilled out into an open area in front of a small church. Ahead of them, the road split into two: the right fork leading off west towards Wintancester, while the left marked the old Roman road to Dover. According to their scouts, it was from the latter direction, that the enemy were expected to come.

But still there was no sign of the enemy, no galloping Norman cavalry with its forest of deadly spear points. Just another wave of frightened villagers fleeing towards them. As he watched, a sudden fleeting glimpse caused his heart to tighten as if squeezed by an unseen hand. A mass of blond curls bobbing up and down as their owner ran. *Surely it can't be?* He looked again but she was lost to him among the throng. *Was his mind playing tricks on him? It can't have been her. No, wait! There she is again.*

"Hild!" Oblivious to any danger, Thurkill sprinted forward, removing his helmet as he did so, so that she would more readily recognise him.

"Thurkill. Thank the Lord and His angels." She launched herself at him with an impact the equal of any he'd ever felt in the shieldwall.

"I can't believe I have found you." She plastered kisses over every inch of his face.

"What are you doing here?" He spluttered when she had at last released him. "Why are you not back in Brightling with Nothelm?"

It was the wrong thing to say and he cursed himself for his lack of forethought as her eyes brimmed with tears, washing away the happiness that had been there mere moments before. "Father's dead, Thurkill. The Normans killed him along with many of the other men in the village before taking our cattle and grain and setting fire to all the houses.

"I didn't know what to do. We couldn't stay and fight, for there were too many of them. Then a few of the others said we should come to Lundenburh as there is a new king with a new army, and that we'd be safe here. And then I remembered you saying you were coming here too, but I hadn't hoped to find you so soon."

"I'm glad you did, my love, but you must cross the bridge as quickly as you can, for the Normans are not far behind you. You'll be safe behind the city walls; I'll come and find you as soon as I can."

Turning back to his men, Thurkill beckoned Copsig forward, the youngest and most inexperienced of his warband. "Take Hild back to the city. Guard her with your life until we return."

Thurkill could tell from Copsig's face that he was disappointed not to have the chance to stand with the rest of them. But he wasted no time in taking Hild's hand to guide her back whence they had come. Thurkill stared after her for a while, his emotions reeling at having to be parted from her again so soon. He wanted nothing more than to go with her, but duty to his king prevented it. With a sigh, he resumed his place in the shieldwall by Aelfric's side.

TWO

The persistent drizzle had now hardened into a heavy, freezing rain from which there was little or no shelter. Thurkill shivered, the cold and wet penetrating his bones through his sodden clothing. As he stood waiting with the others, his mind was filled with images of Hild. Had he really found her again? Could they have a future together?

"Here they come, lads. Stand fast for God and for Edgar."

Aelfric raised his sword high above his head and roared his defiance at the approaching horsemen. Several hundred voices followed his lead. It was a sound that struck fear into Thurkill's heart, so God alone knew what it must have sounded like to the enemy. He tried to count the knights bearing down on them, but gave up when he reached a hundred.

The sound of the horses pounding towards them across the hard-packed earth was now deafening, echoing off the houses that lined each side of the narrow main street. They had chosen their ground well, though. Hemmed in by the buildings, the horsemen were funnelled together, pressed in on each other with little or no room to manoeuvre. Faced by a solid, immovable wall of shields, they were like lambs to the slaughter.

But, despite their disadvantage, the Normans did not lack for courage. They forced their mounts forward, searching for a way through the impenetrable line of defence. But just as had been the case at Senlac, the knights could find no way through. As long as the Saxons held their ground, they could not be broken. Those at the back, unable to engage with shieldwall, launched missile after missile at the Saxons, while those in the front thrust their long spears into the gaps between the shields, hoping to find the smallest amount of exposed flesh. Here and there they met with success. Those warriors - the young, less experienced lads – who carelessly looked out from behind their shield rather than stay hidden, fell prey to a spear point. But their place was soon taken by others who were not so quick to make the same mistake.

The shieldwall was unbending. Even though they had only managed to muster a few hundred men, their ranks were five deep or more, with each side securely anchored against the walls of the flanking buildings. Row after row of horsemen - formed up in small conrois of five to ten men - futilely spent their strength against the wall of wood and iron, like so many impotent waves exhausting themselves against a cliff face.

Thurkill lost count of the number of times his shield shook from the impact of a spear, thrown or thrust, but not once did he fear for his life. They weathered the storm, making no attempt to fight back, content to soak up the pressure of the attack until its force was spent. With heads hidden behind their shields, they encouraged each other with manic grins, a few jokes and the occasional insult thrown at their foe.

"My mother's mother would do better, and she's been dead these ten years."

Thurkill doubted whether Leofric's jibe would be understood by their intended target but they had the desired effect on those within earshot. Roars of laughter mixed with foul curses gave heart to the younger lads, stiffening their resolve to send the enemy back whence they'd come.

Suddenly, Aelfric gave the order to advance. He had noticed that the attack's momentum had waned, and he chose that moment to hit them. The shieldwall moved forward in close order before halting again after five paces. Those in the second and third ranks, finally released from their defensive duties, raised their spears and stabbed them forward into the confused, wheeling mass of horse and human flesh.

The killing was indiscriminate; man and beast alike were gutted as the rain hammered down, washing the blood away. Hooves and feet combined to churn the ground into glutinous mud. Thurkill did not care for the wounded men but the screams of the dying horses were horrendous to his ears.

As horse after horse fell, the sight, sound and smell of their deaths wrought panic among the rest. Frightened beasts reared up, whinnying pitifully, nostrils flared and eyes bulging in fear. Knights fell to the ground only to find themselves trampled by flailing hooves, pounded to death and splattered with blood and shit.

With so little room to spare, there was no escaping the slaughter, no way to pull back out of range of the killing blades. The ground was now slick with mud, blood and gore, so much so that their next advance was almost their undoing. Several warriors lost their footing trying to pick their way through the stricken bodies of man and beast that had spilled their slimy, stinking guts in their path. The stench of blood mixed with human and animal excrement was overpowering, but Thurkill was inured to it, so intent was he now on the conflict. From behind his left shoulder, Eopric's spear blade shot forward, catching the Norman to Thurkill's front in the armpit, just as he had raised his sword to smash down on his head. Screaming in pain, he dropped the sword and bent over his horse's neck in a futile effort to protect himself. Taking a step forward, Thurkill swung his two-handed axe, bringing its edge down a couple of fingers' breadth below the rim of his helmet. A great fountain of blood spurted from the ruined stump where, just moments before, his head had been.

And then it was over. Those horsemen that had somehow survived the carnage were now clattering their way back down the Dover road, stampeding their way through the ranks of their companions who had been too far back to be able to join the fight. A few Saxons broke ranks to pursue them until they were called back by Aelfric.

"We'll need every warrior in the days to come. I can't risk a few hotheads getting themselves killed in these alleys."

Sullenly, they trudged back to their comrades, their blood lust unsated. But even so, their mood was not dampened for long. The exhilaration of the fight, together with the sight of the fleeing enemy, combined to give men cheer in place of what had been doom and gloom not one hour before. Everywhere, men laughed and joked, shaking hands or slapping each other on the back. Others compared kills, each boast becoming more fanciful than the last as the relief of the victory and survival flooded through them.

The retreating Normans had left a scene of devastation behind them. Thurkill estimated there were at least twenty dead soldiers strewn across the road, with a similar number injured. Already, small groups were moving among them, slitting the throats of the wounded. As they carried out their grim work, they also dealt with the animals. It was a blessing to have an end to their needless suffering, but Thurkill knew that their screams would haunt his sleep for days to come. He hated that they were made to endure man's cruelty to each other; they had done nothing to deserve such barbarism.

To distract himself, Thurkill turned his attention to his warband. Mercifully, none had been injured other than a slight graze sustained by Eardwulf. To add insult to injury it had been Eopric who had given him the wound, being a little too eager with his spear when standing behind him. He laughed along with the rest as Eardwulf berated his friend for being more dangerous to his health than the Normans.

With the danger passed, his thoughts returned to Hild. He felt as if a gap in his life had been filled, a gap that has opened like a chasm in his soul since the murder of his aunt and sister. Perhaps he could put the memory of FitzGilbert behind him and find new purpose with her instead?

THREE

Back within the walls of Lundenburh, Thurkill sent Eahlmund and the others to find lodgings for them all. "Watch the price too. Don't let them rob you blind." He yelled at his disappearing back. "I'm not made of money."

Wishing he was going with his men, Thurkill trudged off instead with Aelfric towards Edgar's hall by the abbey of Westminster. The Lord of Huntendune has been ordered to provide a report of the attack to the young king and asked Thurkill to accompany him, though what he would be able to add he did not know.

They were ushered in to Edgar's presence by one of the door wardens. With no time to clear the muck and sweat of battle from their faces, they must have presented an odious sight and smell, especially to the high-born ladies of the court, not least of whom was Ealdgyth, wife of King Harold. Tall, regal-looking and slender, she was standing to the right of Edgar's throne by her kin, Eadwine and Morcar, the Earls of Mercia and Northumbria. Staring at her, idly, Thurkill found himself wondering why her two brothers had not come with them to Suthweca. The two most senior lords in England and yet they were nowhere to be found when it came to the dirty work of slaughter.

To the rear of the king's throne stood a dark-haired brute of a man who, it was said, hailed from the far-off kingdom where Edgar had been brought up in exile. Aelfric had told him that his name was Ladislav, but much more than that was a mystery.

"He's a man of few words, Thurkill, though perhaps this is no surprise for he'll have no mastery of our tongue. He does his talking with his sword instead. When he does speak, mind, his voice is so harsh that, every word sounds like an invitation to fight."

"Well met, Aelfric. A famous victory, I hear?" Looking every inch the boy he was, Edgar was bouncing with excitement, making mock slashing and thrusting moves as if he had been in the thick of the fighting himself. "Come, tell me all. I want to know every detail."

Aelfric bowed stiffly, "There's not much to tell, Lord."

"What? I heard we gave the Norman scum a bloody nose and more."

"That we did, Lord. It cannot be denied. But they only sent a small cavalry force to scout our defences; to test our strength and determination, if you will."

"What makes you say that, Aelfric? The Normans have been sent packing have they not?" Morcar could barely contain his agitation.

"They have, Lord. But I swear to you they numbered fewer than three hundred. No foot soldiers and, thankfully, no archers. It was a hard fight, for sure, but one that was well within our means to win."

"But how many did you kill? Have we not significantly reduced their numbers?"

"The fight was brief, they did not stand for long. They had no need to. We killed no more than twenty, with the same number wounded – all of whom have since been dispatched."

"What about our losses?" Thurkill noted Edgar's face displayed genuine concern, a quality that was becoming of a man who would be king.

"A handful at most, Lord. Fewer than half a dozen if I am not mistaken. We were well positioned and our shields spared us from the worst of their threat. They're stout Saxon lads who fight for you, all good men and true."

"Well, let God be praised. Whilst it may not have been the blow we had hoped to strike; we have nonetheless prevailed with little loss of life. See that the brave men who gave their lives are buried with honour that their kin are cared for from my purse."

"It will be done, Lord." Aelfric bowed once more.

"'Tis all well and good, Lord, but what of our plan now?"

"Speak plainly, Lord Eadwine, I would know what is on your mind."

The earl sighed as if it were obvious to all but a child and Edgar's expression showed that it had not gone unnoticed. "If this was but a small force, there must be many thousands more of them somewhere between here and Dover."

"With more crossing from Normandy as we speak, I daresay," his brother chimed in.

"We also have many thousands of men, especially now that your fyrds have finally arrived." A silence descended over the room as the thinly veiled message of Edgar's words sunk in.

"Your meaning, Lord?" The tone was cold, threatening even. Thurkill glanced at Ladislav. Though his expression was immutable, the Hungarian's eyes were fixed on Eadwine, scanning his face for the slightest threat to his master.

"It is of no matter. I simply meant that things may have gone differently for Harold had he had the benefit of your brave warriors at Senlac."

Despite Edgar's placatory words, it was still more than the earl was prepared to stomach. "Perhaps he should have waited for us then, as I requested. You know how sorely tested our men were against the Hardrada at both Fulford and Stamford. I will not have a young pup like you, with no hair on his chin, impugn their honour. Every one of them has seen more conflict than you."

Edgar's ire was rising now. "I have nothing but respect for your men, Eadwine."

"How dare you," the earl stepped forward, the insult clear for all to hear.

Ladislav growled, his hand falling ominously to his sword hilt. Though the words had no meaning to him, the danger was all too plain.

"Gentlemen, I urge you to calm yourselves. Such intemperance does nothing to help our cause." The latest speaker emerged from the shadows, where he had escaped Thurkill's notice up until now. He was an old man, his tonsured hair the colour of snow. Despite his years, he still walked tall and proud, as a man of some bearing and status. His attire marked him as a member of the church, perhaps even a bishop by the richness of his vestments. But underneath the finery, Thurkill could see that he was stick thin; the hands that appeared from his voluminous sleeves were almost skeletal, while the skin on his face and head appeared almost grey, marked with dark spots that were the sign of great age.

"I did not risk life and limb to bring your father back from the wilds of Hungary to have to listen to his son and his lords squabble like children. Earl Eadwine, you should show your king more respect. It is he who rules here not you, or had you forgotten your oath already?"

The tension broke, like water released from a dam. Ladislav melted once more into the background, his face once again an inscrutable mask. For his part, Edgar hung his head, looking every inch the shame-faced youth that had just been reprimanded by his tutor for failing at his letters. "Your pardon, Bishop Ealdred. Would that my father, Edward, were here instead of me. He would have made a far better choice as king than me."

Though chastened by his rebuke, Eadwine could not, nevertheless, stifle a grunt of derision. Ealdred glared at him, but chose to say nothing further, perhaps fearful of reigniting a still volatile situation.

"Whatever you may wish or think, Edgar, is irrelevant. You are king and a crisis is upon us. At any moment, Norman horsemen could come charging over the bridge to put the city to the sword. Lord Aelfric, pray tell us what is to stop them from doing just that?"

Aelfric smiled. "I think it unlikely, Lord Bishop. Though it was but an advance party, they have learned something of our strength and determination today. I doubt they will try their luck with a frontal assault again. The bridge is the only way to reach the city and we can defend it easily enough. It would be a massacre."

The bishop nodded approvingly. "So, in your opinion, what will the Normans do now? Although I pray for it hourly, I fear they will not simply pack up and go home. Duke William has made no secret of his desire to sit on the throne that young Edgar now occupies. What would you do if you were in William's shoes?"

As Aelfric paused to consider his response, Thurkill began to speak, realising only too late that he had overstepped his mark.

"I would move west, find another place to cross the river."

"Silence, boy! By what right do you speak here in front of your betters?"

"He is here, Lord Eadwine, because I asked him," Aelfric's voice was calm but his tone conveyed an iron resolve. "This boy - as you call him - is Thurkill, son of Scalpi, whom you will recall as one of King Harold's most honoured captains. He has earned the right to speak in this company because he stood by his king to the last, while you were yet making your way south down Ermine Street. What's more, this boy brought down the Viking champion on the bridge at Stamford; for which feat of arms Harold rewarded him with the Viking's great war axe."

Thurkill's face reddened. He was not used to praise, especially not in front of such exalted company. Thurkill felt the heat radiating from his face as all eyes turned towards him. He wished for the ground to open beneath his feet.

"In which case, I say he deserves to be heard. Speak, brave Thurkill. Give us the benefit of your wisdom in matters of war."

Although the bishop hid it well, Thurkill could not help but wonder if his words were intended to mock him. It was too late now in any event; his rash outburst meant there was no retreat without dishonour. Praying for courage, he launched into a hurried explanation.

"As Lord Aelfric says, the bridge here is too stoutly defended to be taken. So, if he can't take the city from the south, William must find another crossing place. He does not have time to build enough boats to ferry his men and horses across, as we grow stronger every day. So he must go west until he finds a bridge or a place where the water is shallow enough to ford."

"Makes sense to me, lad."

Thurkill nodded his thanks at Aelfric. "But it will still take time to journey that far west and then return. I urge that we use that time to summon all the men we can. Then we can meet him in a place of our choosing."

Edgar looked doubtful. "What you say carries merit, Thurkill, but I worry what privations he will inflict upon my people in the meantime. Can we really stand back and allow him free rein across my lands? Should we not sally forth across the bridge

14

and attack now? He would not expect that, I'll wager."

Ealdred smiled, shaking his head slowly from side to side. "It is just such noble sentiments that saw your predecessor meet his doom, Lord Edgar. Had Harold waited for Eadwine and Morcar's fyrd to arrive, he might yet still be sat where you are. But he found he could no longer stand by while William ravaged his lands and so he marched before his army was ready. Do not repeat that same mistake. We must focus on the greater goal. As Thurkill says, use the time to marshal your forces and then let us beat the Norman devils once and for all. With the Lords Eadwine and Morcar in command, I have every confidence that we will be victorious."

"Would we not be better to move our armies further north?"

The bishop stared open-mouthed. "Why ever would we do that, Lord Morcar? The enemy is here."

"But if we retreat to the hills in my earldom of Northumbria, we will win ourselves more time to gather our strength. The land there would also be in our favour; we can use the terrain to our advantage. Hide among those hills and attack the enemy when least expected."

"Yes," his brother added, "we could burn the land as we march, so that the enemy would have nothing on which to live as they follow us north. By the time we attack them, they and their horses would be weak from hunger. Then we'll kill every last one of them."

Edgar rose to his feet once more, his face reddening as his anger rose. "You'd have me abandon my people to the mercy of the Norman scum? You'd have me run away from danger? I will not commit such a craven act, no matter how much you would like me to. As king of all this land, I cannot leave my people in the path of such danger."

"You dare call me craven?" Lord Eadwine started towards Edgar, his hand falling menacingly to his hip where he might have expected to find his sword hilt had he not left it at the door, as custom demanded. With surprising agility for one so big, Ladislav was in front of Edgar, sword in hand, before the earl could take another step. No one spoke as the two men faced each other. Eventually, the impasse was broken by the bishop's infuriated voice.

"Enough!" Ealdred's eyes blazed with anger as he rounded on the two men. "For every moment you bicker, our enemy moves closer to his prize. We must unite if we are to survive. Carry on like this and I promise you William will be lord of us all before the turn of the year."

Having said his piece, the bishop then sought to ease the smouldering tension. "Is that agreed then?" He turned to face the two earls. "Do you, Eadwine Lord of Mercia, and you, Morcar Lord of Northumbria, swear by Almighty God that you will fight for your king and do his bidding until death alone releases you from that vow?"

"Yes." Eadwine hissed as he stepped back, his hands dropping back down by his sides, allowing Ladislav to resume his position behind Edgar.

"I asked you to swear by Almighty God. Both of you."

"Alright, Bishop, we swear by Almighty God. Though we will send Ealdgyth north to Chester so that she is out of harm's way. Assuming that is," he bowed in a show of mock respect, "that it pleases you, Edgar?"

Displaying greater maturity than the man who was twice his age, Edgar chose to ignore the insult. "You have my leave, Lord Eadwine, though be sure not to send all your best warriors as her escort. They will be needed here before too long, I assure you".

"Now that is settled," Ealdred continued, his voice soothing and mellifluous once more, "what is to be done about these damned foreigners in our midst, assuming young Thurkill has the rights of it, that is?"

16

FOUR

Thurkill dragged himself up the narrow wooden stairs to the door of their lodgings, his muscles aching with every step. It had been a long day, what with the skirmish in Suthweca followed by the long and testy deliberations in the king's hall. He longed for his bed and Hild's welcoming embrace.

The shock of their reuniting was still fresh in his mind, though - in truth - she had never been far from his thoughts since he had parted from her in Brightling to go to his father's hall at Haslow. Although but a few days ago, it already felt like a lifetime. Suddenly afraid, he paused outside the doorway. Would she blame him for her father's death? Had he stayed in Brightling, could he have prevented it or would he also be lying dead with the other men of her village? All he knew for sure was he could not stand here forever; he was ready to drop from exhaustion. Steeling himself for what lay within, he pushed open the door, wincing at the loud scraping noise it made as it forced its way over the uneven floorboards. He hoped they had not all been asleep.

"Well, it's about time you showed up." Eahlmund stood in the centre of the compact little room, his hands on his hips in mock anger, playing the role of an irate mother.

Thurkill laughed, joining in the ruse. "But you said I could play out until it went dark."

"Don't cheek me, boy, or you'll feel the back of my hand. I've a good mind to send you straight to bed with no dinner."

The mention of food made him forget his tiredness. He had not eaten since he broke his fast at dawn. He was famished. "Dinner, you say?" His voice was hopeful, verging on pleading.

Eahlmund shrugged. "Don't get your hopes up too much, Lord. It's just some dry bread and a bit of cheese that's seen better days. And there's some apples too. Still, the ale in the jug there is quite passable, and helps to wash it all down. It was the best that young Copsig could lay his hands on at this late hour, given how overrun the place is at the moment."

Thurkill did not care. To his ears, it sounded like a feast to rival anything a king might enjoy. He made his way to the table where the remains of the food lay, looking around him as he did so. His whole warband was there; the two brothers, dozing on a single cot in the corner, lying head to toe to make best use of space in the cramped conditions. Against the other wall, Copsig, Eopric and Eardwulf were bickering about who was going to sleep where; Eardwulf claiming the right of first choice as the eldest. Across the far end of the room, a couple of blankets had been hung to create a screen. Peeking out from one side, he saw Hild's face smiling tentatively at him as if unsure of her welcome.

Eahlmund shrugged. "It was the best we could do, Lord. We thought it best not to waste coin on two rooms, not that we would have found another one nearby. Still, it should be nice and cosy with eight of us in here, eh? Oh, and I've told the lads to keep the farting to a minimum, what with the presence of a lady and all."

Thurkill smiled. "It'll do just fine, my friend. I'm too tired to care about our sleeping arrangements anyway." Holding out his arms, he beckoned Hild over to sit with him as he ate. "I am pleased to see you safe, Hild. I had begun to doubt whether it was really you on the bridge all those hours ago."

Her sibilant laugh awakened memories of happier times together back at her village. He felt its warmth spreading through him, caressing his exhausted body. Seeing his eyelids drooping, Hild took his hand and guided it towards the platter in front of him. "Eat, Killi. You'll need your strength again tomorrow should the Normans return."

No sooner had he demolished what remained of the food and ale, than he collapsed on the straw mattress that he shared with Hild. It was lumpy with age and a little damp in places, but he cared not. Lying there on his back with Hild curled up in the crook of his arm, he felt more at peace than he could have imagined. It felt as if they'd never been apart. Listening to her shallow breathing, feeling the soft caress of her golden hair on his cheek as she stroked his face with her long slender fingers, was all that he could have wished for. In a few short moments, he fell into a deep and dreamless slumber.

***

He awoke to the sound of singing. For a moment he thought he was a child back home in Haslow with his aunt, Aga, going about her morning chores. He half expected his sister, Edith, to jump on his bed in a state of excitement at some new insect or bird she had caught, but it was Hild's face that appeared round the edge of the screen. Though it was a vision no less wonderful, it was also a sharp reminder of what he'd lost.

"I thought I heard you stirring. It's about time you were up, you lazy toad."

Stretching and yawning simultaneously, Thurkill pushed himself up on one elbow to take a better look at her. So fatigued had he been the previous night, that it had all been a blur. She was more beautiful than he'd remembered. Her eyes had lost nothing of their sparkle, set on either side of the most elegantly slim nose. Her cheeks were like two sun-ripened apples, rosy and firm. Awkward under his lustful gaze, she turned away and disappeared behind the blankets. "There's some of that bread and apples to eat and a little of last night's ale left as well."

Sighing happily, Thurkill stretched his arms above his head, feeling the tension ease in his back and shoulders. He dressed quickly before pushing the screen aside so he could fold his arms around Hild's waist from behind. Burying his face in her neck and inhaling deeply of her scent, he mumbled. "Where is everyone?"

"Eahlmund took them off to market to buy more food. Truth be told, I think he wanted to give us some time alone." She blushed, as if fearing her words might be misconstrued. "To talk," she added coyly, turning to look up at him through the curtain of golden curls that hung low over her forehead.

He felt the first inkling of a stirring in his groin. With an effort he forced himself to look away; she was right, they needed to talk. He had news that he had not had the will nor the energy to share last evening, but which he knew he could not put off for long. "Hild, there is much we need to discuss. But first, we have to think of the future. I need to know you will be safe."

Her face fell. "And what of you, Thurkill? Who will think of

19

your safety? Are we not to be together now that we have found each other once more? If not, who will take care of me now that I have no father?"

Thurkill's voice caught in his throat; she looked so alone and so vulnerable. It was true; she had no one now that Nothelm was dead. No brothers or uncle to take her in. She knew no one else in the vast city. His heart ached for her, but he had no choice.

"I will do all that I can to care for you, Hild, even lay down my life for you should it come to it, but I have other duties that I must perform. Duties to the king in the defence of his lands."

"Are there not others that could take your place? Can we not go north to start a new life with our own farm somewhere?"

"I promise you there is nothing I would like more, my love. But how long would it be before the Normans came and took it away from us once more if we don't fight them now? We cannot fool ourselves into thinking they will go home and leave us in peace. They have come to take the kingdom and we must fight to stop them before it's too late."

"But you have already done your part and more. You stood by Harold and nearly died defending him. You told me so yourself."

"And the thought of doing it all again scares me to death, especially now we are together again. But what sort of man would I be if I were to refuse to take my place in the shieldwall? I could not live with the disgrace of it."

Hild turned away, her eyes brimming with tears. "In my heart, I knew you would say this. I only wish I could go with you. Didn't the Vikings of old allow their women to fight?"

Thurkill grinned. "I have heard the same tales, though I know not if they are true; shield-maidens they were called, as fearsome as any man, I'll wager. And having seen you fight back at Brightling, I would be proud to have you next to me in battle."

Reaching out for her, he wrapped his arms around her once more, pulling her lithe but strong body tight against his own. "If we're quick," he whispered, "we could reacquaint ourselves properly before the lads return."

"Thurkill!" She slapped his face in mock outrage. "Take your paws off me. All this talk of maidens holding swords has made you forget yourself." But she had no mind to resist him too much and soon their mouths met in passionate embrace.

Just as Thurkill broke away to focus on the cord that held up his trews, there came a loud stomping noise from without, as several pairs of boots tramped their way up the rickety wooden stairs, making a far greater racket than was necessary. Then Eahlmund's unmistakable voice shouted. "Careful with those jugs of ale, Copsig, I'll send you all the way back to replace any that you spill."

Ruefully, Thurkill smiled at Hild, shrugging as he did so. He kissed her one last time and stroked her soft hair against her cheek. "Another time, my love."

Moments later, there was a loud knock on the door. "Are you, er, up, Lord?"

"For God's sake, Eahlmund, stop this tomfoolery and come in."

Eahlmund's smirking face appeared round the edge of the now half-opened door. "Well, you can't be too careful when two young lovers get back together after a time apart, that's all I'm saying."

Hild laughed. "We don't all think with the contents of our trews, Eahlmund."

"Well, you lordly types must be different than the rest of us then. All I'm saying is that if it had been me left alone with a pretty young lass, I'd have been…"

Thurkill cuffed him round the back of the head to change the subject. "So, what have you brought back from the market? I hope you have spent my money wisely."

"A few loaves, some cheese, two dozen apples and a decent amount of salted pork. The former we'll have to eat quickly but the rest should keep for a good while; enough to see us back here again anyway."

Fool! With a shock Thurkill realised he still hadn't told Hild that he must leave later that very day. Meekly, he glanced at her, hoping she had not been paying attention to what Eahlmund had been saying. But his luck was out. She stood, arms folded across her chest, her head tilted to one side with an expression that reminded him of his aunt Aga when he had failed to do his chores. *Oh Lord, this is going to be difficult.*

Realising his own part in the sudden change in the room's atmosphere, Eahlmund sought for an escape. "Anyway, there's much to do before we go and no doubt you two have things to talk about." He began backing towards the door, shooing the others in the same direction using his hands hidden behind his back.

"Wait there, Eahlmund, if you please. And you others too. I'd be glad to know where you are all off to on this fine day and whether your lord is aware, for he has made no mention of it to me."

"Well, er…" Eahlmund looked imploringly at Thurkill, as if begging him to rescue him. He cursed himself for having slept so late. If he'd risen with the rest of the lads, he might have had time to explain or, better still, gone to the market with them and avoided the whole situation.

"You see, the thing is - as I am sure Thurkill will have wanted to tell you before now - we have been ordered south of the river to find where the Normans have gone…"

"Well, he hasn't and I am astonished that something as important as this has slipped his mind." Though she was talking to Eahlmund, Hild's eyes stared directly at Thurkill, challenging him to respond.

Thurkill shrugged, admitting defeat. "I'm sorry, my love. I was going to explain but I overslept and then the lads came back before I had time."

Hild's cheeks had reddened now, her voice trembling as she struggled to contain her emotions. "Why you? Are there no other men under the this king's command who could not go in your stead?"

Thurkill looked at his feet. "I can't refuse a direct order from the king, can I? He'd have me clapped in irons before you knew it and then where would you be?"

"And where will I be if you get yourself killed?" Her voice was rising, a mix of anger and fear. She turned to stare out of the room's one small window, her shoulders heaving as she fought to regain her composure.

Shamefaced, Thurkill went to her, placing his hand on her shoulder in what he hoped was a reassuring gesture. He pushed his face into the mass of curls until he found her ear which he then kissed gently, something he recalled she had liked when they had first lain together. "Don't worry so, Hild. We're not going to fight the Normans; we're only going to watch what they're doing and come straight back."

Furiously, she rounded on him, pummelling his chest with her fists. "You stupid, thoughtless idiot. You can't just kiss my ear and hope it makes everything better. Get out of my sight before you really annoy me. Go on, go. All of you!"

Eahlmund and the others did not need telling twice. They had been edging ever closer to the door as the situation became more and more uncomfortable and they were through it and gone almost before the first punch was thrown. Thurkill was not far behind, eager to be away from Hild's fury and - at the same time - utterly confused by the whole thing. *Killing Normans is so much easier than keeping a woman happy* was all he could think as he clattered down the stairs as fast as his heavy boots would allow.

FIVE

"In Jesus Christ's name, why doesn't this God-forsaken country know when it's beaten?"

In his anger, Duke William flung his still full goblet across the room where it slammed into the far wall, spraying wine over those unfortunate enough to be within range. Not one person flinched, though; no one dared lift a hand to wipe the dark red liquid from their faces or clothes, such was their fear of the Duke's well-known tantrums.

A brooding silence hung in the air as William stalked back and forth behind the table from which the evening meal had long since been cleared away. He grabbed a new cup from the servant who had rushed forward to provide a replacement, draining it in one gulp.

News of the defeat at Suthweca had not long since been reported to him, turning his already foul mood into an incandescent rage. In the four weeks since his victory at Senlac, all he had to show for it was a few moderately-sized towns in the south east corner of the country. And they had only submitted to him to avoid annihilation. Had he not been promised the throne by his cousin, King Edward? Had Harold, while still Earl of Wessex, not sworn on relics most holy that he would support his claim?

And yet he had been forced to marshal a huge army, secure the support of the Pope, no less, and then risk life and limb to destroy the usurper king. So why now didn't those Saxon lords who still lived prostrate themselves before him? Why didn't they invite - indeed implore - him to take the throne? By rights, they should be begging him for mercy. Instead they had the gall to elect some boy, fresh from his mother's teat no less, to be their king. And by what right was he now king? Because he had been chosen? What ridiculous laws and customs these hairy-arsed barbarians have. That will change, he promised himself.

"Would you, Lord?"

William spun round, angry that his thoughts had been

interrupted. He had not expected or wanted an answer, and yet someone had the balls to offer one. Ah, Odo, his half-brother. A stout fellow who'd been with him at Senlac. As much as he wanted to, he couldn't be angry with the Bishop of Bayeux. He owed him his life, after all. When his men had believed him killed and were on the verge of breaking, it was Odo who had rallied them, sending them back up the hill to crush those Saxons foolish enough to have left the safety of their shieldwall. Without Odo's leadership, the day might have gone very differently.

"I suppose you're right, brother of mine. I had to fight tooth and nail to win Normandy when I was younger. That alone should have taught me that if you want something, you must fight for it. You must not give up until the last breath leaves your body."

"Finely put, William. All that matters is that God and numbers are on our side. The Saxons will struggle to replenish the men they lost at Senlac. Not only did they lose their king, but many of their best warriors fell that day as well. Whereas ships join us from across the water almost every day, attracted by your great victory and the promise of more spoils to come. Have patience, brother; it is just a matter of time."

"Time is what I don't have, though. The longer this goes on the more emboldened this Edgar may become. Today's events have shown they have men still ready to fight; we should not under-estimate their resolve."

"How then should we proceed? That bridge is the only way across this damned river for miles around. There are boats to be had but not enough for our needs. It would take days to carry the army across and the Saxons would slaughter us as soon as each boat emptied its load."

"We have no option but to go west, until we reach Warengeforte where there is a bridge and where we have friends. They tell me the water levels there are shallow enough for us to wade across as well if the fancy takes us."

Odo frowned. "It may be our only option but it saddens me to move further away from Lundenburh and our goal."

"I know, but the time will not be wasted. We shall not simply stroll as if we are taking the air. Rather, we shall wreak destruction in our wake, destroy farms, take livestock, kill any who resist - man, woman or child. We shall sow fear as we go so that the message reaches this Edgar that to stand against me is to invite ruin. He will either have to come out to fight me - in which case I will destroy him as I did the perfidious Harold - or submit to spare his people their suffering. And if I were to wager, I would say he will submit. Beardless boys have not the stomach for a fight in the same way us grizzled old whoresons do, eh?"

SIX

The six men clattered across the bridge about an hour or two before sundown, their horses creating such a racket on the wooden slats that it sounded as if a great army were on the move. Each man was hunched low in the saddle, wrapped about in thick cloaks, though they did little to keep the stinging rain at bay.

Thurkill could have done with the extra man, but Hild's safety was paramount and so he had ordered Copsig once again to remain with her in the city. In the event of any trouble, they were to go north with all speed to Aelfric's estate at Huntendune where the old warlord had promised to take her in for as long as was necessary. Knowing she had a haven to which she could run help salve the guilt he felt for leaving her, and he was grateful beyond words to the old bear for his kindness.

When he'd gone to tell her this news, he feared what she might say, that she might still be angry with him. But she'd welcomed him with open arms and a kiss that seemed to go on forever. Releasing him, she'd then forced him backwards until they tumbled onto the cot in a flailing mass of limbs, made all the more chaotic by their frantic efforts to rid themselves of their clothes. Thinking back to that moment, Thurkill grinned stupidly – uncaring as to how he must look to those around him. That memory would keep him warm until he saw her again.

Nevertheless, Hild remained an enigma to him. She occupied his every waking moment and more than a few of those when he slept too. One moment she was ice and the next, fire. It was hard for Thurkill - who dealt with life with a simplicity he found was common to most men he knew - to keep pace with what was going on in her mind. He had gone there ready to be scolded and yet she had been unable to keep her hands off him. He shook his head, ruefully; it was a mystery he doubted he would ever manage to solve, and he was not sure if he wanted to.

"You look like a dog that's just been given the biggest bone ever. Do share it with the rest of us; we could do with a laugh to take our minds off this shitty weather."

Eahlmund was right; the rain was, if anything, getting worse. It seemed to be coming at them sideways, blown by a stiff north-easterly breeze. Already his cloak was sodden and several times heavier than when dry. And, without any gloves to his name, the fingers of his right hand had turned a whitish-blue where they held the shaft of his spear. His left hand – holding the reins – was thankfully covered by the folds of his cloak. The only thing that could have been worse was that the worst of the weather was behind them, blowing against their backs. And far away to their rear, the horizon bore the faint glimmer of lighter skies, giving hope that the wind would eventually clear the clouds and rain away in front of them. Till then, however, it promised to be a miserable ride.

"Your pardon, Eahlmund. My mind was elsewhere."

"I can imagine where it was too. And I bet the rest of you also wishes it were there with it."

The rest of the men joined in with the tired laughter, a short but welcome distraction from the rain. "So, where are we headed, Lord?"

"South then west. We'll follow the line of the river as far as possible."

"To what purpose, Lord? I'd much rather be tucked up by a fireside in the arms of someone warm and cuddly, so please tell me I'm out here freezing my balls off for a reason."

"That you are, Leofric. Our king has sent out a number of scouting parties to find Duke William's army so we can report on their movements. If we are to have any chance of defeating them, we have to know where they are, where they are heading, what they are doing and how many of them there are doing it."

Leofric sniffed. "I suppose such a task is worthy of my time. But why us? What did we do to deserve such an honour?" The sarcasm was unmistakable, though not unkindly meant.

"I fear - and I should apologise to you all for this - that it is my doing and my doing alone. It was I who suggested to Edgar that the Normans could head west along the river until they came to a place where they might be able to cross. Several of my betters were annoyed that I should speak in their company and I think I have them to thank for this opportunity."

"Sometimes I wonder what it is I see in you, Lord. You need to stop volunteering us for dangerous things like this. That way we may all live a bit longer."

"Ah, but think of all the money you save by being out here with me, Eahlmund. No beer to buy, no games of chance to lose, no women of dubious repute to favour."

Eahlmund looked up at Thurkill from where he was hunched miserably over his saddle. "That's not helping."

They stopped for the night just as the light was fading. As fate would have it, the rain finally abated at about the same time. By now, they were all soaked to the skin, hungry and thoroughly foul-tempered. The only thing that saved their mood was the fact that they had reached what looked to be an abandoned farm, next to which was a newly-built barn. Thurkill doubted whether the Normans could have come this way, else it would surely have been destroyed, if only as a demonstration of their power.

Once settled inside, he allowed the men to break open their rations but forbade a fire to be lit. There was no way of knowing how close the enemy was and, besides, the barn was full of straw and grain dust; it would not take much for a spark to set the whole place alight. After some half-hearted grumbling, the others acceded to his demand; the sense of it could not be denied after all. Soon enough, they were settled in amongst the straw which provided both comfort and warmth, despite the increasing chill as the night came on.

Taking the first watch, Thurkill sat by the open door, shielded from the wind but still able to see and hear all that went on outside. He had arranged a few bales of straw so that he could sit propped up in some comfort, while staying alert. Looking up, he could see a multitude of stars beginning to twinkle as the skies freed themselves of cloud and darkness came on. It was going to be a cold night, he thought, pulling his still-damp cloak tighter around his shoulders.

***

Sure enough, he awoke the next morning to find a thick frost covering the ground. Eopric, who had taken the dawn watch, was stamping his feet and flapping his arms about his body to stay warm. Thurkill smiled; he was chilled to the bone himself but at least he had benefitted for the last few hours from the shared heat of the jumble of bodies sprawled together in the straw. He might not have been able to sleep much, what with the continual snoring, arse-scratching and other assorted disturbances but at least he had been quite cosy.

"Any news?"

"Nothing, Lord. Quiet as a mouse. Speaking of which, there seems to be a small army of the little bastards scurrying around in here. How you lot managed to sleep through that, I'll never know."

"Can't have been as bad as Eahlmund's snoring, though. Who needs a fire to let the Normans know where we are when they could hear that?"

"Hey, I don't snore and anyone who says otherwise is a filthy liar."

Loud guffaws broke out on all sides. "Your pardon, Eahlmund, perhaps it was a herd of pigs that joined us during the night, then."

Before long, they were back on the road, heading west, walking alongside the horses at first to shake the stiffness from of their limbs and generate some much needed warmth. By mid-morning they were back in the saddle, spirits much improved. But despite their stiff pace, and the miles they covered, they saw no sign of the enemy. They passed several villages along the way, none of which had news of the Normans. Everywhere they went, it was the same story.

By mid-afternoon, Thurkill was becoming uneasy. What if he had been wrong after all? What if the Normans had not gone this way? Even now, they could be readying for another attack on Lundenburh and he was not there to protect Hild.

Just as their route meandered, following the twists and turns of the river, so his mind wandered in every direction as he fretted about what might befall her should Duke William unleash his men against the city. They had all heard what had happened to the people of Dover for closing their gates to the invader. Angered by their show of defiance, William had torched the fortress, killing many of its inhabitants in the process. Lundenburh would suffer the same fate were it to block his path for too long.

But all that changed just as dusk began to fall on the second day. They had not long since turned south, following yet another change in the course of the river, when Leofgar – who was riding some distance to their front – came thundering back.

"Lord, fires glow yonder, to the west. A settlement burns."

Thurkill followed Leofgar's pointing finger, slightly to the right of their direction of travel, but could see nothing beyond the trees that screened the view. "You sure it is not the setting sun?"

"Yes, Lord. The light dances against the sky. That can only mean flames and lots of them."

Thurkill nodded. "Right. This may be what we have been sent to find. Let's ride there so that we might find the cause of it. If it is the Normans, we need to know if it's their full force or just a raiding party. Stay close to each other and, above all, stay vigilant. At the first sign of danger, we head back whence we came, to the bridge at Suthweca."

Grim-faced in the growing gloom, each man grunted his understanding, their minds now focussed on what lay ahead.

"Remember, we come to observe, not to engage. We must avoid contact with the enemy at all costs. If we fall, we fail in our duty to report what we have seen to the king."

They had not gone more than a mile when they encountered a stream of people, making their escape from the burning town. Most had nothing with them but what they stood up in, but here and there one or two of the more enterprising souls dragged carts on which they had loaded as many of their possessions as they could. It made for a sorry sight and reminded Thurkill of the recent scenes back at the bridge. He had a feeling that it was a sight that might become all too common in the coming days and weeks.

Most of the refugees did not spare them a second glance as they trudged – lost in their misery – along the churned-up track, made boggy by the rain of the previous day. Thurkill suspected they had no goal other than to move as far away as possible from the destruction that lay behind them. Bedraggled, most looked broken as they plodded, heads down, staring at the ground in a mixture of shock and despondency.

Thurkill had no wish to add to their woes but he needed information. Standing up in his stirrups, he peered through the growing darkness. Sure enough, about a hundred paces ahead, he what he was looking for. A family group comprising two waggons, piled high with chests, food and other items as well as what appeared to be the female members of the family. Alongside them, walked a guard made up of a dozen or so spearmen, while leading the group were two men on horseback who, from their features and respective ages, looked to be father and son. Kicking his heels into the flanks of his mare, Thurkill trotted forward until he was level with the two men, whereupon he greeted them warmly.

"Hail and well met, fellow travellers. What is the name of the town that burns and what fate has befallen it? Some accident perhaps?"

"It is Redding, good fellow, and have you not heard? An army has come to our town and put it to the torch. For no other reason, it seems, than the desire for wilful destruction."

"You did not resist? I see a dozen good warriors here."

The older of the two bristled, as if angry at the insinuation of cowardice. "There was no time. They were upon us before we even knew they were there and in more numbers than we could count. The gates were open and they simply rode in. Some carried firebrands which they tossed through windows and onto thatched rooves, while others lay about them with swords and spears. Scores were killed wantonly and we were lucky to escape with our lives."

Despite his initial feelings of sympathy, Thurkill could not resist a barbed jibe. "Though you had time to gather a couple of carts and most of your possessions by the looks of it."

"A few trinkets and some food and a handful of men to see us safe on the road. There was no time for anything more. We would have been killed had we stayed longer."

"Hmmm. An army you say? What makes you so sure? What were their numbers?" Thurkill knew that, when goaded by panic, men often over-estimated the size of the threat.

"My son, Bassa, here was at Senlac. He knows what he saw and I trust his judgement."

Thurkill manoeuvred his mount closer to the younger man so that he could reach out to grip his forearm, a newfound respect in his expression. "Greetings from another who stood with Harold on that day. With whom did you stand?"

Bassa lifted his head and straightened his back, pride returning to replace the stooped shoulders of defeat. "Godric of Fyfield, Earldorman of Berkshire was my lord, but he gave his life there and is no more. And you?"

"I stood with my father, Scalpi. King Harold was our lord. I was with him at the end and bear the scars. Thurkill swept his unkempt mane away from the left side of his face to reveal the ugly scar where his ear had been. "Quick, tell me all that you've seen here, for we ride as scouts for the new King Edgar and must report back with news of the Normans."

"As we were leaving, I could see their whole army, drawn up to the west of the town's ramparts. Although they only sent a few hundred horsemen against the town, there were many thousand more outside. They never even sent messengers forward to offer surrender. It was as if they were sending a message." The anger and hurt in the young man's face were plain to see, even as he cast his gaze down towards his feet.

Thurkill gripped the man's shoulder, forcing him to look up at his face. "There's no shame in what happened here, Bassa. There is nothing any of you could have done to stop it, else you would've all been killed for no reason. Better that men like you survive to fight on. Do you know where they are heading next?"

"I don't. But it is not hard to work it out. It is a short march north from here to Warengeforte where a man may wade across the river without fear of his life, though there is a narrow bridge too if I am not mistaken. If the Normans mean to reach Lundenburh, that is where they must head."

Thurkill smiled. "Well, perhaps we can reach the town before the Normans to warn them. There may be time to prepare the defences. If we can stop them from crossing, for a while at least, we may buy time for Edgar to muster his army."

Bassa's father interjected, his tone still pompous and

bombastic. "A fine strategy, but one I fear that is doomed to failure."

"How so? What knowledge of war and strategy do you possess to be so bold in your claim?" Thurkill's irritation was visible to all.

"Well I know for one that Wigod, Lord of Warengeforte, has friends among the Normans. He is kin to the old King Edward, of blessed memory and he had friends among the Normans from many years spent in exile there. It's said that Lord Wigod has invited Duke William to make free with his town and to cross the river without impediment."

Thurkill released Bassa's shoulder from his grip, and slumped back down in his saddle. "Then I fear we are lost."

SEVEN

They continued their journey, heading north to Warengeforte, passing the still burning ruins of Redding to their right. There were but five of them now; Eardwulf riding hard in the opposite direction, carrying reports of William's army and its intentions. News of Wigod's treachery had to reach the king as quickly as possible. If they did not stop to rest at the river ford, the Normans could be at the western walls of Lundenburh within days.

Rather than turn back, however, Thurkill had decided to press on, to try to learn more of the enemy's plans. He reasoned that the more information they could send back to Edgar, the better prepared he would be. If Warengeforte would not prevent the Normans from crossing the Thames, their chance of victory had receded, but while there was still hope, Thurkill knew he must do all he could to help.

So they made for Warengeforte. It was risky but there was no other choice. To help them, Bassa had directed them to his cousin's farm, which lay a short distance from the town's earthwork defences. They could not very well march into the town as warriors, for that would invite nothing but a quick death. Rather, they intended to assume the appearance of traders so that they might mingle more readily with the other townspeople

By the time they reached the farm, it was pitch dark. A heavy bank of cloud had rolled in during the afternoon blocking any light by which to navigate that the moon might have offered. The farm was deserted; Bassa's cousin having abandoned it earlier that day in the face of the advancing Normans. Those fears had proved unfounded, however, as the place seemed to be intact; it had not been ransacked or looted in anyway as far as he could tell. The prospect of a good night's sleep under a solid roof with plentiful food to eat warmed their hearts as much as their bodies. Thurkill even allowed Eahlmund to light a small fire in the hearth in celebration of their good fortune.

They rose at dawn and made ready to enter the town. Keeping only their short handled seaxes, they left their mailshirts, shields and swords hidden at the back of the woodshed. Thurkill felt naked without his weapons and armour, but he knew they must avoid arousing suspicion whilst within the town's walls. There would be Normans everywhere and they could do nothing that might encourage any of them to give them a second glance.

To add to their disguise, they found a handcart behind the barn which they proceeded to load with piles of cheeses and apples from the farm's abundant supplies, no doubt stockpiled in readiness for the winter months. Having wares to sell would seal their status as local merchants. Thus equipped, they set off to cover the short distance to the southern gate.

Warengeforte was shaped much like a square. Earthworks from the time of King Alfred protected three sides, whilst the fourth - the eastern side - backed on to the river, which was much narrower here than it was in Lundenburh, several miles to the east. The street pattern mirrored the walls with the main street passing from the southern gate to the north, crossing an east-west road which it met in the middle of the town where the church and market place stood. Taking a right turn at the crossroads would see you arrive at the river where a narrow bridge spanned the fast-flowing waters. In summer it would have been a simple matter to ford the river, whereas now, following the heavy autumnal rains, though the ford was still passable with care, the bridge was by far the safer option.

But Thurkill was not bound for the bridge. In the north-east corner of the town, stood Wigod's hall, surrounded by a second ring of raised, earthwork defences from where it overlooked both the river and the bridge alike. It was there where William would, doubtless, be found and Thurkill had a hankering to set eyes on the Duke close up. He had caught glimpses of him back at Senlac but they were fleeting and far off. But here, in the confines of Wigod's hall, he would be able to take the measure of the man. It crossed his mind that he might even try to kill the Duke, should he be able to get within arm's length, but he quickly dismissed the idea as futile. Surely, he would not be allowed to come that close and certainly not with any kind of weapon. And besides, what would Hild say were he to get himself killed on some foolish quest? Still, he had to admit that the notion was tempting to say the least.

Reaching the hall proved to be anything but simple, though. It seemed the whole Norman army had taken over the town and the place was heaving, accompanied by every sound and stinking smell that went with it.

Once past Warengeforte's main gate, Thurkill led his little party down the first road on their right to avoid the swirling masses on the main street. They soon found a parallel, albeit narrower, road along which they were able to reach the centre of the town after a walk of no longer than the time it would take to saddle a horse.

But there, they were once again thrust into the bustling maelstrom of an army on the move. Like a river flowing inexorably to the sea, so the Normans - archers, foot-soldiers and mounted horsemen alike - moved ever eastwards towards the river. The stench of unwashed bodies mixed with urine was overpowering as men and beasts relieved themselves where they stood rather than lose their place. It was a slow-moving log jam heading for a single narrow exit.

Looking down towards the river, Thurkill could see a good number of men and horses in the water on either side of the bridge; those too impatient to wait their turn had decided to chance the ford instead. He doubted whether he would have risked it, but then the Norman mounts were bigger and more powerful than those he was used to riding and were, perhaps, better equipped to deal with a river in spate.

While Thurkill watched as the Norman army passed before him, Eahlmund finally lost patience. "This is no bastard good. We'll be here forever waiting for these whoresons to pass. Leofric, Leofgar, get behind the cart and start pushing." With that, he stepped forward into the throng, holding his arm out to stop the nearest soldier.

Thurkill's heart jumped into his mouth. He was about to reach out to drag his friend back, when the incredible happened. Rather than resort to violence, the soldier simply stopped to allow Eahlmund to pass, though not without uttering what sounded to be a particularly foul-mouthed curse in his direction. Thurkill grinned to himself, it seemed that soldiers were used to following orders whatever their tongue. Shrugging with his best apologetic expression, Thurkill bent his shoulder to the cart's rear wheel and began to push. Amazingly enough, two or three of the waiting Normans lent a hand as well; whether out of kind-heartedness or anger at being held up made no difference to Thurkill. Nodding his thanks in their direction, he renewed his efforts. In no time at all, they were across and into the wide open space of the market area.

As his heart rate returned to normal, Thurkill took stock of their surroundings. Ahead of them, Wigod's hall stood on its banked plateau from where it dominated the rest of the town. All around them, stall after stall had been set up selling all manner of wares, taking advantage of the presence of several thousand soldiers.

Spotting a gap between a man selling horse tackle and another with a cart stacked high with earthenware pots, Thurkill directed Eopric and the two brothers to set up shop. "May as well try and make a bit of coin, lads. Especially after the way you lot were spending it back in Lundenburh. Oh, and be sure to charge a good price to any Normans - more than you would if you were selling to good Saxon folk. Eahlmund and I will take a look up at the hall."

The ground rose steeply on the path up to the plateau, so much so that Thurkill was panting by the time they joined the queue to pass through the gate set into the palisade that surrounded the hall. It was a recent construction, the wood had yet to weather from continued exposure to the elements and, here and there, sticky, sweet-smelling sap still oozed from where side branches had been lopped off.

When they reached the front of the queue, they were greeted by two Normans who barred the entrance with their crossed spears.

"State your business, Saxons."

Thurkill froze, cursing himself for not having given a moment's thought to what he might say if challenged. He was on the verge of panic when Eahlmund came to his rescue.

"We're scouts with news of Lundenburh."

Satisfied, the Norman nodded, stepping to one side to wave them through. *Thank God Eahlmund's wits are sharper than mine.*

As soon as they were beyond earshot, Thurkill whispered from the corner of his mouth. "Good work, friend. You may just have saved our skins there. Though it was a novel idea to actually tell the truth. I hadn't considered that."

"Well, I didn't say whose scouts we were, so I suppose no one can call me liar. My conscience before God remains clear."

Thurkill grinned. "Now, let's see if we can stretch our luck a little more by being allowed into the hall itself."

This time they were met by a Saxon, a man by the name of Hartha, who immediately apologised for the presence of Normans. "I wish it were not so but Lord Wigod, has made his peace with Duke William and there is nothing I can do about it. Anyway, you're scouts you say? With news from Lundenburh? How goes things there? Is it true a new king has been acclaimed? Someone from the old line of King Alfred no less?"

"Aye. 'Tis so, Hartha. The boy, Edgar, sits on the throne now, with Earls Eadwine and Morcar at his side. Even now, they gather men to stand against this Bastard of Normandy." Thurkill tried to sound more confident than he felt; though whether it was to scare Hartha or give him hope was hard to tell. The man certainly seemed to be conflicted between the wishes of his lord and what lay in his own heart.

"Still, there's no point you telling me, lads. We'd best have you inside to see Wigod. Leave your weapons here, and I'll usher you within."

Before they could move, however, a great commotion broke out behind them. Fearing their identity had somehow been uncovered, Thurkill swung round in alarm to see a group of a dozen or so heavily armed knights marching through the palisade gate through which they'd come, shoving aside any who blocked their way. Eahlmund and he were directly in their path and a confrontation seemed almost inevitable until Hartha grabbed each of them by the sleeve and pulled them out of the way.

It was as well that Hartha intervened as they were rooted to the spot, staring open-mouthed at the lead knight. Turning to look at each other, no words were exchanged but their expressions said it all. The same shock of dark hair, the same thick eyebrows which almost met in the middle and the same slightly hooked nose. All that was missing was the scar. It was as if the ghost of Richard FitzGilbert walked among them.

EIGHT

"Who was that?" Thurkill tried to keep his voice neutral, though his pulse was racing.

Hartha looked up at the knight who was now barging his way into the hall, closely followed by the rest of his escort. "Who? Him? I've heard him called Robert Fitz-something. I can't get my tongue round some of these Norman names. A thoroughly unpleasant fellow by all accounts, though. It's said his brother was murdered over in Kent not long back. He has sworn to kill whomever was responsible."

I know his name, Thurkill thought. *FitzGilbert. Richard must have had a brother. It seems I am not yet done with this family.*

Thurkill and Eahlmund exchanged glances once more, the latter snorting in a derisory manner. "Well I wouldn't like to be in that poor sod's boots when Robert Fitz-whatsit catches up with him. You'd die of fright just looking at his ugly face before he laid a hand on you. I've seen better looking pigs, slept with a few too when I was younger."

Hartha threw his head back and laughed uproariously. "Don't let him hear you say that. He has a temper on him that one. I'm sure he would be happy to add you to his list of Saxons to be killed. I say whoever did it did us all a favour, though. Imagine having two of the bastards roaming around."

Thurkill risked one more question, hoping not to invite suspicion. "Does he know where to find the culprit?"

"He doesn't know the name, just that it was a young huscarl who fought with Harold at Senlac. Beyond that, I can't say. Though... having said that..." He paused, as if remembering some half-forgotten detail.

"Said what?" Thurkill's heart began to beat faster once more.

"I'm sure it's nonsense. Forget it."

"Out with it, man. Piss or get off the pot." Eahlmund's impatience had worn thin.

Hartha shrugged. "Well. I've heard that the man he looks for has but one ear."

It took a monumental effort of will to stop himself from touching the side of his head. Instead, Thurkill bunched his hands into fists by his side, praying that this face did not betray him. Richard's brother had come to England to seek vengeance against the killer of his kin. Fault or blame were not material; this was a matter of honour. Thurkill would have no option but to kill this man or be killed by him.

"Anyway, I think it's about time we saw you into the hall to deliver your news." Thankfully, Hartha had not noticed anything untoward. But, FitzGilbert's arrival had cast new doubt in Thurkill's mind. Did he really want to risk standing in front of the man who'd sworn to kill him?

"Will they not be too busy now that this Robert has arrived? My news can wait until later."

"Nonsense, they will be keen to hear talk of this Edgar. Now then, what did you say your name was, so I may introduce you?"

***

Hartha pushed open the door of the hall and the two men followed him inside. Thurkill's nose and eyes were immediately assailed with the acrid sting of smoke rising from the huge fire that burned in the central hearth. His heart was thumping so hard, he feared it would burst forth from the confines of his chest. For all he knew, his life hung in the balance; not only was he about to go before Duke William - King Harold's killer - but he would do so in the presence of the man whose brother he had slaughtered only a few days ago. What had seemed like a clever ruse now felt like the height of stupidity.

"Lord Wigod, may I present to you Assa, recently returned from Lundenburh with tidings." Thurkill felt the flat of Hartha's hand in the small of his back, gently propelling him forward. He adjusted his hair for probably the fourth time since he had entered the hall, making sure that the unsightly wound was fully covered.

"You are welcome, Assa. I fear I know you not, though. Who is your lord?" Wigod was a fat, balding man, close to his forties. Beads of sweat stood out on his forehead while the armpits of his tunic bore dark stains. As he spoke, his fleshy jowls wobbled in a way that made Thurkill feel queasy.

Thurkill bowed before offering an apologetic shrug. "I have no master, Lord. Not since Senlac."

The fat man nodded. "Many good men were lost that day, and all for what? To fight for a king who broke a solemn oath, sworn not two years previously on the holiest of relics, to support the claim of my good friend here, Duke William. Many might yet live were it not for his avarice. But enough of the past, what news do you bring of the present, Assa. Has Edgar come to his senses and decided to submit?"

As he spoke, Wigod gestured to the man sat to his right who Thurkill realised must be William. Though similar in age, the Duke was an altogether more imposing figure; broad of shoulder and taller than most. Muscular, too, by the looks of it, but perhaps carrying a little more weight around the middle than he would have in his youth. Like all of his kind, William wore his hair in the Norman fashion; shaved back and sides, with a thick thatch of dark hair on top. He was dressed in a luxuriant red tunic with a green and gold cloak draped over his shoulders to keep out the chill. Everything about him spoke of power and authority; from the piercing green eyes that even now bore into Thurkill's soul, to the way he sat, leaning forward, his chin resting on his hand as he weighed the man who stood in front of him. It was nothing short of intimidating.

Beyond the Duke, Thurkill could see FitzGilbert, slouched in his chair with one leg draped casually over the arm, booted foot swinging back and forth, apparently bored by everything that went on around him. The Devil's spawn wasn't even looking at him.

Taking his courage in both hands, he spoke with a clear voice, praying that his fear would not be visible. "Would you, Lord? Would any of us? Edgar may still be young but he is proud. He comes from a long line of Saxon kings, right back to Aethelstan and his grandfather, Alfred, before him."

"All that you say is true, Assa, but the boy should accept the truth. Harold - the best war-leader that England had - lies dead along with many of his greatest lords and warriors. For how long can Edgar hope to resist? He should welcome our Norman cousins with open arms as we have. You've seen the market?

Our traders prosper. To do otherwise is to invite destruction. The people of England will not thank him for his stubbornness."

"This is all very interesting, Wigod, but I want to hear what Assa has to say about Edgar's plans. How many men does he have? What are his dispositions? What can we expect him to do next?"

Thurkill had anticipated the Duke's question, yet it still filled him with dread. How to answer without betraying himself or his king? "Edgar has summoned the fyrd and waits for it to assemble in Lundenburh."

"Whence come the men, though? How many are left to fight after Stamford and Senlac?"

"The army which faced you at Senlac was but a portion of the forces that England can call upon. There are those who say that, had Harold but waited another week, he would have faced you with twice as many men."

The Duke's brow furrowed. "I had hoped that England had been stripped of its best warriors. Are they not but old men and children that remain?"

"No, Lord. The Earls Eadwine and Morcar will have many men under their banners, and there are other shires north of the city who have not yet been called upon."

"What does it matter?" FitzGilbert yawned, stretching his arms behind his head. "Whoever turns up will be no match for us. We will destroy them once again."

The Duke rounded on him. "Do not presume to instruct me in matters of war and strategy, FitzGilbert. What do you know of the Saxons? You did not face them at Senlac. It was a closer affair than you think. They are staunch warriors; I doubt I have ever faced braver men in battle."

The knight was sullen but respectful in the face of the all too public rebuke. "Your pardon, Lord. I meant no offence. I am simply impatient to see you take your rightful place as king of these people. Tell us what you would have us do? Surely, we should bring them to battle before they become too strong."

"I know your mind, man, however much you try to hide it. Your only goal is to hunt down whoever killed your brother. Though, if you ask me, I think he brought his fate upon himself.

Still, it's your business and I'll not stand in your way – but not until we have secured our victory. Understood?"

FitzGilbert bowed his head in obeisance, though Thurkill could see the man still smarted. There was much of the brother in this man, the same insolence, arrogance and, doubtless, the same harsh cruelty. Thurkill knew there would be no end to it until one of them lay dead at the other's feet. Thurkill swore to himself that it would not be him that was found wanting.

"But to your point, FitzGilbert, what to do indeed? We are seemingly no closer to our goal. I had hoped that Edgar would fold like a house built on sand, but it appears he has stronger foundations than I thought. In fact, if we are to believe our friend, Assa, here, the Saxons grow bolder and stronger each day. We must make our point a little more loudly in case we cannot be heard from this far away."

"What do you propose, Lord?"

"What I suggest, my dear Wigod, is that we send a message to this Edgar that it does not do to stand against me. FitzGilbert, take horsemen to ravage to the west and south of here. There are rich pickings to be had between here and Wintancaester. You must take that city too for it has great meaning to this line of kings and its loss will not go unnoticed. On your return, we will march on Lundenburh, burning and harrying as we go. Edgar will reap the rewards of defiance; his people will suffer, their homes will be razed to the ground, their livestock taken from them and their ploughs destroyed. I mean to hear my coronation mass in Edward's Abbey at Westminster before the year is out."

NINE

It did not take long for the Duke's plan to bear fruit. The first significant move of the pieces on the game board happened when Stigand, Archbishop of Canterbury, arrived at Warengeforte to swear fealty to William, having not long since acclaimed Edgar. Thurkill could barely conceal his contempt as the churchman passed through the market, surrounded by a small army of monks and other retainers on his way up to Wigod's hall. At a time when Edgar needed all the help he could find, one of the foremost lords of England, the head of the English church in fact, had abandoned him. Thurkill wondered what he had been promised in return?

Thurkill decided to dwell on it no further. He needed to report back to Edgar and his council. They were about to leave when Thurkill saw Hartha heading towards them. Something in his expression told him that all was not well. Turning back to the others he whispered. "Be ready, lads. I don't have a good feeling about this."

"Ah, Assa, there you are."

"Well met, Hartha. You are lucky to find us. We were just on our way."

"Fortunate indeed, but I am not sure for whom. The strangest thing just happened and I thought you should know soonest."

"Your pardon, Hartha, but we are in a hurry."

"It won't take but a moment and it may be to your advantage." The look in Hartha's eyes told him all he needed to know. As he had suspected, the man was not a friend of the Normans, unlike his master.

"The Lord Archbishop Stigand of Canterbury has not long since arrived to bend the knee to Duke William."

"Is that who that was? I thought he looked important." Thurkill was determined keep up the pretence for a while longer, just to see on which side the dice fell. He had already begun to piece together the various pieces of the puzzle in his mind, though.

"Indeed. He swore that he had just seen one of Harold's huscarls, and one who is now King Edgar's sworn man, here in Warengeforte. And what's more, he seems to be running a market stall selling cheese and apples."

It all fell into place. Stigand had recognised him from when he had been standing close to Harold in Lundenburh, back before Senlac. He had never considered his remarkable size to be a disadvantage, but now it may just have sealed his doom.

Thurkill decided to take a risk, hoping he had judged the man correctly. The risk of capture followed by a slow and painful death at FitzGilbert's hand was great but his need was greater.

"Hartha, you seem a stout fellow to me, and I'd like to think I can trust you. I am the man of whom Stigand speaks. I have come here at Edgar's behest to learn what I can of William's plans. To my shame, I had not thought the old bastard would recognise me. If I had kept my wits about me, I would have concealed myself as he passed by, but it is too late for that now. Now, I must place my life in your hands if I am to survive. Will you help me and my companions escape before it is too late?"

Hartha stood silent, expressionless, his eyes flickering from Thurkill to those around him, as if weighing the options. Would his duty to his lord outweigh his dislike of the Normans? Thurkill could only pray that the latter burned more fiercely than anything else. Eventually he reached a decision.

"I shall declare to Wigod that I was unable to find you. I shall cite witnesses who saw you go east across the bridge not one hour since. I presume your route will actually see you head south?"

Smiling, Thurkill clasped Hartha's forearm. "If it is ever in my power, I shall see you well rewarded for your kindness. Your service to me will be made known to the king."

"Do not trouble yourself on my part, Assa, or whomever you are. Although, I fear England's fate may be already sealed, I am partial to a game of chance, so I would see the odds evened a little."

"My thanks, friend. You have, at least, earned the right to know my name. I am Thurkill, son of Scalpi, proud huscarl in the service of the true King of England."

47

Thurkill released Hartha's arm from his grip and turned to the rest of his men. "Leave the cart, it will only slow us down. Make your way back to the farm as quickly as you can, and go singly for they will be looking for a group of us. Quick, go now. We must hurry for they'll send horsemen after us both east and south despite what our friend here tells them."

As he spoke, Thurkill lifted a sack containing their provisions over his shoulder. In doing so, the cloth brushed against the side of his face, sweeping the hair back. Irritated, he shook his head to untangle it, but not before Hartha saw.

"Your ear."

There was no turning back now. "You are mistaken, my friend. There is no ear to be seen."

***

Eahlmund was already in the barn saddling the horses, when Thurkill arrived. Straightaway, he lent him a hand; they could not afford to waste a moment. The Normans would be after them almost immediately, especially if news about his ear reached FitzGilbert. Several bystanders had witnessed his exchange with Hartha and, whilst he did not recall any of them being Norman, it was reasonable to assume that news of such an oddity would soon travel.

By the time all five horses were ready, Leofric, Leofgar and Eopric had also arrived, allowing Thurkill to breathe a sigh of relief. Quickly, they donned their mailshirts, strapped their sword belts around their waists and slung their shields over their shoulders. Then they were ready to begin the long trek back to Lundenburh. It was late afternoon, but the sky was clear and the weather, for once, calm and mild; they would make good progress.

"We need to put a good few miles between us and Warengeforte before nightfall. I've no doubt there will be men on our trail before the sun goes down, so let's not make it easy for them."

They set off at no more than a fast trot. It made no sense to tire the horses out too soon; they might need their strength before long. They decided not to follow the river too closely for this was the most direct route and the one the Normans would surely expect them to take. Instead, they struck further south, skirting the still smouldering ruins of Redding on their left, until they picked up the old Roman road that headed south west from Lundenburh to the coast.

By now the sun was low on the horizon, presaging the onset of night. Not wanting to be found close to the road, Thurkill led them a few hundred paces along a narrow path that took them further south into a small close-knit copse of beech and alder. It was far enough from the road to shield them from prying eyes, and yet close enough that they could see any who passed that way. They tethered the horses to the trees that were furthest from the road, making sure the mast beneath their hooves was plentiful amongst which they could forage aplenty.

Following a brief meal of the remains of the fruit and cheese they had grabbed from their market stall, the five of them settled down for the night. With no fire to warm them, they huddled as close to each other as possible for shelter from the breeze and to share what body warmth they had.

Thurkill took the first watch, taking up a position with his back up against a tree which, whilst a few paces back from the edge of the copse, allowed a sweeping view of the road in both directions. As he sat there, willing himself to stay awake, his thoughts turned to Hild. Eardwulf would have reached the city a few days ago and he hoped he had managed to send news to her about the army that had now crossed the Thames and stood poised to descend on Lundenburh. In his heart he did not know whether Edgar's army would survive the coming onslaught. And then who knew what the Normans might do to the city and its inhabitants were they to be victorious?

Would Edgar try to defend the city or would he march out to meet them on open ground? Thurkill wondered what he would do were it his decision? It was hard to know in truth; he was no strategist after all, just a fighter, albeit a good one, with a fire in his belly that would not fade until the every last Norman whoreson had been killed or sent homewards.

His thoughts were cut short by a tug on his sleeve. Looking up in a state of mild panic, he saw Leofric leaning over him. It must be time already to change the watch and yet it seemed he had only just sat down.

"Get some sleep if you can, Lord. We'll wake you come the dawn."

"My thanks, friend. It's quiet here. With luck it will stay that way."

TEN

A hand on his shoulder shook him awake. Instinctively, he grabbed for his seax which he always kept within reach.

"Hush, Lord. Enemies afoot."

He recognised Leofgar's voice in the darkness and let go of the knife. It was still dark, the only light coming from the thinnest sliver of moon. He reckoned it would be some hours yet before the first flush of dawn crept over the eastern horizon.

Stifling a yawn, he whispered. "Whither?"

"Yonder." He followed the direction of Leofgar's outstretched arm, which pointed back up the road along which they'd come the previous day. In the distance, he could see small pin pricks of light against the black canvas of the night. Two, or was it three? It was hard to tell this far away.

"Fires, Lord. Three of them by my reckoning. They sprung up not long since."

"An enemy you say? How many would you reckon?"

"Who else would be travelling in the dead of night and have the balls to go about lighting fires? Three or four men to a fire would mean ten to a dozen, I'd say."

Thurkill nodded in agreement. "Wake the others, Leofgar. But quietly. We must leave without delay. Hopefully they've settled down for the night and don't know of our presence close by. With luck we can fool them."

They walked the first couple of miles. It was too dark to ride safely; a horse might easily break a leg. Leaving the copse behind them, they struck out east across open meadows. Thurkill would have liked to have re-joined the road, but with the Normans on their trail, it was a risk they could not take. It irked him though for he was desperate to be back with Hild. His place was there, protecting her, not walking through a meadow in the wrong damned direction.

A few hours later, they reached a narrow stream, where they halted briefly to let the horses drink and to replenish their own skins. In the distance, the first signs of the new day were beginning to show as the horizon was lightening little by little. Thurkill doubted they would see much sun, though, as a thick, forbidding bank of cloud had rolled in, sealing off what little light had come from the moon.

With both horses and men refreshed, Thurkill gave the order to mount up. As the darkness receded with every step, the danger of a horse missing its footing was much reduced. *At last,* Thurkill patted his mount's neck, glad to be on her back once more with the prospect of much quicker progress to be made. He was not familiar with the land through which they rode, but he reckoned that they would soon come across another road leading to the city. He knew many roads led there, like the spokes of a wheel connected to its hub. It was only a matter of time before they found one.

It was close to midday when he was finally proved right. Creating a steep ridge, they found the road in the valley below. It was not as wide or as well-kept as the last one but it still had the look of Roman engineering about it, stretching off into the distance, hardly deviating from its rigid course. Thurkill smiled to see it for he knew that Lundenburh and Hild lay at the end of that road.

"Lord!"

Twisting round in his saddle, Thurkill saw Eahlmund, ashen-faced, staring back down the slope. Looking past him, he saw what had caused his friend's outburst. No more than two miles back, a small group of horsemen - surely the same as those whose fires they had seen last night – were riding hard, pushing their horses to close the gap between them. Thurkill did a brief count; ten. They were outnumbered two to one. They could not stand and fight, at least not for now. They would have to try to outrun them or else be slaughtered.

As he watched, he saw the lead man point in their direction and give a shout, the echoes of which reached him faintly on the wind. They had spotted their quarry. Immediately, they urged the poor beasts to even greater efforts with vicious looking jabs of their heels into their flanks.

"By the Devil's hairy scrotum, how did they get so close?"

"God alone knows, Eahlmund, but we must stay ahead of

them. Come on!" Without waiting to see if they followed, Thurkill yanked his mare's head back round and surged forward down the slope towards the road. He had no idea what he was planning to do. He did not even know if they could outrun the enemy. Could he really hope to reach Lundenburh ahead of them?

At first the gradient helped, lending speed to their flight. But after a short while, the ground became uneven forcing them to slow the horses for fear of injury. As often as he could, Thurkill glanced back to keep track of the distance between them, all the while wracking his brains for some sort of plan. If they could try to match the pace of their pursuers, they should stay ahead for a good while, perhaps even until nightfall which was only a few hours hence at this time of year. Darkness would help even the odds for sure.

The thudding of their horses' hooves filled his ears. His thighs ached with the strain of keeping a tight grip, while every joint vibrated with the jolting motion of the hardy little beast as it pounded its way over the grass, ears flattened by the wind. Thurkill's long flowing hair flicked at his face as the air rushed past them, forcing tears from his eyes. He'd lost count of the number of insects he'd swallowed as he sucked great gulps of air into his lungs.

Reaching the road, Thurkill looked back for perhaps the sixth or seventh time. And now, finally, he saw the enemy. They had reached the summit, pausing for a moment to allow their horses to recover following the sharp ascent. By his reckoning, the gap had not closed much, if at all. But the glimmer of hope that rose in his heart was dampened by the knowledge that the Normans' stronger horses would give them the edge on the road.

"What's the plan, Lord?" Eahlmund spoke in breathless gasps, his face red with exertion.

"We keep going as best we can. With luck we will reach Lundenburh ahead of them, but if all else fails, we hold them off until the sun goes down. Then we stand and make a fight of it somewhere that suits us."

"I'm not sure I like the odds."

"Neither do I, Eahlmund. But the least we can do is take as

many of them with us as we can, if we cannot escape them."

His friend did not reply, but the look on his face told Thurkill all he needed to know.

They set off down the road, pushing their horses as hard as they dared. At first they seemed to keep an even distance ahead of their foe, but as soon as the Normans reached the road, they began to close with alarming speed, just as they feared. With the wind coming from behind, Thurkill could hear the shouts of encouragement with which they were urging each other and their horses on to yet greater efforts. They knew they were going to catch their prey. It was like sport for them, like hunting wild boar in the forests of Normandy.

Scanning the road ahead, Thurkill's heart jumped as he saw a dark smudge on the horizon. It was hard to be sure but he felt certain that it must be the start of a great forest, perhaps even the western edge of the Weald which stretched from the Kentish coast all the way almost to Hampshire. If they could get in amongst the trees, they might yet be able to lose their pursuers or at least slow them down. It was time to make a decision. Looking back once more, he could see that the enemy was even closer than before. *That settles it,* Thurkill thought. *There's no way we can outrun them, not unless their horses drop dead from exhaustion.*

Thurkill gave the order. "Head for yonder trees. We'll make a stand there and use the land to even the odds a little."

Leofric growled. "Good. I've had enough of running. It's time to make the bastards pay."

Whether he was scared or not, it didn't show and Thurkill was grateful for the show of defiance as it helped embolden the others. He was under no illusions, though; it would be a miracle if any of them were to survive. The thought of these brave men's deaths weighed heavily on his mind. It was a responsibility he knew he would never get used to.

"I'm sorry lads. I had hoped it would not come to this. I would understand it if any of you wanted to use the cover of the woods to run. You might not make it, but it might increase your chances."

Eahlmund's response was immediate. "Bollocks, Lord. You

don't get to kill them all by yourself." A chorus of approvals greeted his words. Thurkill found himself humbled with pride. They might not be the best-trained warriors but what they lacked in skill they more than made up for in heart and determination.

"To the trees, then, and be quick about it."

They swerved off the road, hitting the tree line a good thirty lengths ahead of their pursuers. Immediately, Thurkill felt his hopes rising. The trees - whilst closely packed together - were not so dense that they hindered their progress too much. Their small, sturdy ponies had no difficulty twisting and turning through the trunks, whereas he knew that the much larger beasts behind them would be more severely hampered.

Although it gave them an edge, Thurkill did not for one moment believe it would be enough. They would have to stand and fight sooner or later. But the trees would, at least, win them time to find a place suitable for an ambush. It would be the only way to swing the odds in their favour.

They trotted on in single file, Thurkill at the front, looking left and right for inspiration. All the while he listened for signs that the Normans might be getting closer. The soft earth under foot meant that they had no hope of losing them; the trail would be plain as day despite the growing gloom.

And then he saw what he'd been looking for. The path suddenly dove down into a narrow gully winding its way between a series of boulders that rose up to about the height of two men on either side. The gully was short - no more than fifty paces long - but the height of the rocks meant that there was no way out until you reached the end. It was as good a place as they were likely to find. Holding up his hand to halt the others, Thurkill barked out his commands. Time was critical; they had to be in position well before the Normans arrived.

"Leofric, Leofgar get yourselves up on top of those rocks on that side. Eahlmund and I will do likewise here. Eopric, take the horses and tether them out of sight down the path and hurry back here with your spear and shield. I need you to block the end as best you can so they cannot escape. Don't put yourself in any unnecessary danger, though. If it looks like you're going to be overwhelmed, get away from there as best you can."

Leofric grinned; the thrill of the impending fight animating his face, masking any fear he might have felt. "What would you have us do, Lord?"

"Grab rocks. When they are all within the gully, we'll take out as many as we can with them before dropping on them with our knives. It'll be tight down there with not much room to manoeuvre, so swords and shields are pointless. It'll be dirty work, lads. You'll have to stick them up close; close enough to feel their breath on your skin and to smell their shit as they soil their braes in fear. Can you do it?"

"Aye!" They answered as one.

They had to move fast; they could already hear their prey forcing their way through the undergrowth, cursing and shouting as they came. As instructed, Eopric ran off, leading all five horses off into the trees. The rest of them seized what rocks they could find before scrambling their way up the boulders.

In his rush to complete the climb, Thurkill scuffed his shins at least twice before breaking a nail as he missed a hand hold, the sharp pain almost causing him to cry out which would have given away their position. He reached the top, just in time. From where he lay, with Eahlmund just to his right, he could now see the line of horsemen approaching the gully.

To his relief they appeared to be unaware of the impending threat. Doubtless, they assumed the Saxons would simply keep on running ahead of them. He allowed himself a thin smile, the plan appeared to be working so far. Lifting his head a little, slowly so as not to alert the enemy with any sudden movement, he glanced over to the other side to check on the two brothers. Sure enough, they were ready and waiting, focussed on the enemy below with wicked looking lumps of rock clutched in their hands.

The Normans were close enough now for Thurkill to hear their voices. Though he could not understand what they said, their tone betrayed no anxiety. *Perhaps this might just work,* he mused. At last, the rearmost horseman entered the gully. All the while, Thurkill prayed they would not be discovered. They were so close that one slight noise, one careless scrape of blade against stone, would be enough to give the game away. Finally, it was time. Leaping to his feet, he yelled "Now!"

All four men stood and hurled their rocks as hard as they could. At that range, they could not miss and nor could helmets save their victims. Each missile found its intended target and soon four men lay sprawled on the ground. With good foresight, they had targeted the men at front and back, so that the six still ahorse were now boxed in, unable to go forward or back in the narrow confines of the rock formations. The horses at the rear were unable to turn, whilst those at the front found their path blocked by Eopric standing behind his shield, spear point thrust ahead. It was a better result than Thurkill could possibly have hoped for. Panic was beginning to set in among the six remaining soldiers as they twisted this way and that, trying to sight their enemy. It was time to end it.

"Finish it, lads. Slaughter the bastards."

They needed no encouragement. Their blood-lust was up, drunk on their early success and eager for more. Releasing their seaxes from their belts, each man, steadied himself for a heartbeat before jumping down onto the men below.

Thurkill timed his leap to perfection. With his knife reversed in his right hand, he landed on the back of the horse closest to him, simultaneously plunging his blade into its rider's exposed neck. Blood fountained from the wound, drenching his face and arms. The soldier screamed briefly before crumpling to the ground.

Casting around to gain his bearings, Thurkill saw his next target and just in time. One of the remaining knights had drawn his sword and was using it to urge his horse forward as best he could in a desperate attempt to escape the gully. In his path stood Eopric, whose complexion had turned as white as the snow that fell in winter. To his credit, the young lad stood his ground, though he must have feared for his life. The smell of blood and death had panicked the horse, its eyes staring with wild abandon and its nostrils flaring. Like its master it, too, was desperate to be away from the carnage.

Thurkill knew he could not reach the man from where he was. But he had to do something; the next few seconds could determine Eopric's fate. He urged the horse forward, raking its flanks with his heels. But the poor animal was wedged fast between the rock wall on its left and another horse to its right. Reluctantly, Thurkill did the only thing he could; he stabbed down into the other horse's flank. It was not a deep cut - he did not want to injure the animal too much - but it was enough to achieve the desired result. Whinnying in terror, it surged forward, kicking back with its hind legs to clear itself a path.

As he hoped it would, Thurkill's own mount took fright and followed its lead. With an unlooked for stroke of luck, the wounded beast then careened into the soldier's horse, causing him to lose balance just as he was about to bring his sword down on Eopric's bare head. It was now or never, Thurkill knew, he would not get another opportunity. He launched himself at the Norman, not caring whether he managed to stab him. Even if he could just knock him to the ground, then Eopric would be saved.

He took the man full in the back, forcing him out of his saddle. Thurkill held on tight to him as he fell. As they tumbled to the ground, Thurkill was vaguely aware of a cry of pain but he had no time to wonder whence it came, for the Norman was now snarling at him, writhing to be free from his grip.

He had lost his seax in the fall, the impact causing it to be sprung from his grip. Now as he straddled the man, he was lost in indecision without a weapon to hand. His hesitation gave the Norman the opportunity he needed. Wrenching his right arm free of Thurkill's grip, he managed to punch his mailed fist on to Thurkill's nose. The bone cracked with a sound like a dry twig breaking under foot. Dazed, he felt his vision blurring while hot, tangy blood flooding his mouth.

The knight immediately followed up his advantage with a further flurry of blows to the face. If it had not been for the narrow confines of the gully restricting the power of each punch, all would have been lost.

Any thought of trying to find his seax had gone; he had but one hope left if he wanted to survive. Shaking his head to clear the fug that threatened engulf him, he roared with anger and frustration. Then, he reached down with both hands to grab the soldier's ears and began smashing his head back and forth against the ground. The Norman did his best to knock his assailant off, but he found his way blocked by the Saxon's muscular arms clamped to either side of his head. After the second blow, the his helmet flew off, leaving the back of his head exposed. With each thud of skull striking earth, the punches became fewer and less powerful until, finally, he lapsed into unconsciousness. With one final effort, Thurkill lifted the limp form up and rammed his own forehead into the unprotected face for good measure.

For a moment, Thurkill remained knelt over him, his chest heaving, until the thumping pain in his head got the better of him and he slumped to one side, exhausted. Around him, the sounds of fighting had ceased and he prayed his men had been victorious. If not, it would be but a moment or two before he felt a knife slashing across his throat, ending his life.

But the next face he saw belonged to Eahlmund, his expression full of concern. "My God, Thurkill, that fellow has made a mess of your face. Spoiled your good looks, he has."

He tried to laugh but the sound that came out was more of a croak that caught in his throat. Sitting up, Thurkill hawked and spat out the mix of blood and snot that had filled the back of his throat. His ruined nose still dripped with blood. Gingerly, he prodded the area with his fingers, wincing with pain as he did so. His vision was becoming more and more hazy; *my eyes must be puffing up* he realised. He hadn't taken a beating like this since old Aelle the farmer had caught him in his barn with his daughter.

"Don't worry though, Lord. If Hild can't bring herself to lie with you now that you're as ugly as a dog chewing on a bee, I would consider it my duty - no matter how painful it would be - to step in on your behalf."

"I would be indebted to you, Eahlmund, were that ever to prove to be the case. But if I could drag you back to the moment, should I take it from your welcome presence that we have won the day? How fares everyone?"

Eahlmund's face darkened. "Aye, Lord. Every one of the whoresons is dead, except one who managed to slip the net. The brothers have slit the throats of those that we knocked out, the rest we managed to kill. Even young Eopric took one before…" His voice caught and he dropped his gaze to the ground.

"Before what, Eahlmund?"

Tears filled his friend's eyes as he spoke, his voice barely audible. "It was the bravest thing I ever saw, Lord. He stood his ground against one of the bastards as he rode the lad down. I shouted to him to stand aside and let the devil go, but whether he heard me or no, I cannot say. All I know is that he faced down man and beast and did not flinch, even as the sword took him in the neck. As far as I could tell, he died instantly; he would not have felt a thing."

"What of the Norman?"

"Oh, Eopric got him alright. Stuck his spear right through his gut. He goes to meet his Maker in the knowledge that he did his duty."

Thurkill bowed his head, his mind flooded with emotion. Young Eopric was the first of his warband to die. Though the fight could not have been avoided, he knew his death would prey on his mind for months to come.

With heavy heart, Thurkill pushed himself to his feet and walked groggily over to where the body lay. The poor boy was a mess, but he forced himself not to look away. In the last two months, he had seen more than his fair share of bodies with all manner of grievous wounds, but few had hit him as hard as this. The sword had caught Eopric where body and neck joined, leaving a deep gash that must have killed him instantly; a small mercy, thought Thurkill. It was a small consolation that, not six feet away, lay the Norman he had killed, the spear point still buried deep within him.

Uncertain what else to do, Thurkill knelt before him and bowed his head. Before long Eahlmund, Leofric and Leofgar joined him in prayer. He had never been one to pay too much attention in church; the only words he knew were those that Father Acha had recited every Sunday in his little church at the end of each interminable service. It had stuck in his mind because he knew it meant that he would soon be released to fill his afternoon with whatever pleasures he had planned with his friends. The words came to him, filled with memories of happier times. He felt a tear forming in the corner of his eye as images came flooding back to him of his childhood; a childhood which he imagined must have been similar to Eopric's. *It will have to do*; *I know no other...*

"Our Father, who art in Heaven..."

The prayer completed, Thurkill rose to his feet, cuffing his eyes with his sleeve. He had to put the sadness behind him, though, as they were still some distance from safety. They still need to reach Lundenburh to warn Edgar before it was too late.

"Eahlmund, fetch the horses. Leofric, Leofgar, wrap Eopric in his cloak and lay him across his horse. Be sure to tie him on securely. We will take him back for burial."

ELEVEN

"You dare return empty-handed? Did I not tell you I wanted him brought back to me alive?"

The hapless knight recoiled as Robert FitzGilbert punctuated every other word with a blow from his gloved fist. He was the sole survivor from the ambush, considering it his duty to report back to his lord. It was a decision he was already regretting.

"Tell me again, de Lacey, how ten heavily-armed and well-trained knights allowed themselves to be bested by a handful of peasants."

With blood now streaming from his cut lip, the miserable man allowed the words spew forth. "They led us deep into the forest, into a narrow gully where the devils were waiting for us in ambush. Amery managed to kill one before he himself was killed, but everyone else died without landing a blow, such was the skill of their trap. I only escaped because of Amery's brave sacrifice."

"I care nothing for Amery, you or any of the other fools who perished there."

FitzGilbert's fury was so fierce that flecks of spittle sprayed from his mouth, coating de Lacey's face with a fine sheen of saliva. He knew better than to react or attempt to wipe it away, though. He dare not antagonise his lord yet further.

"I sent you to do a simple job, to bring back my brother's killer to me that I might have my vengeance. My mother could have accomplished it with ease. And yet it proved too much for you. It would appear that I sent boys in place of men."

FitzGilbert turned away towards the fire where he stood, brooding in front of the flames for a few moments. Then – without warning – he turned, drew his dagger and strode back to the soldier, plunging the blade deep into his gut. So sudden and unexpected was the attack that de Lacey had no time to defend himself. He stood there helpless, held upright by FitzGilbert's hand which gripped his throat, as his life ebbed away into the matted rushes on the floor of the hall.

A hush fell across the room; no one moved or said a word. Eventually, Duke William stood up from where he had been lounging in Wigod's chair and yawned. "Robert, could I ask you to refrain from killing any more of my soldiers? You've already cost me nine in your hare-brained scheme and now this? I indulged you in this matter as a favour to your father who served me well in my youth, but there are limits and you would do well not to push me beyond them. Now, with your permission of course, might we finally put this matter behind us and continue with the more pressing business of taking the throne of England?"

"But, Lord, the Saxon cur still lives, and I cannot rest while that remains so."

"Yes, he lives and doubtless he does so in Lundenburh even as we speak. You had your chance and you failed and that is an end to it. If it was that important to you, perhaps you should have gone yourself - that way you'd at least have no one else to blame. Instead you have cost me ten good men - including this poor fellow here whose guts are even now making a mess of Wigod's floor."

Robert's eyes burned with anger, his cheeks reddening with a mix of embarrassment and anger but he chose to challenge the Duke no further. Not for the time being at least. "As you wish, Lord."

"I do wish. So, let that be an end to it. Once we have secured Lundenburh and with it the throne, then I care not what you do. Until then you are under my orders and will do my bidding. Clear?"

When FitzGilbert nodded, the Duke continued. "Now that little distraction is dealt with, perhaps we might resume our march on the city?"

"What are your orders, Lord?"

"I see no reason to part company with our current strategy. The more fear and misery we create, the more likely it will be that Edgar will seek terms. The most powerful man in the English church has already come over to our cause and today, emissaries from Edward's wife, the former Queen Edith, have surrendered Wintancaester and its royal treasury to us. The tide is turning for sure, we just need to apply a little more encouragement to finish the job.

"I will split the army into two. I will lead the greater part north and then eastwards, whereas my brother, Robert of Mortain, will take the rest along the river. Between us, we shall cut a swathe through this land, pillaging and burning as we go. With luck, we will force Edgar's hand."

"What if he comes out to fight, Lord?"

William grabbed a goblet from the table in front of him, draining its contents in one draught, before replying. "Then we shall destroy him, like we did his predecessor. Our losses have been replenished twice over and we have nothing to fear. If he has any sense, though, he will seek peace and spare his people further suffering."

TWELVE

Dusk was falling at the end of the next day when the first buildings on the outskirts of Suthweca came into view. Four exhausted, emotional riders led a fifth horse across which lay a body closely wrapped in a pair of torn and bloody cloaks. It made for a pitiful sight. As they trudged along the narrow road, men and women paused to bow their heads in respect, even though they knew them not.

They made their way over the bridge, eager to reach the king's hall before the gates were locked for the night. With luck, Thurkill thought, his business with Edgar would be finished promptly so that he could seek out Hild before too long. He ached to see her, to take comfort in her arms. The pain of Eopric's death hung over him like a forbidding black cloud, heavy with rain.

He left the brothers just north of the bridge, with instructions to find a priest to make arrangements for the lad's burial. Meanwhile, he and Eahlmund made their way west. There was no danger of them losing their way among the narrow, criss-crossing streets as the abbey's tower rose to a great height. It was said it could be seen wherever you stood within the city.

For the first time since the ambush, Eahlmund managed a smile. He had never been inside a royal hall, let alone met a king, and he was excited for the experience.

"Just try not to say anything. Only speaking when you're spoken to was one of the first things my father told me when I accompanied him to Harold's hall. I know it will be difficult for you – against your nature even – but try not to draw attention to yourself for once."

Eahlmund grinned foolishly but said nothing, leaving Thurkill even more worried than he had been before. His head still ached from the beating he had received and waves of nausea washed over him from time to time. He had hoped it would have faded by now as he felt he would need his wits about him in front of Edgar's court.

As soon as they were ushered into Edgar's presence, however, Thurkill knew that something was amiss. The atmosphere was as thick as the smoke-filled air. Gone was the gaiety, the laughter, the cheer. All around men stood in small groups, talking quietly behind their hands. Several turned to watch him as he walked, making him feel more and more self-conscious.

To his relief, he spotted a familiar face standing with a small group close to the left wall. Steering Eahlmund gently but firmly by the arm, he greeted Aelfric warmly, genuinely pleased to see the old warrior.

"Well met, Lord. What news can you tell me?"

Aelfric's response was muted at best. "Greetings, Thurkill. I was going to ask you and your friend here the same, but, by God, what has happened to your face? You look like you've taken on the whole Norman army on your own. And by the smell of you, I'd say you've ridden hard to get here, too. What you have to say must be of some import."

"It is, Lord. Eahlmund and I come from Warengeforte where we watched Duke William and his whole army cross the Thames at the invitation of the turncoat Wigod, lord of that town."

Aelfric snorted. "I fear this may be old news, my lad. Word has already come in from the shires to the north of the river; the Normans are on their way. Still," he shrugged, "I am glad to see you and your man safe and well all the same."

"I wish I could say that for all those who went with me." In response to Aelfric's quizzical look, Thurkill continued. "I lost a good man two days' ride to the south and west of here."

"How so?"

"In Warengeforte, I saw the brother of the man I killed after Senlac. He come to these shores to seek vengeance against me. My identity became known to him and he sent men to take me. With God's help, we managed to deal with them, but not before they had killed one of my men; a young lad by the name of Eopric."

Aelfric clapped his bear's paw of a hand on the younger man's shoulder. "I'm heartily sorry for your loss, Thurkill. These things are never easy. I fear there may yet be many more brave warriors who will give their lives in defence of Edgar and this kingdom before we are done."

A silence fell between them, each man alone with his thoughts. True to his word, Eahlmund said nothing, though Thurkill could sense him shifting from foot to foot, craning his neck to see all that went on in the hall, especially up on the dais where Edgar was deep in conversation with a number of lords, among whom Thurkill recognised Archbishop Ealdred of York but few, if any, others.

"Tell me, Lord, what is the king's mood? Has the fyrd been mustered? When do we march out to fight the Norman scum?"

Before answering, Aelfric looked around him as if to see who was in earshot. Then, leaning in close, he whispered. "All is not well, lad. Day after day, reports arrive of atrocities inflicted upon the people by the Normans. There are many now who begin to say that it might be better to submit than risk destruction. There seems to be little confidence in our new king; few believe he can lead us to victory. On top of which, we hear daily that Norman boats arrive at the coast, growing his numbers while ours dwindle."

"What do you mean, 'dwindle'? Surely the fyrd has mustered? We need to attack now before their strength increases yet further."

"I'm with you, Thurkill, you know that. God knows it is the only option if we are to save the kingdom from the Norman whoresons, but there are too many others who do not share our view."

"Such as? Who are these craven scum?"

Aelfric lowered his voice still further, making it hard for Thurkill to hear over the background noise. "Earls Eadwine and Morcar for two."

"What?" Thurkill's outburst caused a few heads to turn, making the colour flush to his cheeks. He continued more quietly. "I wondered why they were not here. Where are they?"

"They've gone north, taking their men with them. It's a grievous blow as their warriors accounted for nigh on half our numbers. Without them, I fear all hope is lost."

"Bastards!" He hissed. "Why did they leave?"

"It's not known for certain, they made no announcement. They left under cover of night; went north of the city to where their men were camped were gone by dawn. If you ask me, though, I'd agree with your earlier assessment. They have no stomach for the fight; no intention of risking all on a single throw of a die."

"They have no master but themselves. They disobeyed Harold's orders at Eoforwic and were soundly beaten for their pains. And they made little effort to reach Lundenburh in time for the battle against William. On its own, that may have cost the king his life. And now this." Once more he found his voice had risen in his anger, but this time he had attracted the attention of the king.

"You there. Come forward and share your news. What can you tell me of William's movements?"

Abashed, Thurkill walked into the centre of the hall, where he dropped to one knee before Edgar.

"Your pardon, Lord King. We are returned from Warengeforte where Duke William has crossed the Thames with his whole army. I am sorry to tell you that he was aided in this endeavour by Lord Wigod."

Bishop Ealdred nodded. "So, it is true what we have heard? Wigod never even tried to stop them?"

"Quite the opposite, Lord. He invited the Normans into the town and freely replenished their supplies from his own stores."

"I always had my doubts about that man, but I never thought he would betray his country so readily. Was he so desperate to save his own skin that he would openly side with the enemy?"

"There is more to tell, Lord. Shortly before I left, Bishop Stigand arrived. And though I did not see it with my own eyes, I am told he has sworn fealty to the Duke."

"By God I will have his hide for this! Did he not stand in this very hall and acclaim me king? It did not take him long to change course; no longer than the time it takes the wind to change from east to west. I will see him strung up in the market place and have ravens peck at his eyes while he yet lives."

Ealdred offered a more conciliatory tone, perhaps eager to steer the conversation away from the threat of committing atrocities on the head of the English church. "I wonder what inducements Duke William laid before him? It is no secret Stigand is a lover of coin, so I can only assume he has been promised great wealth for his allegiance. William will be thinking ahead - he knows he needs at least one of us to preside over his coronation were it to come to that. William must have been planning this for some time."

Thurkill was growing impatient. A question had been gnawing away at him since he had entered the hall. In the end, it got the better of him; he cared not what punishment might be forthcoming.

"But will we do now, Lord? Duke William could be here within a few days. Give the order to send the army out to face him. Every moment we delay strengthens his hand and weakens ours."

Edgar's expression showed how rash he'd been. "Don't you think I know that? I may be young but I do not need lessons from a jumped-up country boy such as you. It is only respect for your father's name that stops me from sending you packing with my boot up your arse."

Suitably cowed, Thurkill bowed his head, before Aelfric spoke up to spare his blushes. "Lord, I pray you pardon young Thurkill's intemperance. He merely wishes to help you rid the country of the Norman invader. Youthful enthusiasm gets the better of him, is all."

Edgar grunted, though Thurkill could not tell whether his apology had been accepted or not.

"But the boy's point still stands, Lord. Whither now for us, especially now we are shorn of the support of the Lords Eadwine and Morcar?"

Edgar visibly flinched as if Aelfric had landed a punch on him. "I'll thank you not to mention those bastards in my presence again, Aelfric."

"Your pardon, Lord, but the fact remains; their loss has hit our cause hard."

"Lord King, I think it is time we face facts. The race is run and I fear we must accept we have been found wanting. I urge you to seek terms for the sake of your people."

Thurkill did not recognise the new speaker. He was the only man in the hall, other than the king, who was seated; the result of wounds that had presumably been sustained at Senlac. He wore no tunic, but instead his torso was tightly wrapped in thick linen bandages which were, nevertheless, stained red where the blood still oozed. To keep the cold at bay, he wore a heavy cloak around his shoulders, over which several animal pelts were also draped. His face was pale and he grimaced as he spoke, as though every word caused him physical pain. Thurkill was amazed that the man yet clung to life; a testament to an iron will that few men possessed.

Edgar went to his side. "Noble Aesgar, do not exert yourself. You have already given much in the service of your country. You must rest so that you may recover to serve me once more."

"You are gracious, Lord, but my time has gone. And though it pains me to say, I fear yours may also have passed before it could begin. With the northern earls, we had a chance to defeat William but now what would we have? Half their numbers? Two thirds at best? Even on ground of our choosing, we would be overwhelmed by their horse and archers. I saw it at Senlac to my cost, and there we were more evenly matched. I beg you to think of your soldiers and their folk at home. Do not commit them to a fight they cannot win."

So this, Thurkill realised, must be Aesgar the Staller, the man to whom Edgar had entrusted the defence of Lundenburh. It was said he had taken a spear to the belly during the final moments of the battle around Harold's Wyvern battle standard.

Thurkill burned with indignation at Aesgar' words. He would never dare call Aesgar a coward - the man had proved himself beyond doubt, that much was apparent to all - but that did not stop his feelings of rage and frustration. Surely things were not as dire as the great man painted? If it were, though, it would be no one's fault but Eadwine and Morcar. He cursed their names under his breath, hoping that he might one day have the chance to confront them for their perfidy.

Edgar was speaking once more. "I thank you for your words, Lord Aesgar, and do consider them most closely, for they are freely given and honestly intentioned. But what sort of king would I be were I to surrender so meekly? Do the people not depend on me to defend them to the death?"

"They do, Lord, but I fear we face a foe whose means and resources outweigh ours. Your people also depend on your for their safety. To endure another defeat more damaging than Senlac could not be countenanced before God, if we have no hope of victory"

As always, Archbishop Ealdred's honeyed words sought to soothe the king's mood. "Continued resistance would only lead to more bloodshed and much loss of life; lives which could be spared if a peace could be agreed now. We have all heard the reports of wanton destruction that have accompanied William's march across the land, and it is plain to me that he will not cease in his efforts until he is victorious."

Thurkill could see the indecision that tore at the king's soul. The weight of history told him that he must emulate his ancestors and fight. Had not his grandfather, the mighty Edmund of the iron sides, fought back against the Dane, Cnut, giving his life in that cause? How would he stand before his ancestor in the afterlife if he did not fight for his country?

But then, were he to do so, the odds were better than even that they would be slaughtered to a man. Could he knowingly commit his men - the farmers, blacksmiths, farriers, coopers and all manner of other tradesmen - to what amounted to almost certain death? Thurkill gave thanks it was not his decision to make. His gut told him that if it were, he would choose to fight. He couldn't bear the thought of kneeling before a foreign oppressor.

He also knew that Edgar had not grown up expecting one day to be king. He had been born hundreds of miles away in a land where few outside the ruling families would have even heard of England. He had been brought back - along with his father, Edward – to play their part in the game of chance that was the English throne. His father's sudden death and Harold's defeat had conspired to lead him to this day where he, a boy of fourteen - or was he now fifteen? - was being asked to make a decision on which hung the fate of hundreds if not thousands of his people.

For what seemed an age, Edgar paced up and down the dais under the watchful eye of his champion - the almost-mute Ladislav. Finally, he came to a halt. Decision made, the look on his face was grim but resolute.

"Ealdred, summon the emissaries. I would send word to Duke William that I would have peace between us."

"Lord, for clarity…"

"Yes, yes," he was almost impatient now, perhaps eager to be done with it all. "I mean that I will place myself and my people in his care."

THIRTEEN

On his way back to their lodgings, Thurkill purchased bread, meat and several wine skins to share with Hild and the others as a way of commemorating Eopric's passing. It was while they were drinking to the boy's memory that Thurkill also shared the news that Edgar had decided to submit to William. It was all over, he said; their struggle, Eopric's death, it had all been in vain.

"But we held them off at Suthweca, surely we can do so again?"

"Would only that it were so, Leofric. Now their whole strength is north of the river and approaching the city across the flat lands of Berkshire, that makes for a different game altogether. What's more they are reinforced with fresh men from their homeland while our numbers fall through betrayal and cowardice. I fear we have no choice as much as it riles me.

"What's more, many have already followed Stigand's lead. Seeing such an important man submit to William has given others the courage to do likewise - as if the actions of that coin-obsessed worm are any sort of model to follow. Good Saxon men are going over to William like flies to a dead pig. And it can only get worse. Without the northern earls..."

"Bastards..." Eahlmund hissed angrily into his cup.

"Without the northern earls, we no longer have the strength to stop the Normans. There is no option but to respect our king's decision."

Sometime later, when the two of them were snuggled under their woollen covers, Hild asked the question that had long been nagging at the back of his mind. "But what next for us all? What sort of treatment can we expect from this Duke William?"

Thurkill shrugged, yawning sleepily. "I cannot say, my love. But I do believe that it can suit no one if he were to be hell bent on destruction and chaos. My father always used to tell me that England is the richest kingdom in all Christendom. He will want that wealth for himself and will not want to ruin her by excessive deprivations."

"Yes, but what does that mean for us?"

"I don't know, Hild, but I think it would be wise for us to leave the city for a while, if not for good."

Though he did not wish to alarm her unnecessarily, he could not shake off the image of FitzGilbert's snarling face and the knowledge that he was now one step closer to his goal.

Once William was crowned king, what would stop him from avenging his brother? As long as FitzGilbert lived, he would have to keep one eye open the whole time. Could he really subject Hild to a life such as this? It hardly seemed fair. At the same time, he feared to discuss it with her in case she chose to abandon him for the risk he posed to her safety. What sensible woman would want to live in fear the whole time? He knew he was no coward, but why run towards danger if there was no need? Where could they go that was beyond his reach?

"Perhaps we should take Aelfric's offer and go north to his lands?"

"You would do that?" The look of hope in Hild's eyes settled things in his mind.

"Why not? It's a few days' journey north of here so hopefully would be far enough away from trouble for the time being. I'd have to discuss it with Eahlmund and the others; give them the choice whether to continue to follow me or not, but I think they would agree."

Hild pressed her body against his, burying her head in his shoulder. "I was so worried while you were away, afraid I might never see you again. But this way, we can put such things behind us and have a life together once more. We can ask Aelfric for a small plot of land, enough for us and the rest of your boys. Together we can build our homes and farm the land. We can find a blacksmith and other tradesmen we might need and before long we'll have our own little village; the perfect place for our children to grow up."

She drew back so that she could look at him the way she did with her head tilted to one side, a smile that turned up just the one corner of her mouth and eyes that twinkled with humour and mischief in equal measure. It was one of the first things

Thurkill had loved about her and it melted his heart every time. Eagerly he hugged her back just as fiercely until she squealed in mock agony to be released. Laughing with her, he was glad to put thoughts of FitzGilbert and the Normans to the back of his mind, if only for a short while.

***

Thurkill awoke the next day with a foul head and a mood that was little better, neither of which were helped by the sharp sunlight that streamed through the window and directly into his eyes. He hadn't realised how drunk he was, fooled perhaps by the happiness he had felt with Hild by his side. Her idyllic view of the world with their little village and innumerable brats running around his ankles, was something he dearly wanted - for her as much as for himself - but, in the cold light of day, he knew there were many hurdles to cross before it could become a reality.

The first of which, he knew, was the reason for his foul mood; the thought of bending the knee to William. Emissaries had been sent to carry Edgar's offer to the Duke's camp and they were expected back with a day or two. At that point, Edgar – together with those great lords who still stood with him – would have to present himself at the appointed place to swear fealty.

This would be humiliating enough but was made immeasurably worse because Aelfric had ordered him to accompany the royal escort. He could not refuse as Aelfric was, to all intents and purposes, his lord now and - besides which - his respect and love for the old warrior was such that he would not willingly do anything to anger him.

To clear his mind, Thurkill dunked his head in the bowl of water that stood on the sideboard on the far side of the room. It was freezing, causing his whole body to shiver as the drips cascaded from this face and hair down his chest and back. It did the job, though, as he felt marginally more awake afterwards. He was just pulling on his boots when he heard shouting from the street below, followed by screams and the sound of running feet. Sticking his still damp and dishevelled head out of the window, Thurkill tried to find news, though his worst fears and suspicions were already aroused.

"Hie! What's happening? Is it the Normans?" It took three attempts before he managed to stop any of the panicked townspeople long enough to answer him.

"Run, you fool! The Normans are at the north gate." The wretch could not be made to wait any longer, no matter what curses Thurkill rained down on his fleeing back. His hangover forgotten, Thurkill lurched back into the room, gathering up his axe and shield as he did so.

"Hild, wait for me here. Bar the door and do not move from this place - promise me." Reassured by her nodded acceptance, he turned to the others. "Grab your things and follow me. I don't care if Edgar does plan to submit, he has not done so yet and so we will defend our city - with our lives if necessary. Come on!"

Outside, the narrow street was filled with people milling about in all directions, unsure where the threat came from. Knowing no more than what the fellow had told him, Thurkill headed off north and west as much as he could. He hoped the others would stay with him as he pushed and jostled his way through panicked throng coming in the opposite direction. He set a punishing pace, barging past any that failed to get out of his way in time, until they emerged onto a wider thoroughfare; the main route that led to the great gate to the north of the king's Westminster hall. At last he began to feel he was heading in the right direction as the numbers of townspeople were now outweighed by warriors, all hurtling as fast as they could towards the perceived danger.

As he ran, Thurkill prayed that the whole Norman army was not waiting for them as there seemed to be pitifully few warriors running to meet them. Unless there were thousands already there, it promised to be a slaughter from which few would escape. The shouting and sound of metal clashing against metal and wood was growing louder with each pace. This was no false alarm at least.

Breaking through the final group of fleeing citizens, Thurkill skidded to a halt. His five warriors were still at his side, even young Copsig who had flat out refused to stay behind this time. With Eopric gone, Thurkill was grateful for the extra shield so he had not argued the point for long.

He took in the scene before him; it did not look good. Several Normans had managed to breach the gate and more were pouring into the streets with every passing moment. He could not reckon the total number, but this was clearly no mere raiding party. They surely would not have risked pressing home their attack so deeply otherwise.

As for the Saxons, they were disorganised and under pressure. Step by step they were being pushed back by the ever-increasing numbers coming through the gate. If something were not done soon, they could be overrun, leaving the rest of the city at the mercy of the marauding knights. All around him, small groups of warriors stared in confusion, unsure where to go for the best. It was not until Eahlmund spoke, that Thurkill realised what he must do.

"Lord, what would you have us do? It's a massacre up there."

Thurkill realised there was no one else there ready to lead. Only him. He prayed that his youthfulness did not hinder his ability to sway others to his command.

"Form the shieldwall, Eahlmund. We'll round up others as we go. We have to push them back through the gate and have it closed; else all is lost."

Decision made, they began to put the plan into action. He had not really considered what it was to lead a large group of men before, thinking it was something that only older, more experienced men did and not something that should concern him. But whether it was five men or fifty, he supposed it made little difference. As long as they were close enough to hear his orders, it should be within his grasp.

Steadily and purposefully, the six of them trotted forward, shields overlapping and weapons held at the ready. As they went, Thurkill yelled at all those within earshot to join. At first, many just stood there, non-plussed, as if paralysed without a lord they recognised to follow, but soon enough the message began to sink home. Warriors began to attach themselves to either end of the line while still more began to form a second rank. In twos and threes at first, and then in greater and greater numbers. After thirty or so paces there were well over fifty of them in two even lines.

To help maintain their tight formation, Thurkill had them shouting "Ut" on every other step, combined with banging their spear hafts or sword hilts against their shields in unison.

It looked and sounded impressive enough to Thurkill, but would it be enough to hold back the Normans? They were barely twenty paces away now, hammering away at the steadily crumbling line of defenders. Dead Saxons lay all around; many more wounded men were trying to crawl or drag themselves away from the killing ground. So far, the defenders had managed to contain the enemy within a short radius of the gate, but it was plain they could not hold out much longer. It was going to be close as to whether they reached them before they broke.

As if to confirm his fears, the two men holding the centre of the line fell, simultaneously cut down by vicious sword cuts from above. Immediately, the Normans began to surge forward into the gap. It was now or never; the city's survival hung by a thread. They had to throw caution to the wind.

"Charge!" Trusting to fate and hoping that his companions would follow his lead, Thurkill broke into a run, closing the gap to the enemy as quickly as he could. Moments before impact, he lifted his shield and bent his shoulder against it to add extra weight. All along his little shieldwall, men followed his example. It was a tried and trusted technique that had worked countless times over the ages and it did not let them down now. The impact of sixty or so men all hitting the line at the same time was as sudden as it was immediate. Everywhere, horses reared up, unable to withstand the pressure coming from below. Man after man tumbled to the hard ground, as their mounts reared in fright.

"Ut, Ut, Ut". With every roar, Thurkill pushed another step forward, yelling at those on each side to do likewise. The rhythmic chanting of the growing number of Saxon warriors was pounding in his ears, half scaring him to death - so God alone knew what it must be like for the enemy. At first the going was tough but steady - the resistance coming from the enemy soldiers fierce and unflinching. But soon the unity and strength of the defenders began to reap its rewards.

And all this time, Thurkill made no attempt to use his axe. There was no need; not only was it almost impossible to reach any exposed flesh, but the shieldwall on its own was having the desired effect. Men were falling to the ground and being trampled under hoof or foot. Here and there a warrior armed with a spear managed to skewer an unfortunate horseman in the face, neck or groin, but beyond that, there was little need to try to kill the enemy. It was tiring work though. His shoulders ached where they bore the brunt of the pressure against his shield while his leg muscles screamed at the effort of holding fast his position. Despite the chill in the air, beads of sweat poured from his forehead, stinging his eyes until he blinked them away.

By his side, Thurkill could see that Copsig was terrified. To his credit, the lad was giving his all, but this was his first taste of battle and the fear was etched on his face for all to see. Thurkill found himself thinking back to his first time at Stamford - a few short weeks ago - how his bowels had turned to liquid and he had almost shat himself when the blood fest began. It was nothing less than a horrible, deeply shocking experience that he would not wish on anyone. He knew it was only the presence of familiar faces on either side of him that kept Copsig steady; the fear of letting his closest companions down was worse than the fear of the enemy. He would never be able to face his friends again for shame if he turned and ran. It was better to die in the thick of the fighting than to live as a coward. Catching his eye, Thurkill gave him what he hoped was an encouraging nod. "Hold on, lad," he grunted through gritted teeth. "They'll not stand for much longer, I'm sure of it."

The horsemen broke without warning. One moment there were pressing hard against the immovable wall of shields and the next there was nothing but empty space. One order, shouted loud enough to carry across the breadth of the conflict, and the knights wheeled their mounts away from the melee and fled.

Spent, Thurkill leaned on the edge of his shield, his chest heaving with the effort. "Quick! Shut and bar the gates," he wheezed. "Do not let the whoresons back in."

As men rushed to do his bidding, others worked their way

across the ground to complete the grisly task of finishing any that yet lived. There was to be no mercy; they were skewered or gutted where they lay despite their outstretched arms and begging eyes. Others looked to the Saxon wounded and began to treat those who stood a chance of recovery as well as they could.

By his side, the sound of retching made him turn; with the skirmish over, Copsig was reacting to the experience in the only way he could. Smiling, Thurkill laid a comforting hand on his shoulder, much as he remembered his father doing to him after his first fight. "You acquitted yourself well, Copsig. You should take pride in that. Being afraid carries no shame and any man who tells you otherwise is either a fool or a liar. Trust me when I say, though, it will become easier. The first time is always the worst."

Copsig spat the last remnants of bile onto the ground before wiping his mouth with the back of his hand. Grinning sheepishly, he thanked Thurkill. "It was an honour to stand with you today, Lord. I am pleased to have not let you down."

"There was never any danger of that, lad. I knew you would do your duty well. I am only sorry that your first taste of battle had to be a defeat."

"Defeat, Lord? Did we not send them packing with their tails between their legs?"

"Aye, they may have retreated but they had no need to stay. This was just another probe to let us see their strength. Look around you; are there not many more of our slain than theirs? I'd reckon there are five or six dead Saxons for every Norman. Even though Edgar intends to submit, we cannot afford to carry such losses."

Copsig's shoulders slumped. *Damn me for my insensitivity,* Thurkill rebuked himself. *I did not need to be quite so negative.* Slapping the poor lad on the back, he tried to repair the damage. "Still, all that is for others to worry about. We need to find a tavern to drink to the first step in your career as a mighty warrior. The time will come when friend and foe alike will hear the name, Copsig Normans'-bane, and quake in their boots."

"With laughter more than fear though." Eahlmund roared at

his own joke, punching Copsig hard on his arm for good measure. "Come on, lad, forget Thurkill and his miserable bellyaching; let's go find ale and women, and hopefully vast amounts of both."

***

Thurkill left them to it after the first two cups, though he threw them a handful of coins with which to avail themselves of several more. He would have loved to stay, to bury his head in ale to wash away the emotions of battle, but he had other, more pressing, matters to attend to – not least of which was to make sure Hild was safe and not worrying for his welfare. With more than a little regret he left his five companions at a tavern not far from their lodgings with orders not to make Copsig too ill. As well as it being his first taste of conflict, his youthful looks suggested that he might also be new to the idea of excessive drinking. Thurkill chuckled as he imagined what the rest of the lads had in store for him; he doubted the poor boy would be up before sunrise at any rate.

Hild greeted him at the door to their lodgings, relief apparent in her eyes. "Thank God you're alive. All I've heard since you ran off is people screaming, running past the window, yelling that the Normans are in the city and slaughtering everyone. I didn't know what to do for the best; whether I should stay put and wait for you, or run with the rest of them."

Thurkill took her in his arms and hugged her hard, so hard that she grunted as the wind was forced from her lungs. Releasing her, he ran a hand through her hair, pushing it back from her face, to better take in her beauty. In the thick of the fighting, he'd not had time to think of his own safety or of Hild being left alone to fend for herself without him, but her words brought home to him just how close he had been to death. Kissing her forehead, he sought to reassure her and - if truth be told - himself.

"It's true the bastards managed to breach the north gate, but we arrived in time to put a stop to them. We pushed them back through the gate and barred it behind them. Young Copsig did well, too, for his first time."

Hild smiled for she had genuine affection for the lad. "Where is he now? I would offer my congratulations."

"It may be a while before you see him and, when you do, his head will be sore. Eahlmund and the others have taken him off to drink to his coming of age. I fear they mean to leave him with a woman too."

Hild stared open-mouthed in outrage. "He's only just sixteen is he not?"

"Just two years younger than me, you'll find. Besides, in these days, he may as well enjoy himself while he can as who knows what tomorrow may bring?"

Rather than dwell on such unsavoury matters, Hild changed the subject. "How did the Normans manage to get in? And why are they attacking when you tell me that Edgar is going to surrender anyway?"

"I can't say for sure; I can only assume that they took the gate wardens by surprise. Perhaps those men had also heard that Edgar planned to submit and assumed there was no danger of attack. But it would appear that no one has yet told the Normans, or perhaps they wanted to send a message to make sure that the king does not change his mind."

"Is that likely?"

"I'd say not, especially not now. I'm afraid the game's up, Hild. We're cooped up in Lundenburh and what strength we do have is pitifully small; far too small to have a chance of stopping Duke William and his army of Norman sheep dung. As much as it pains me to say it, we must prepare ourselves for life under these foreign bastards."

FOURTEEN

It was still dark when Thurkill pushed open the door to Edgar's hall. A sharp frost carpeted the ground and it was perishingly cold, so he was overjoyed to find that a well-stoked fire was already burning in the central hearth. Making for it, he elbowed himself a space amongst the others who had already gathered there. He stood with his hands stuffed under his armpits and stamping his feet to force warmth back into his extremities. Sure enough, his hands and feet soon began to tingle, painfully at first, as sensation slowly came back to them.

"Well met, Thurkill my lad. I wish it were under happier circumstances though."

Despite his poor humour, Thurkill smiled as Aelfric pushed his way in close to him, shooing the previous occupant to one side. Whatever his mood, Thurkill always felt lifted in the older man's presence. Even the prospect of kneeling before Duke William seemed less bad than it had when he had woken that morning.

"Well met, Lord. We can but smile and hope the day goes without incident."

Thurkill stifled a yawn. He had been up half the night polishing his helmet, mail shirt, belt buckles and every other bit of metal, great and small, until they shone. Hild had stayed up with him, sponging the dirt from his clothes and mending the little tears and blemishes as best she could. If he had to prostrate himself before his enemy, he would do so with pride and bearing.

He wondered if FitzGilbert would be there. It seemed a strong possibility. Although, Duke William had promised a truce for the duration of the assembly on pain of death, it might not be enough to stop a sly knife between the ribs before or after. He was sure FitzGilbert would not shrink from such a perfidious act should the chance present itself. He would have to be on his guard at all times and not stray too far from Aelfric's side. The old man's protection and the strength of his retinue should be enough, he hoped.

"What do you know of this place where we are to meet?"

"Beorhthanstaed? It's a small place set amidst a birch wood to the north west; about two to three hundred souls, so I am told. I know of no reason why William has chosen this site other than it's close to the city and sited on a river. As good a place as any for his army to set up camp, I suppose."

Thurkill snorted, unimpressed. "Explains the early start, I suppose. If we set off now, we should be there before the sun goes down."

***

Dusk was, indeed, falling as they arrived at the town. The sun had shone brightly all day, causing the frost and ice to sparkle on the trees like so many spear points; spears which, Thurkill thought ironically, he would have dearly loved to have with them now. They should be marching to battle, to bring death to the Normans, not bowing meekly before their lord, offering him the crown.

All the same, their party numbered over two hundred men; enough to show the Normans they were not afraid or humbled, but a paltry number considering the forces that King Harold had called on just two short months before.

They were met a mile from the town by a group of horsemen sent to escort them to the camp. Thurkill could not help but admire the knights; each man wore a matching dark blue cloak that hung down below his knees and was equipped with helmet, long kite-shaped shield, full length mailshirt, sword and spear. In unison, they wheeled around the Saxon delegation, forming up in two equal columns on either side of them. It was a practised manoeuvre that was executed to perfection. It spoke to their exceptional horsemanship; not a single word had been spoken, no command given, just absolute faith in each other's ability to be in the right place. *How did we think we could beat these people?* Thurkill wondered. *These men have been schooled for war since before they could walk, whereas we fight with farmers, blacksmiths and fishermen.*

There were further surprises in store when they reached the settlement. Apart from the sheer size of the Norman camp, with tents stretching as far as the eye could see in all directions, hundreds of men were scurrying around shifting vast piles of earth from the ground and piling them into a huge defensive earthwork that ringed an area to the north east of the town. In those places where the earthwork was already the height of a man, other soldiers were busy sinking long wooden posts into the soil and lashing them to each other to form a solid, impenetrable palisade.

Eahlmund spat to one side. "I see they waste no time making themselves at home. Bastards."

Aelfric, riding just in front of them, turned in his saddle. "They're building a castle, lad. No doubt the first of many we shall see in our lands. I hear Normandy is riddled with them. This is the start of their subjugation of our land. Soon they will have them all over the place, each one garrisoned with soldiers. Of course, they will tell us they're there to keep the peace but I fear that just means putting us Saxons in our place."

Eahlmund said nothing, but spat once more; a huge gobbet of phlegm passing inches from one of their escorts, who scowled at the Saxon no doubt yearning to curse him – or worse – but under strict orders to cause no trouble ahead of the meeting.

They halted at the edge of the construction site. Edgar, along with Archbishop Ealdred, Aelfric and the other lords, were then ushered through what would doubtless eventually become the gateway to the castle. As he walked, marvelling at the scale of the enterprise, Thurkill saw it for what it was: a thinly veiled attempt to strike awe into the minds of the hall-dwelling Saxons.

Edgar did not speak as he walked. He held his head high, looking neither left or right as if determined not to appear cowed in the presence of his conqueror.

They strode on towards a huge tent, much larger than all the others, which had been erected in the middle of the enclosure, presumably to protect the Duke from the worst of the winter weather. The flaps on either side had been pinned back so that Thurkill could see within, despite the gathering gloom. The interior was illuminated by several huge candles which cast their light on to an ornately carved wooden chair that had been set in the middle. On this chair, wrapped in furs, was the Duke, his dark hair newly cropped close to his skull. He was bareheaded but for a narrow gold band, the symbol of his ducal rank.

As Edgar with his dozen or so companions – Thurkill included – ducked under the low entrance, William made no effort to rise, emphasising his authority over his visitors. As he watched, Thurkill saw fury in his features and grew afraid. *My God, he's angry with us for keeping him waiting this long for the throne.*

But then, Thurkill's blood froze. He was grateful for the shadows within the tent so that none might see the colour had drained from his face. There, just behind and to the right of William, stood FitzGilbert; his features - so similar to his dead brother - unmistakeable. In that same moment, the Norman also caught sight of Thurkill and all hell broke loose.

So many things happened at once that it was almost impossible to piece together. Apparently oblivious to his surroundings, FitzGilbert lunged forward, drawing his knife as he came. Immediately, Ladislav, the mountainous bodyguard who rarely left the king's side, stepped into his path, no doubt fearing an attempt on Edgar's life. He had no weapon – all blades having been surrendered already – so in one swift movement, he drove his gloved fist with every ounce of his upper body strength into the Norman's face. No man could have withstood such a blow and FitzGilbert found himself sprawled on the ground, his right eye already puffing up and blood streaming from his nose.

And while all this was going on, William finally rose to his feet. "FitzGilbert! Hold, damn you!"

The whole tent was in uproar as men on both sides shouted the odds at each other. Those with knives had them drawn ready to defend or attack. For a moment, it seemed as though a great slaughter would ensue until William took control of the situation, his booming voice dripping with menacing authority.

"Hold! Hold I say. There'll be no killing here today; I have given my word that the safety of our guests is guaranteed and I will not have any of you honourless scum prove me liar."

Turning to the still sitting FitzGilbert, he continued. "Get out of my sight, now. Rest assured, though, we will have words about this later."

Groggily, the knight rose to his feet, still staring at Thurkill, his eyes like daggers. "But, Lord, this is the worthless pig who murdered my brother. I have sworn vengeance on him. I cannot allow my oath to go unfulfilled."

"I don't care if he is King Solomon himself, while you are in my presence, you will do whatever I tell you; oath be damned. If I command you to stick that knife in your own gut, you will do it or I will find someone else who will. Now get out before I grow yet more weary with you."

Sulkily, FitzGilbert forced his way through the throng, pushing people out of his way without a care.

With order restored once more, the duke resumed his seat. "Lords, allow me to apologise for this intolerable incident. I had made it clear you were all under my protection while you were in my camp and FitzGilbert will be punished for his transgression. There will be no repeat. Though if I were you," the duke fixed Thurkill with a look that burned into his soul, "I would stay out of his way. He has taken a dislike to you which rules his emotions to the exclusion of all else. In my presence you will be safe but I cannot vouch for him when I am not around to hold him in check. It was unwise of you to come here."

"Lord," Aelfric stepped forward, bristling with indignation. "Thurkill is my sworn man and as his lord, I am honour bound to protect him. Your FitzGilbert will do well to remember that if he harms my man in any way, I will seek redress accordingly."

William nodded. "It is understood and accepted. If he breaks my peace, he must be prepared for the consequences. Your laws in such matters are not so different to ours. Which brings us to the reason for our being here today, does it not?"

There was a brief pause while each of the dozen or so men in the Edgar's party looked at each other, awaiting the first move. Eventually, Ealdred stepped forward, bowing his head before the duke.

"Indeed so, Lord. We have come here for two reasons: firstly, to submit to your authority and secondly to invite you to accept the throne of England in accordance with our traditions and established practices."

William nodded approvingly; his scowl slowly being replaced by something approaching a smile. "You would wish me to become your king? To rule this land, to set its laws, to dispense justice in accordance with those laws?"

Edgar hung his head, shame clearly burning a hole in his heart. If he had been in Edgar's place, Thurkill would have wanted the ground beneath his feet to open up to swallow him whole. Anything to put an end to the ignominy of the moment. He could see the young man's fists clenching and unclenching in a stoic effort to remain in control of his emotions. He felt a wave of pity for the boy whose reign was being so cruelly cut short less than two months after it began. More than anything, however, he felt sorrow for his people. Who knew what lay ahead for the Saxons under Norman rule?

"Yes, Lord. We place ourselves in your hands. The kingdom is yours to rule. We ask you do so fairly and justly as befits the duties of a lord over his people."

"I want to hear it from Edgar."

"Is my word as Bishop of York not enough?"

"No. With all due deference to your eminence, I would have the man who would be king in my place submit and swear fealty to me now. Step forward, Edgar, prince of Wessex." These last words were spat contemptuously, as if he refused to recognise the boy's authority or title in any way.

Thurkill looked at his erstwhile king; his whole body seemed to squirm with awkwardness and anger. But to his credit, perhaps remembering his role and status amongst those he represented, he straightened his back, cleared his throat and stepped forward proudly. Stopping before William, Edgar then knelt and clasped his palms together as if in prayer. He then reached forward so that his hands hovered above the Duke's knees. Whether to humiliate or to add to the drama of the moment, William made no move, until finally enveloping the boy's hands in his own much larger, shovel-like paws. "Proceed."

With a voice that did not waver and which belied his tender

years, Edgar then made his oath, loudly enough for all to hear. "I promise on my oath that I will be faithful to my lord, never to cause him harm and will observe my homage to him completely against all persons, in good faith and without deceit."

The duke nodded approvingly. "Now, I call upon Ealdred, Bishop of York, and my own half-brother, Odo, Bishop of Bayeux, to witness this act. May they call for your excommunication from God's holy church should you ever break your word. Now rise, Edgar, loyal subject of the new King of England."

The two men then rose and embraced each other, before the duke pulled back to hold Edgar at arm's length. "I too was left without a father at a young age and had to fight for my right to rule. Though my fortune has fared me a little better, perhaps, I hope you will not rue your decision for too long and that you may - in time - come to love me much as you would a father. Let us put these things behind us and go forward hand in hand together."

It was a remarkable moment. In truth, Thurkill had not known what to expect of this meeting and, after FitzGilbert's rashness, he had feared the worst. But he had not thought to see such warmth and such a genuine desire for reconciliation from the duke. Whether it was sincerely meant or not, it was a canny move designed to wrong foot the English nobility. To rebel against William now would be a clear breach of trust.

"If we might now turn to other, equally important matters, we should discuss plans for my coronation; for not until then can I truly call myself King of England. For that reason, I would have it done sooner rather than later. I would be pleased for the ceremony to take place in King Edward's abbey of Westminster. It seems fitting that I should be crowned in the church that was built by the man who promised me the crown of England, don't you think? It would also seem right for it to take place on the feast of our Saviour Jesus Christ's birth, one week from today.

"Lord Ealdred, can I rely on you to make the arrangements?"

FIFTEEN

"Come on, Hild. We need to get there early to have any hope of finding a decent place. St Peter's abbey only holds a few hundred souls and there are going to be thousands that want to be there."

Hild's muffled voice sounded from behind the cloth screen where she had - for what seemed like hours now to Thurkill - been getting ready for the coronation. "But as Aelfric's man, your place is guaranteed is it not?"

"Only if we get there before he goes in. He will not wait for us as he, too, will want to secure the most advantageous spot. Have you not got that dress on yet?"

"Alright, alright. It's easy for you, you don't have to bother with jewellery or your hair – or at least I assume you don't, judging by the appearance of that great shaggy mane of yours. How many birds had made their nest in there at last count?"

Despite his frustration, Thurkill could not help but laugh. He was still chuckling when she pulled back the drape and stood before him. Thurkill's laugh died in his throat as he stared at her in awe. She stood in front of the room's narrow window through which a piercing shaft of sunlight caught her full in its beam. Her golden hair shone in the light forming what looked like halo around her face. *She is more beautiful than any angel,* he thought.

Hild blushed, embarrassed by his scrutiny. "Close your mouth before something flies in, for goodness sake. It's not as if you've never seen me before."

"Not looking like that I haven't," he mumbled. Not knowing what else to say he shuffled towards her, arms held wide to embrace her. Laughing, Hild pushed him away.

"Keep your hairy paws off me, you great big oaf. It took me hours to look like this and I'll not have it ruined by you crushing my dress and hair in one of your clumsy bear hugs."

When they finally arrived outside the abbey, Thurkill found, to his relief, that Aelfric had not yet gone inside. He had fretted every step of the way as the crowds along the road that ran from east to west had been had slowed their progress. In the end he had taken to walking in single file with him in the front to barge a path through the throng and Hild tucked in behind. On arrival, he instructed Eahlmund and the others to find a tavern close by and wait. "I'm sorry you cannot also attend, but there is simply not room to fit everyone in."

Eahlmund grinned. "Don't worry, Lord. A few ales to toast the new king is far more our kind of thing, rather than what promises to be a dull, boring affair with lots of bishops gabbling on in Latin."

"When you put it like that, I think I may join you," Thurkill laughed.

"Over my dead body, you will." Hild grabbed his one good ear and pulled him away from the others towards the great doors in the east end of the Abbey.

Wincing as he was dragged away, Thurkill grinned. "I'm sorry, my friend, you will just have to drink without me this time."

Inside, the abbey was already more than half full. Aelfric bustled forward as far as he could go but it was no further than two thirds of the way along the nave; the front section having been reserved for Norman lords and their families or retinues. Still, Thurkill was pleased with their position, in the second row of Saxon nobility and on the end of the aisle so that they would have an unencumbered view of William as he processed along the nave. Everywhere he looked there were Norman soldiers, stationed at short intervals along the grey stone walls of the church. Outside, hundreds more were positioned in a kind of protective cordon around the open area that surrounded the abbey and the adjacent king's hall. Whether they expected trouble or not, they were certainly prepared for it.

Thurkill pushed such thoughts to the back of his mind. Surely the day would pass peacefully? Of course, there were those that were not happy, himself included, but what was the point of getting yourself killed over some foolish act of protest?

As far as he was concerned, he had already decided his future. He had spoken to Aelfric a few days back and he had been offered a small village on his lands not far from his own seat at Huntendune. The previous lord had been killed at Senlac along with most of his followers and so the villagers needed someone to replace him.

"Who better than you, Thurkill?" He'd said. "Think it over, talk to Hild about it, but I hope you will accept my offer."

In fact, there had been little to discuss. Hild had jumped at the chance, flinging her arms around him and smothering his face with kisses. Since she had been forced to leave her own village following her father's death, Hild had felt lost in the world, with no home and no friends or neighbours to turn to. The prospect of having a new home, and being the lord's woman to boot, had filled her with new joy. It had warmed Thurkill's heart so much to see her so happy once more that he'd rushed back to Aelfric to tell him. There was just the small matter of the coronation to endure and then they would be on their way. Aelfric had already declared that they would be travelling north the day after the ceremony.

Eahlmund and the rest of the lads had been equally happy with the idea. They were farmers at heart and they too wished for a simpler life tilling the fields, away from the death and misery of the last few weeks. Doing so on land owned by their lord just made the prospect even more appealing.

Thurkill's mind was dragged back to the present by a commotion from the back of the abbey. While his thoughts had been elsewhere, the space had filled up such that there was no longer any empty room whatsoever. People were crammed in on all sides and it was only the line of soldiers along the central walkway that kept that area clear for the procession. Using his extra height to good effect, Thurkill craned his neck back towards the entrance. Sure enough, things looked to be finally getting under way; he could see people filing in through the great east doors now.

Nudging Hild, he bent down to whisper in her ear. "Here we go, the Duke is on his way now."

Hild's eyes lit up; she'd never seen so many people dressed so richly all in one place. It was some time before they saw William, though. At the head of the royal party came Bishop

Ealdred of Eoforwic, who would be officiating at the ceremony, followed by a several other bishops, one of which - Aelfric had said - was from Coutances in Normandy. After them came any number of priests followed by more monks than Thurkill had ever seen gathered in one place. As they walked slowly up the nave, the monks sang psalms in such wondrous harmony that Thurkill felt sure that Almighty God in heaven must be looking down and smiling on what he heard and saw.

Finally, Duke William was there in all his finery, already bareheaded in readiness for the crown of England to be placed upon it. He was accompanied by his two half-brothers, Robert, Count of Mortain and Odo, Bishop of Bayeux. After them came a long line of other Norman lords and Thurkill swallowed nervously as he spied Robert FitzGilbert passing by. Fortunately, the Count's attention was elsewhere and he strode past without a sideways glance.

When all the participants were finally settled, the service began. With some sadness, Thurkill realised they were in for a long slog as everything was first being said in Norman before being repeated in English so that all present might follow. Church services had a habit of being interminably long without everything having to be done twice.

Sighing, he steeled himself for what was to come, praying that his bladder would not let him down. He would not be able to force his way out of the church so he would have to piss himself where he stood were it to come to it. He felt sure that Hild would not let him forget such a disgraceful act.

After a good while, Thurkill watched as Duke William lay down on the cold stone floor in front of the high altar. His body formed an approximation of the cross with his legs pressed firmly together and his arms stretched out wide on either side. Standing over him, Ealdred spoke numerous prayers and exhortations in Latin, which Aelfric explained were intended to call upon the Duke to promise to be a fair and just king over his people.

"It's known as the promissio regis - or king's promise in our tongue," Aelfric whispered. "This same promise has been used for the last hundred years or so since Bishop Dunstan, of blessed memory, first used it in the coronation of King Aethelraed Unraed. In short, the king promises to preserve the peace, to forbid robbery and all unrighteous things and finally to use justice and mercy in all judgements. Only in such a way can the people be sure that they will be ruled fairly and justly." He finished by raising his eyebrows, as if doubting the how much they could trust words so easily given.

The promise completed, Ealdred then directed William to take his place on the throne where he proceeded to anoint his head with holy oil. Then, he solemnly placed the crown upon his head, while the Norman bishop handed him the symbols of office: the sword, sceptre and rod. Whilst the duke sat perfectly still, showing the proper respect due for such a moment,

Thurkill could have sworn he saw a slight smirk play across his lips, perhaps in recognition of the successful culmination of his long-held ambition to add the throne of England to his Norman dominions. There would be few in Christendom who would be more powerful.

With the ritual completed, Ealdred then turned to the congregation and called upon them, in a voice that boomed across the whole church, reverberating off every wall, whether they would have William as their king. The response was deafening; hundreds of Saxon voices shouted their support, perhaps eager to have an end to a year that had seen so much upheaval and bloodshed.

Though Thurkill also wished for peace, he could not bring himself to shout with the rest. By his side, Hild noticed his silence and squeezed his hand. She understood how he felt. The Normans had taken his father, sister and aunt; he was not ready to forgive just yet.

SIXTEEN

Something was very wrong. As the sound of the acclamation slowly died away, Thurkill realised that he could still hear shouting, but not from within the abbey. Around him, heads began to turn as folk tried to discern the origin of the noise. Whispered conversations flew up and down the rows of people as rumour and supposition began to fly as to the cause of the hubbub. Before very long, however, things took a frightening turn for the worse.

"Smoke." Thurkill lifted his head and sniffed deeply. It was unmistakable. The smell of burning wood was drifting from the back of the church, causing more and more people to look back over their shoulders in alarm. *What's going on out there?* Thurkill wondered as he reached down for Hild's hand to reassure her. Surely the Saxons outside had not chosen this moment to launch an attack? If so, it was nothing to do with Edgar; up in the front of the congregation, Thurkill could see he looked as non-plussed as everyone else. It would be a few rogue elements if anything; a few hot-headed fools who saw the coronation as an opportunity to cause mischief or even to attempt to kill the new king.

People at the back of the abbey were now leaving in their droves; some running, some screaming as fear spread throughout the crowd. The threat of being burned alive, trapped inside the church, was a ready-made recipe for panic. Soon, the rush became a stampede, goaded by the shouts and screams that echoed off the bare stone walls.

Grabbing Hild and holding her tight to protect her from the onrushing people, Thurkill fought to make his way towards one of the side entrances. Keeping his left arm close around her shoulders, he had to use all his strength to keep his footing as the hordes tried to push past, round or through him in their eagerness to escape. Here and there, a few unfortunate souls fell to the ground with a cry. If they were lucky, there was someone on hand to haul them back to their feet before they were trampled underfoot, otherwise a dreadful fate awaited them.

Eventually, he reached the exit. The heavy wooden doors had been flung wide open as people forced their way outside. Through the opening, Thurkill could now see the flames. All around the abbey, houses, inns and shops were burning. *What in God's name is going on?* In the confused melee around him, he could make no sense of it. There seemed to be no sounds of any fighting; no tell-tale noise of metal clashing against metal or wood, no screams of the wounded or dying. What he could see, however, were hundreds of Norman soldiers running in all directions. His thoughts turned to Eahlmund and the others. He'd left them drinking in one of the nearby inns, quite probably one of those that now burned fiercely. Silently, he mouthed a prayer that God might keep them safe.

As soon as he was outside, he began to cough. The smoke here was thick and billowing, fed by the wind-assisted flames that even now threatened to engulf the thatched rooves of the nearby houses. He could see those buildings were doomed unless water could be brought quickly.

Just as the thought occurred to him, scores of people arrived in the square, all of them carrying wooden buckets in each hand. Watching them for a moment, he spotted a familiar face amongst those who were trying to organise them. Still holding Hild's hand, he powered his way towards him, pulling her along behind him. "Come on, they need our help."

By the time they had covered the short distance, Eahlmund had the men arranged into two lines leading from the burning houses back down towards the river. Buckets were being passed back and forth with incredible speed as they fought to douse the flames. The desire to save their homes and possessions lent the people an urgency and strength that meant they did not tire in their efforts. Bucket after bucket came to the head of the line where their contents were thrown where the fire was fiercest, before being passed back to be refilled.

Elsewhere, people ran in all directions, screaming or crying. Other folks ran to and from their burning houses carrying what meagre possessions they could rescue. It was brave but foolhardy; several times one or two emerged with their clothes on fire where, if they were fortunate, friends or neighbours covered them in blankets or threw water over them until the flames were put out.

Without ceremony, Thurkill grabbed hold of Eahlmund's shoulder, spinning him around. "Where are the others? Are they safe?"

Silhouetted against the burning buildings, the whites of Eahlmund's eyes shone brightly, contrasted against his soot-blackened face, giving him an almost devilish look. "They're fine, Lord. The brothers are down by the river looking after that end and the others are somewhere back along the line. Grab a bucket and help. We need every hand we can get."

"What in God's name happened? Is it Saxon or Norman doing?"

Eahlmund growled. "It was the Norman bastards."

"What could have provoked such an outrage? Were they attacked?"

"Not in the slightest. It's confused but, as far as I can tell it all began after that great shout in the church. Maybe they were looking for a fight anyway and that just gave them an excuse; you know what bored soldiers are like and there were enough of them in the square here. But once they heard Saxon voices raised inside the church, they began to push and shove people. A few fists were thrown, in self-defence, I might add," Eahlmund looked at his shoes, revealing that he had been one of those involved, "and then it all went mad. Before you knew it, the soldiers were grabbing burning logs from the braziers all around and setting fire to the buildings. I don't know, perhaps they thought that there was some kind of attack happening, what with the shouting and everything."

Thurkill thought back to the coronation. "The acclamation!"

"The what?"

"The moment when Bishop Ealdred called upon the people to accept William as king. There was such a great shout that the sound of it would have carried far beyond the walls. Perhaps they mistook that for some kind of uprising?"

"Whereas actually everyone was shouting in favour of William?"

"Yes," the irony was not lost on him. "Let's just hope not too many are killed in this confusion. Where have all the soldiers gone now?"

"Those that have not disappeared off down side alleys on the lookout for loot or women went into the abbey, presumably to protect their lord."

"Well, it seems quieter now. Let's put these fires out. Hild, stay cl…. Goddammit, where's she gone?" Thurkill looked around frantically, hoping she had not been taken by soldiers, panic rising in his heart with every passing moment.

Eahlmund laughed. "Worry not, Lord. She's over there, putting you to shame."

Thurkill followed the direction in which his friend was pointing to see Hild organising the women and children, sending the older children to join the line of bucket carriers and making sure the younger ones found their mothers safely. Thurkill looked on with pride. *Far more of a lord's wife than I am a lord,* he thought ruefully. *I should have seen to those tasks already.*

***

It took most of the rest of the day for the fires to be extinguished. Many buildings had been saved, but many more had been destroyed and would need to be rebuilt in the coming days. Fortunately, not many of the townspeople had been killed, which was a blessing considering the chaos that had reigned. To their credit, the Norman captains had managed to bring their men under control quickly once it became apparent that there was no threat to the new king's life.

Wearily, Thurkill climbed the stairs to their room behind Hild, too tired even to admire the shape and movement of her hips. Entering the small room, he yawned and stretched, hearing his shoulders crack as he loosened off his aching joints. "I confess I'll be glad to put this place behind us, Hild. I've had enough of cities for the time being."

Hild reached up behind him, massaging his aching shoulders. "As, indeed, have I. I long for the peace of the countryside. Things may never be like they once were when I was growing up, but they must surely be better than they are now. I hate the stench of the city: so many people living on top of each other; so much noise all day and all night; human waste flowing in the streets. It's horrid."

"Well, soon we'll have our own place, Hild. Something we've never had before, a home we can call our own."

"I cannot wait. What do you think it will be like?"

"I don't know, but Aelfric says it's a nice little village, settled in a valley by the side of a stream, so we shan't want for fresh water. There's plenty of fields, a large wood and a good number of cows and pigs. We'll have everything we need."

"It sounds perfect. And there'll be room for Eahlmund and the others too?"

"Aye, there will. Aelfric tells me a good number of the menfolk were lost at Senlac. Their lord was one of those that went down the hill after the fleeing Normans, only to be killed when the bastards turned and fought back. So, they have desperate need for men to come to the village before the spring so that they have enough hands to help plant the crops. Without the five of them, the villagers could starve next winter."

"And who knows," Hild winked cheekily, "Perhaps they too may find love there."

Thurkill playfully pushed Hild back on the bed, nibbling her ear as he knew it annoyed her. "Who knows indeed? Though I doubt that anyone would find Eahlmund attractive. Perhaps he would be better suited amongst the pigs?"

Hild laughed. "You're the pig, Killi. And keep your trotters to yourself. We have to be up at dawn to be ready to leave."

SEVENTEEN

Thurkill woke coughing, his lungs still affected by the acrid tang of the smoke. The noise roused Hild from her slumber too, though she bounced out of bed, oblivious to the chill within the room. "Come on, lazy bones. Today's the day we start our new life."

Still wheezing, Thurkill swung his legs out onto the floor. "You know it's three to four days' journey to the north, my love?"

"Yes, but every step is a step toward our new home and happiness. Stop being a misery and help me pack."

Thurkill smiled, her enthusiasm was infectious. It gladdened his heart to see her so happy; he had worried for her continually since her father had been killed. She never spoke of what she saw that day and he was content not to intrude on her private grief, but he could not help but worry what dark thoughts dwelt within her soul. But for days like today, he could banish such worries to the remotest recesses of his mind and allow himself to be caught up in her joyfulness.

"Come on! They will be leaving without us."

"Alright, woman, would you rather I walk the streets with no trews?"

"It would not matter if you did my love, it's so cold that your modesty would be protected."

Pulling on his boots, Thurkill gave Hild's arse a slap as she passed in front of him. "Cheeky mare. It's lucky for you we're in a hurry or I'd put you over my knee to teach you who's the lord round here."

Hild dropped a little curtsy, winking at him at the same time. "Promises, promises, *my Lord.* Besides, everyone knows who wears the trews in this relationship."

Before the abbey bells had even sounded for Terce, they were on their way. What with Aelfric and his retinue and Thurkill's own warband, they made for a sizeable party, numbering almost fifty souls and five carts. The pace was necessarily slow, though, as they did not want to leave the ox-drawn waggons too far behind for fear of bandits on the road.

As they trotted along, Thurkill had plenty of time to survey the damage from the previous day's conflagration. Several homes had been destroyed completely while many more showed significant signs of fire damage and would probably have to be torn down. Here and there, blanket-covered lumps lay between the houses; the bodies of those who had perished, mostly from the effects of smoke, or killed by Norman soldiers as they ran amok.

Thurkill could feel his ire rising; his face set like thunder. Had not William promised to rule with justice and mercy? Had he not promised to protect his people from wrong-doing? Well the Saxons were his people now, just as much as the Normans and hardly had the words come from his mouth, than his own soldiers were burning houses and killing townspeople without check. Whilst he accepted the fact that they might have believed that the shout from within the church meant there was trouble brewing, a small voice in the back of his mind that could not be silenced told him they were looking for an excuse, any excuse, to cause mischief.

"Best of the morning to you, my lad." Thurkill looked up as Aelfric reined in his horse to walk alongside his. "A sorry business, eh?"

"Aye, Lord."

"Not the best start to King William's reign." As if reading Thurkill's mind, Aelfric continued. "I had truly hoped that we could trust this Norman once he became king; trust him to be fair and just to all his subjects. But events like this give me pause."

"What are you saying, Lord? You may speak plainly with me." Thurkill was on edge. Was Aelfric talking rebellion so soon after the coronation?

"Just that the king has my loyalty... for now. But he does not yet have my trust. He will have to earn that with more than words. And, in the meantime, I shall be watching."

Thurkill nodded as he realised Aelfric was right. England might have a new king, but that king would have to prove himself to be worthy of the position. He had no idea what he, Aelfric, or anyone else for that matter, could do if it came to it but knowing that Aelfric thought the same way as him was comforting.

"Anyway, enough of this sour talk; we have better things to look forward to, do we not? Like introducing Gudmundcestre to its new lord, eh?"

"Is that its name? Gudmundcestre? What more can you tell me about it? How many people live there? What crafts are undertaken?"

"Whoa, lad. One question at a time. My old brain cannot keep pace with your young tongue. Yes, the place is called Gudmundcestre. It's a short distance south - an hour or two's walk, no more - from my own hall in Huntendune, both of which lie on the banks of the river Ouse. There's been a settlement there for as long as anyone can remember, right back to the time of the Romans. In fact, it lies where two Roman roads meet, which, what with the river, probably explains why the place exists.

"Used to be a fort there, I'm told, but no longer. Probably had its stone robbed for other buildings, including the church which stands in the middle of the village, I've no doubt. There's a small earthwork of sorts around the village which provides some protection from bandits. You may find that you want to improve those defences. These are uncertain times in which we live after all."

"But what of its people? How many souls will look to me as their lord?"

"Fewer than there were, Thurkill, fewer than there were. Not one of the ten or so men that joined the fyrd to stand with Harold at Senlac ever came back." Aelfric's brow furrowed as he thought back to that day. It was clear that he felt the loss of his people deeply, like a wound to his own flesh.

"But there remain a good number, nonetheless. I'd say a hundred or so in total, though it's hard to keep track as the women there seem to be very fertile. There always seems to be a new child coming along almost every week. Anyway, must be something in the water in those parts, eh? Perhaps you and Hild will soon be blessed?" He chuckled to see Thurkill's embarrassment.

"Hey, Alwig, come here a moment." As he waited for the man in front to turn his horse, Aelfric continued. "Alwig is my Steward. He knows all there is to know about my lands and holdings; far more than I do. In fact, he's probably forgotten more than I know. Isn't that right, Alwig?"

Alwig grinned with not a little pride. He was a tall, skinny man with a studious air, almost as if he were a priest or monk by calling. His appearance did nothing to challenge this perception as he was bald save for tufts of black hair that sprouted above his ears and in a ring of sorts which ran round to the back of his head. His voice, when he spoke, was nasal and high-pitched. "It's kind of you to say so, Lord. What would you have of me?"

"Thurkill here is asking about Gudmundcestre, the little village I have entrusted to him as replacement for old Siward. I said I thought there are about one hundred folk there, is that right? What else can you tell him? Even though it's close to Huntendune, it's been a while since I've ventured there and, to be honest, one village looks much like another to me."

Alwig lowered his head in a show of respect. "If I recall correctly, Lord, Gudmundcestre is home to just ninety-five souls last time I checked. It is a thriving little settlement in a fine location on the banks of the river. I would need to check the precise details but, I believe there is land given over to crops, sufficient for around twenty-five ploughs. In addition, there are," he ticked them off one by one on his fingers. "Over one hundred and fifty acres of meadow on which grazes a well-stocked herd of cattle; fifty or so acres of woodland with more than three dozen pigs; and - I think - three water mills, two of which are used for grinding wheat and the other for fulling cloth. Lastly there is a tavern, a blacksmith and a church whose priest is named Wulfric. He's quite a character as I recall."

Aelfric beamed widely. "A little tip for you, Thurkill; a Steward like Alwig is worth his weight in gold. With so much knowledge trapped in one head, there's little that gets past him. No one can escape paying their dues as he knows what each man owes and what he's paid down to the last penny. Anyway, how does that sound? That enough for you to call home?"

Thurkill attempted to bow from where he sat in his saddle. To say it was an ungainly gesture for one who was no expert in horse skills would have been putting it mildly, though - to his credit - Aelfric kept a straight face.

"You do me great honour, Lord. It is more than I could ever have dreamed of. You can be assured that Hild and I will serve you with loyalty and distinction."

"Nonsense, lad. You served your king well and I am proud to be able to stand in place of your father to see you properly rewarded. Besides, I am grateful to you. It does not pay to have profitable holdings like Gudmundcestre unmanaged for too long. The people get out of the habit of good discipline and, before you know it, you have a bugger of a job to collect your taxes."

"Even so, you will not regret your decision, Lord. My sword is yours for all time."

"I thank you, Thurkill, though I pray I do not need to call on it for many a year."

***

The road that led to the village was lined with people. Thurkill imagined the whole population must have turned out to welcome their new lord, perhaps keen to get a first look at what sort of man he was. Self-consciously, he straightened his back and adjusted his cloak so that it was no longer bunched around his middle where it had been keeping him warm against the chill wind. He tried to think back to when he was a boy and how his father would have dealt with such an occasion and found himself, not for the first time, wishing Scalpi were there to guide him. With such thoughts spinning around his mind he did, at least, have the presence of mind to nod, smile and wave at those that hailed him as he passed by.

They came to a halt in the centre of the village where the two roads met just, as Aelfric had said, outside the small stone church. The townsfolk had followed them into the square, forming a loose ring around them. Thurkill could feel the colour rising in his cheeks as he realised that every eye was upon him.

Everywhere, he could see folk digging each other in the ribs and having whispered conversations.

Just then, he remembered what his father had told him; first impressions count, so speak with authority and confidence and that will see you more than half the way home. Half smiling to himself, he silently thanked Scalpi for this small piece of wisdom that had come, unbidden, into his mind. *If only I knew what sort of man my predecessor was, though,* he thought. *If he was the most generous, fair and protective lord there has ever been, then I am doomed before I begin.*

"Well met, friends, well met," Aelfric held up a hand to greet the crowd. "Allow me to apologise for my long absence from these parts; these are difficult times in which we live. Indeed, I return here today bearing tidings of great import for you all."

The whispering and nudging had now all but stopped as, every man, woman and child waited to hear what their lord would say. It was not often that they saw someone like Aelfric and so everyone wanted to hear every word spoken.

"We have a new king. Duke William of Normandy, slayer of King Harold and conqueror of England was crowned in King Edward's new West Minster at the hand of Bishop Ealdred of Eoforwic, just five days ago."

This news was met with angry rumblings which spread up and down the assembled lines, until Aelfric held up his hands for peace. "However sour we may feel, it was properly done according to the sacred observances and laws of this land. The boy Edgar of Wessex stood aside and swore allegiance to the Duke, so William is now our rightful king. I have also sworn my allegiance to him and I will say no more on the matter.

"In happier news, I am pleased to present to you Thurkill, son of Scalpi," Aelfric laid his hand upon Thurkill's shoulder in a clear and unequivocal gesture of support, as if the touch symbolised the transfer of his authority to the younger man. "Thurkill fought bravely at Senlac where he defended King Harold to the last. Had he not been knocked unconscious at the last, he might yet have saved the king's life. He barely escaping with own his life as it was.

"Thurkill lost his father at Senlac and has no hall to call his home any more. In the same way that you lost your father - the Lord Siward - at that battle so it pleases me that I now commend him to you as your new father. Knowing his character as I do, I have no doubt he will serve you well in all things. All I ask is that you serve him well in return."

Silence greeted Aelfric's words. Once again, Thurkill felt his cheeks redden as he realised that everyone was waiting for him to speak. In a sudden flash of inspiration, he remembered the words that William had spoken at his coronation the previous day. *If they were good enough for William, they'll do for me now too,* he smiled to himself. Clearing his throat, he stood up in his stirrups so that all might see him clearly.

"Lord Aelfric does me great honour by naming me lord of Gudmundcestre. I have heard many great and wonderful things about this village and its people on my journey here and I am proud and privileged in equal measure to be given this opportunity.

"I swear, in front of you all now and before God as my witness," he nodded towards the priest who stood, arms folded, in front of his church, "that I will give you peace so that you may prosper in safety, I will forbid robbery and banditry in all its forms and I will exercise justice and mercy in all judgements brought before me. These three things I promise to you faithfully as your lord."

He was pleased to see that, as he spoke, several of those listening to him turned to their neighbours and nodded, muttering what he hoped were complimentary comments. Several more smiled back at him, from which he took great encouragement. Just as he was hoping he had gotten away with it, however, the priest pushed his way forward to the front of the throng.

"Those are fine words, Lord, but may I ask how you can promise protection? You are but one man and the town lost not only its master at Senlac but also ten of its best fighting men. We stand here today with little or no protection from bandits and brigands. Already we hear whispers from travelling merchants that word has reached the outlaws who dwell in the forests that surround us that Gudmundcestre lies undefended."

Thurkill nodded, acknowledging the virtue of the priest's point. Many of those around him murmured their support too. Thurkill knew that safety and security were paramount for these people, many of whom owned nothing more than their ploughs and their cattle. Losing either of those would see them destitute but for the charity of others.

"A fair question, Father Wulfric." The priest looked surprised, and not displeased that he knew his name. "Let me reassure you that I do not come here empty handed." He waved his hand towards his companions who sat patiently as his side. "I bring five staunch warriors with me, men who are proven in combat. Together, we will fill the gap left by those who did not return from battle. Not only will I and these men keep you safe, but they also come from good farming stock. I intend to put them to work on the ploughlands left empty by your sad losses. They will grow the crops that their predecessors would have, so that none may starve next winter. If you will have them?"

A chorus of loud "ayes" greeted his question, causing Thurkill to smile broadly. He was winning them round. Even Aelfric clapped him on the back, congratulating him on his speech.

Seeking to build on his advantage, Thurkill continued. "I have seen on our approach today that this place is protected by an earthwork."

"Yes, but it's neither use nor ornament. A child of six could scale it without difficulty."

"Exactly my thinking, too." Thurkill smiled. "If I am to protect you from brigands, then this will have to change. Therefore, I will promise here and now that my first task as Lord of Gudmundcestre will be to improve its defences."

"And I will lend men from Huntendune to help you." Aelfric's intervention was perfectly timed. Great cheers went up from the crowd as they saw that their new lord's promise to improve their lot had been backed by the great Lord Aelfric. As the cheering continued, Thurkill dismounted so that he could make his way around the assembled throng, shaking hands as he went, ruffling the hair of snot-nosed children who stared wide-eyed at this newcomer who towered over everyone else.

As he moved past a little girl who stood barefoot but proud in front of her father, he felt her tug at his sleeve. "Are you married?"

Embarrassed, her father clipped her round the ear with the flat of his hand. "Quiet, Elspeth. Do not presume to question our lord so. It is none of our business."

Elspeth's face reddened, tears beginning to well in her eyes. Thurkill's heart went out to her; she reminded him of his sister, Edith. The same bright eyes and ready smile, the same confidence to speak up in front of so many. Dropping down to his haunches, he wiped a tear away from her cheek with a grimy finger, leaving a dirty streak in its place.

"Where are my manners? I thank you, Elspeth, for reminding me of them. I am not married, but I do bring with me a lady whom I hope will one day become my wife. Would you like to meet her?"

Elspeth nodded, sniffing back the tears. Thurkill rose and held his hand down for the young girl to take hold. She had to reach up above her head to be able to do so and her tiny fingers were engulfed in his huge shovel of a hand. Still, she was not frightened. Not once did she look back to her father for reassurance but, rather, she allowed herself to be led through the group of strange, armed warriors towards the lead cart of the five that had arrived in the town.

As they arrived, Thurkill let go of Elspeth's hand so that he could reach up to help Hild down. "Hild, I would like you to meet my new friend, Elspeth."

Hild allowed herself to be carried to the ground. As she watched, Elspeth's mouth opened to form a round O of astonishment. "You're beautiful."

Hild smiled warmly. "No more so than you, Elspeth, though I thank you for your kind words. I am pleased to hear you are Thurkill's friend and I dearly hope you will be my friend too. I am sure there is much we can talk about."

The young girl beamed happily. But then her face suddenly turned into a frown, as if remembering something important. "Are you going to marry Lord Thurkill?"

Hild laughed, only mildly abashed by Elspeth's directness. "Well, I don't know. He has not asked me, so I am unable to offer an answer. What would you do if you were me, Elspeth? Would you marry him?"

Elspeth paused and turned to stare appraisingly at Thurkill who looked embarrassed and uncomfortable at the scrutiny of the two women. "I think I like him. He has been kind to me and I think that means he would be kind to you too."

"And kindness is important if two people are to be together, isn't it? Is your father kind to your mother?"

"He was, but I have no mother now. She died last winter of a fever." There was no sadness, no weeping. It was a mere statement of fact as if it were the most everyday thing, but Hild's heart melted. Though it was a fact of life for so many, it was still painful to see one so young suffer such a loss. Hild, knelt in front of the girl and hugged her close, enveloping her in her fur-lined cloak. "In which case, we should definitely be friends so that you have another woman to talk to whenever you want. Here…" Hild reached inside her sleeve to retrieve a small, bone comb, one of several that she had bought in the markets of Lundenburh before they had left. "Take this, Elspeth, I have others. Later, perhaps tomorrow, we can comb each other's hair until it is shiny?"

Elspeth took the gift with great reverence. Doubtless she had never seen, let alone held, such a thing as finely wrought as this. Mumbling her thanks, she ran back to her father, showing him the comb and babbling excitedly.

Once again, Thurkill could have hugged Hild right there and then. Whilst he had made good strides in appealing to the menfolk with his promises of security and protection, Hild had built a bridge directly to the women of the village. Seeing how gracious and kind she was with Elspeth and how she carried herself with assurance and poise, it was immediately apparent that this was someone to whom they could look to as lady of the lord's hall.

EIGHTEEN

What was I thinking? Thurkill groaned as he woke up, wintry sun dancing across his face in time with the wind's movement of the drape that hung over the window of his lord's chamber. To welcome the new lord and lady properly, Aelfric had arranged for a feast to be held on the night of their arrival. Alwig the Steward had been sent ahead to make arrangements for everything to be ready, which explained why the whole village had been expecting their arrival. It had proven to be a resounding success, not least because of the seemingly never-ending quantities of ale that Aelfric had seen fit to provide.

It was yet another reason for him to be grateful to his lord, as man after man clapped him on his back and wished him well, while their ladies had complimented Hild on her dress, her jewellery, and her hair. Even Wulfric had made merry, perhaps a little too much by the end as Thurkill had last seen him vomiting copiously into a bucket held by a grimacing thrall.

The priest was a short man, barrel-chested – almost as round as he was tall – whose red face seemed to be permanently bathed in rivers of sweat. He had a voracious appetite for bread, meat and ale, all of which he devoured with great gusto, punctuating every other mouthful with immense belches that reverberated around the hall. It took Thurkill by surprise at first – he had never met a priest who was anything other than pious and restrained in his habits – but he soon found himself warming to him.

Eahlmund had already become fast friends with him, finding a kindred spirit in his enjoyment of ale and food. They spent most of the feast sat together swapping ribald jokes and songs, behaviour that seemed very unbecoming of a man of God, although was very much in keeping with Eahlmund's character.

Thurkill had also drunk heavily. He had told himself not to, wanting to present a good and sober example to his people, but as the night wore on so his defences came down, so happy was he to be there. Though, he kept a tight rein on his behaviour, he was deep in his cups by the time the night came to an end.

As the fire in the hearth had died down to its embers and the last of the people either went to their homes or simply curled up on the floor in their cloaks, he had sat – or rather, slumped – in his lord's chair just smiling to himself. Forgotten, for the moment, were the deaths of his family, forgotten was the fact that England had a new, Norman, king and forgotten was the fact that he had, in FitzGilbert, a sworn enemy who would like nothing better than to gut him as he himself had done to his brother. For now, he was simply happy. Happy to be away from the turmoil of the city, happy to have his own hall and, above all, happy to have his Hild at side.

This morning, however, was a different matter. His head was thumping as if many little feet were stamping in unison inside his skull. His tongue felt twice its normal size and seemed to be plastered to the roof of his mouth. Opening his eyes, he quickly shut them again as the low sun burned directly into his soul, making his head hurt even more. Over from the corner of the chamber, which was screened off from the rest of the hall by a thin wattle and daub wall, the sound of Hild's laughter mocked his sorry state. "I said you would regret that last cup of ale or, should I say, the last several cups."

Forcing himself up onto one elbow, Thurkill rubbed his other hand over his face, feeling the rough scrape of his wiry stubble. "Shush, woman, and bring me a cup of watered ale to freshen my mouth."

"Ha, you can go yourself. The sooner you remove your stinking hulk from this chamber, the sooner I can have it smelling nice once more. These flowers that Elspeth brought have already wilted under the onslaught of your foul stench. Besides, you boys have a wall to build or did you forget your fine promise?"

"Oh God, yes. Well it seemed a good idea at the time is all I can say."

"Go on with you, Killi. The exercise will do you good and will help to clear your head. Oh, and mind you jump in the river before you come home. I won't have your sweaty, muddy carcass ruining our nice chamber. Go on, be gone, I have work to do to make this place into a home and I promised to help Elspeth with her hair. I have a mind to appoint her my maid if you are agreeable?"

"Is she not a bit young for that? And what about her father? Will he not have need of her on his farm?"

"He has three older sons who already work with him. He has more than enough hands for his plot."

"In which case, if it pleases him and you, I have no objection."

***

Outside, the blast of cold air hit him like a stinging slap in the face. Beating his arms around himself to drive warmth through his body, he was eager to be about his business if only to stave off the cold. Over by the earthwork, he was pleased to see the others already waiting for him. True to his word, whilst Aelfric had departed at dawn for his own hall, he had left a score of men to help with the works. With the six of his warband plus another score of men from Gudmundcestre, Thurkill reckoned they would make quick work of the task, though with the short daylight hours at that time of year, it still promised to be three to four days' work at least.

He divided the men into two groups. To the first and larger of the two, he instructed Eahlmund, Eardwulf and Copsig to issue shovels and ordered them to begin work on the ditch around the outside of the earthwork. He wanted it to be deeper than the height of a tall man, more than six feet in truth. The earth that was dug out was to be piled up on the bank so that – once complete – the combination of ditch and bank would be a formidable barrier to any would-be attackers.

The second group was given hatchets and sent, under Leofric's and Leofgar's guidance, into the surrounding woods, with orders to look for young straight trees, of which there were plenty in these parts. They would need a hundred or more if they were to build a palisade on top of the earthwork that would stretch all the way around the village. He had seen how it had been done at Warengeforte and hoped to be able to recreate a similar structure here. Each log, once cut, would need to be stripped of its branches, cut to a consistent length and then tapered at each end so that it could be sunk into the soft earth to a depth that would keep it rigid. The upper end would also be sharpened to a point as a further deterrent to any that might chance their luck by trying to scale the wall.

With the men thus dispersed, Thurkill divided his time between both groups, overseeing and encouraging, lending a shoulder wherever it were needed. He planned to help as much as he could, not only to show that he was not going to be sort of lord that expected others to labour on his behalf, but also because the bitingly cold temperatures demanded that he not spend his time being idle. He envied Hild staying warm inside the hall. Yes, she had plenty of work on her hands helping to prepare meals to feed them all while they worked, but at least she could do so next to the raging hearth fires, stirring the thick vegetable stew that simmered in the huge iron cauldrons and baking the flat, round loaves to dip in it.

The work proceeded swiftly. Everywhere, the men worked hard, as if eager to impress him. As they laboured, they swapped tales and sang songs that were usually either funny or crude, often both. The camaraderie kept their spirits high and helped them forget the cold, their aching joints and straining muscles. Regular bowls of hot stew in which large lumps of fresh bread floated also helped.

Everywhere Thurkill went he smiled to see the effort that the villagers were putting in to the project. He was also starting to pick up a few names here and there, so he was able to congratulate and thank those individuals as he passed. He could have sworn that each time he did so, the man in question worked that little bit harder or stood that little bit taller as a result. He resolved to learn as many names as he could, aware of the effect it had on a man's morale to be praised by his lord.

By midday on the third day, work on the ditch and earthwork was complete. Breathless, the men leaned on their shovels, admiring the result of their labour. It was an impressive sight and testament to the enthusiasm and collaboration of all involved. Even Aelfric was impressed, having made the short journey from Huntendune to check on progress. "I'll have need of you in Huntendune too, if you can achieve this much in fewer than three days. Truly admirable. I congratulate you all."

For the rest of the day, work centred on building the palisade. Those that had been digging the rampart swapped their shovels for adzes as they began shaping the logs ready to be dug into the ground. Those who had been chopping down the trees now formed themselves into smaller groups who took each trunk as it was finished and drove it deep into the soil so that half a man's height was buried beneath ground while still leaving a good eight feet above. Progress was slower now, not least because Aelfric had recalled his men for other tasks for which he had need of them. Nevertheless, the wall still began to take shape as post after post was slotted into place on top of the earthen bank. Thurkill calculated that another two days, at most, would see the job done.

"What do you think?"

Eahlmund stood next to him, covered almost from head to foot in cloying mud. "It's not a look I particularly favour, if I'm honest, but I am sure it will wash off."

Thurkill punched him good-naturedly on the arm. "Oh, you mean the defences? A fine job, if I say so myself. I didn't think we would achieve so much this quick, Lord."

"Me neither, but that just shows what can be done if everyone pulls together, eh? Whilst I am glad to have the wall – its value to the village is beyond doubt – the real benefit is what you can't see."

"How so, Lord?"

"Look at the people, Eahlmund. They labour willingly for their lord with a smile on their face. New friends have been made, new songs have been created, new bonds made. We cannot forget the womenfolk in this too. Hild's marshalled them as well as any captain of war might, so that we've not wanted for food and drink during the whole time. This is a group of people who are more close-knit now than they have ever been. We've achieved more than I could have hoped."

Eahlmund was about to reply when an horrific scream rent the cold air. Eahlmund was first to react. "Quick! It came from the woods, from the logging camp, I'd say."

As they ran, any number of terrifying scenarios flowed through Thurkill's head. Were they under attack? If so, from whom? Normans? Bandits? Perhaps it was a wild boar or a wolf? Aelfric had said some had been known to come close to settlements in the winter when hunger drove them to take greater and greater risks. He wished he had his war axe with him but, as it was, he would have to meet whatever danger awaited them with just his seax. He had already pulled it from his belt as he sprinted towards the sound. Several others were running from all directions, drawn to the pitiable sounds that continued to rip into Thurkill's soul.

As soon as they arrived at the logging camp, it was immediately obvious that there was no enemy; human or beast. But, amidst the chaos, it still took Thurkill some time to work out what had happened. Pushing through the gathering crowd, he finally reached the source of the commotion.

One of the carts they had used to move the hewn trunks from the woods to the village had lost a wheel and in doing so had collapsed onto a young lad by the name of Toki. Thurkill had spotted the cart a couple of days previously, noting that it seemed older and more decrepit than the others; but it was too late now. Thankfully, the wheel had broken while the cart was unladen, and this had probably saved young Toki's life. He had been standing by the cart when it collapsed and had been knocked to the ground as it fell. He now lay on his back, his right leg pinned beneath the waggon.

The poor lad's face was as white as Thurkill's tunic. He was shivering partly through cold but mainly through shock which had now supplanted the extreme pain, meaning that his screams had subsided. It was clear, though, that he had to be moved quickly. Thurkill was about to send back to the village for ropes and tackle with which to create a pulley to winch up the load, when Toki groaned horrendously. The pain was starting to return. There was no time to wait for the equipment; he had to act now.

Removing his cloak, he lay it over Toki's chest to try to keep out the worst of the cold. "Come here, Eahlmund."

Together the two men, helped by another two of the villagers, braced themselves on either side of the upturned cart with their backs to it. Squatting on their haunches they were able to get their shoulders under the lip of the planks which formed the side wall.

"On three, straighten your legs. Whilst we may not be able to shift the cart completely, we can hopefully lift it a hand's breadth or two; just enough for you others to drag Toki clear. Is everyone ready?"

Another two men came forward and bent down, placing their hands beneath Toki's armpits, ready to heave him out from where he lay. As soon as they were in position, they nodded. They were almost as white as the stricken woodsman. Toki groaned once again; it looked as if he was slipping into unconsciousness. God alone knew what damage his leg had sustained under all that weight. Thurkill feared their actions could make things worse but to do nothing was not an option. The boy could die where he lay if they delayed any longer. With that thought uppermost in his mind, Thurkill began the count.

"One, two, three, heave…" Slowly, but undeniably, the cart began to move. At first it was almost undetectable, though the effect on Toki's leg was immediate as the pressure eased. Then, as the four men strained yet further, pushing as hard as they could until they could finally lock their legs in an upright position, a small gap appeared.

The effort was so intense, Thurkill had no strength to yell at the two men to act, but they needed no such order. He just hoped they could extract him before they had to let go of the immense burden that bore down on their shoulders.

"Clear!"

Exhausted, they let the cart drop, all four men sinking to their knees where they stood. Thurkill found he was momentarily deaf due to the noise of the blood rushing in his ears. It sounded like he was standing beside a raging waterfall. Gradually, his senses began to return and his thoughts turned to Toki. The pain of being moved had caused him to pass out, but he was alive, though his breathing was laboured and fitful. At least there was no blood that he could see so perhaps the injuries were not as bad as he had first thought. The bone would no doubt be broken but at least it had not penetrated the skin. There was hope it could be reset without there being too much permanent damage.

Pointing at the two men who had helped pull Toki out from under the cart, Thurkill ordered. "Take him to Wulfric as quick as you can. I hear he has some skill with broken bones and his wife, Raeda, has knowledge of herbs that can dull pain. He'll be in good hands there. But do it gently; let's not cause the lad any more distress than we have to."

As they left, Eahlmund came over to his side. "I pray he'll recover well. I must admit I didn't think we would shift that weight. Do you know how heavy those things are?"

"It's remarkable what can be done when there is a need to, Eahlmund. Though I thank God for granting us the strength to save him. I doubt we could've done it without His help."

***

The next evening, Thurkill hosted a feast to celebrate the completion of the village's defences. It had taken the whole five days in the end but he was by no means displeased. Other than Toki's broken leg, there had been no other serious injuries which was, of itself, a minor miracle. As for Toki, Wulfric had tended to him as best he could and professed himself happy with the results. He declared that, though he might walk with a limp for the rest of his days, he would at least walk. Now the boy rested, slept mostly – with the aid of Raeda's potions – allowing the bone to set and his strength to return.

So pleased was the lad's mother that she had marched straight into the hall that night, walked right up to Eahlmund and Thurkill and wrapped them both in a bear hug, planting a huge kiss on both their faces. The two men had been struck dumb by the sudden, unexpected onslaught and they could only stare in bewilderment as she marched back out again to the sound of raucous laughter and cheering from everyone else present.

But more important than the wall itself, was the spirit amongst the villagers. Thurkill and his men had been accepted, of that there could be no doubt. They had proven themselves with hard work, courage and leadership. It was still early days, but Thurkill could not have hoped for a better start. He felt sure that he had at least begun to repay Aelfric's trust in him.

As he sat listening to a travelling bard recounting tales of battles and deeds from times long gone, he realised with a start that he had been so busy these last several days that he had not even thought about William or the Normans. It was as if the last few weeks had not happened, despite the fact that it was the death and destruction dealt out by the invader that had led him to this place. Perhaps he could make a new life here with Hild and the people of the village after all? Away from William and his bloodthirsty, rapacious soldiers? Turning to his left, he looked at Hild, enjoying the strong lines of her face in profile. Conscious of his gaze, she turned to face him, a look of indescribable happiness spreading across her face. He felt his heart swell, so proud was he to have succeeded in making a safe home for her after all she had been through.

The sound of loud applause caused him to turn back. The bard had finished his tale of the noble Lord Brythnoth who had once given battle against Viking invaders at Maldon, not far to the south east of where they now sat – only to lose his life in the thick of the fighting, leading to a terrible defeat for the Saxons. It was an heroic tale, full of bravery and heroism which had reminded Thurkill of the battle at Senlac in which King Harold had lost his life. It was a sad tale, but yet one of courage and hope as well. *Who knows*, he thought, *perhaps we will rise again one day and rid ourselves of William and his foreign whoresons*?

For now, however, his thoughts remained focussed on Hild. Rising to his feet, he offered thanks to the bard, tossing him a silver penny in payment for his efforts and ordering that food and ale be provided as he had now sung for his supper. The singer bowed deeply, earning himself another rapturous round of applause. Eventually, the acclaim died down as the audience realised that Thurkill had remained on his feet. He had not done speaking.

"My friends, I thank you all for the welcome you have shown to me, to Hild and to those who came with us. I did not know what to expect when I came here and I'll wager you too had your doubts. I, for one, however, could not be happier. You have all shown yourselves to be strong of arm and heart and I am proud to be your lord. But there is one thing that remains amiss, and has been for far too long. One thing that I must correct before all can be well here."

A hushed silence fell over the room. Heads turned nervously to neighbours, wondering what it was that could have displeased their lord. Who had incurred his wrath that he might need to take action so publicly?

"It shames me to stand before you here as a lord that has no wife. This situation cannot be allowed to continue and so it is that I ask – with you all as my witnesses – my beautiful Hild whether she will consent to be my bride."

No one spoke or moved as all eyes turned to Hild who sat open-mouthed, completely taken aback by the unexpected proposal. Her cheeks reddened furiously as she became aware of almost one hundred sets of eyes staring at her, not to mention Thurkill standing before her, an anxious – yet hopeful – look on his face.

Slowly, she rose to her feet and curtsied before him. "Gladly, Lord. It is my most heartfelt desire to be wedded to you."

Like a wave crashing against a cliff, the relief of those watching erupted in shouts, laughter and cheering. They had another feast to look forward to.

NINETEEN

They set the wedding for the following Sunday, just three days hence; they both agreed that there was little point in waiting any longer. There were no complicated negotiations to undertake between the two families as there were no parents alive to have them. It was to be a simple agreement between two adults who loved each other.

Wulfric had beamed with delight when Thurkill asked if he would marry the two of them. He'd warmed to the curmudgeonly old priest over the last several days, not least because he'd mucked in with the rest of them during the building of the defences.

Thurkill had seen how well liked he was by everyone in the village. He was very much treated as one of the lads – the only concession to his office being that the jokes and songs became marginally less ribald in his presence, at least until Wulfric joined in anyway. His strength and endurance had been astonishing too. When all others were flagging towards the end of the day, he was still there hefting his axe or shovelling earth, whilst whistling the tune of some psalm or other as if he were merely out for a gentle stroll.

Aelfric was also overjoyed to hear the news when Thurkill and Hild made the short trip north to Huntendune to seek his permission. Though it was but a formality, it was still their duty to seek their lord's blessing for their match. "It's about time you made an honest woman of her, Thurkill. Can't have you two living in sin, as Wulfric might put it. I look forward to it and, what is more, I would be honoured to stand in place of your father, Hild. If you would have an old goat like me that is? A girl should not be left with no one to give her away, I think."

Hild said nothing, but simply burst into tears and hugged Aelfric there and then, burying her face in his shaggy beard. Aelfric, who would have been about the same age as her father, Nothelm, was left feeling awkward and unsure what to do. He settled on patting her on the back in what he took to be a fatherly way whilst mumbling, "There there, my dear" over and over until she had recovered her composure.

Once back in Gudmundcestre, Hild shooed Thurkill out of their chambers. "Be gone with you. The wedding is only three days away and there is so much to do and if you don't get out from under my feet, it won't be done on time."

"What on earth is there to be done, woman? Do we not simply turn up at the appointed time, stand in front of Wulfric, say the right words and then go and get so drunk that you can't even see?"

"God preserve us from men in all their forms!" Hild yelled, hurling a wooden bowl at his head which only narrowly missed as he ducked. He ran from the room, laughing uproariously as he went.

***

On the morning of the wedding, Thurkill awoke with a feeling of nausea so strong that he had to rush outside to puke behind the house. When he came back in a few moments later, it was to the sound of laughter from Eahlmund.

"I thought you could take your ale, Lord. You must be going soft in readiness for life as a married man. You won't be allowed out drinking with us lot again, you mark my words. She'll have you tied to her apron strings and doing her bidding in no time, you'll see."

Thurkill smiled half-heartedly. He'd not had that much to drink, not least because Hild's warning had rung in his ears all night when she'd packed him off out of the hall, saying it was bad luck for the groom to see the bride on the morning of the wedding. "And don't you go getting so drunk that you're ill on my wedding day."

This must be nerves, he thought to himself. Thinking back, he recalled feeling very much the same before his first battle at Stamford. He shook his head, marvelling at how he could stand in a shieldwall and confront death more easily than he could face a day such as this.

"By my faith, Eahlmund, I drank in moderation. You were with me all night and could swear to it if asked. You heard the words Hild spoke to me as I left. No one would dare disobey such an order."

"'Tis true enough, friend. So, this is fear then, pure and simple. I've seen men look less pale than you just before a fight. They often shit their britches too, so I'd thank you to go back outside if you feel that might happen."

"Your compassion for my plight does you credit, my friend."

"You're not the one that would have to live with the stench all day. Anyway, it all goes to prove why you won't catch me getting wed. Women are more trouble than they're worth if you ask me. All those rules about what you can and can't do and being scolded for things you don't even know you've done wrong."

"Aye, but is it not worth it for that loving face that greets you when you come home and a warm embrace on a cold night. Or is that why you like pigs?"

"Huh. Even they won't have anything to do with me. If you ask me it's some kind of conspiracy against me by all females of every type. But that's fine by me. I'm happy being my own master."

"Right you are, Eahlmund," Thurkill nodded, winking to show his friend just how much he did not believe him. "Anyway, we'd best get moving or we'll be late. And then we'll both have no doubt what we're being scolded for."

An hour later, the pair of them were waiting in the front pew of the church. Thurkill didn't think he'd ever looked smarter or cleaner, not even when aunt Aga had scrubbed him for what had seemed like a whole week before he'd gone with his father to court for the first time. He certainly didn't remember ever having spent so long on his appearance. It had helped having Eahlmund with him, though, for his friend had inspected him minutely before allowing him to leave his house, walking slowly round him several times, stopping every now and then to pick loose hairs or tiny specks of dust or dirt off his best tunic and trews.

As he'd stood there, Thurkill could not help feeling like a kitten being washed and groomed by its mother, so close was the care and scrutiny that Eahlmund exercised over his appearance. Such was the emotion he felt at that moment, that neither his father or mother were there to witness this day, that a tear had escaped, unbidden, and rolled slowly down his cheek. Self-consciously, he'd cuffed it away with the back of his hand but not before Eahlmund had seen the movement and guessed at its meaning.

Eahlmund had straightened up, his task completed, and then embraced Thurkill. "They would be proud to see you here today, my friend. They'll be watching you, though; have no fear of that."

Thurkill had to swallow back the big lump that threatened to choke his throat before replying. "That's as may be, but stop crushing my tunic will you, you big oaf? We've just spent forever making it to look half decent."

Eahlmund had released his grip but held on to his friend's shoulders, looking him up and down for any final blemishes. They caught each other's eye and smiled, nodding at each other; the look saying far more than any words could.

Turning away, lest he too be overcome with emotion, Eahlmund had whispered. "You'll do."

The little church was full to overflowing. Every space in every row was taken and yet more people were standing against the walls along the side and back as well. The whole village had crammed inside its walls to witness the spectacle. If that were all, there might have been enough room, but there was also a sizeable contingent from Huntendune including Aelfric and his wife, Aelfgifu. Neither of them was anywhere to be seen, though. Aelfgifu and her two maids had rushed straight to the hall, on their arrival, to help Hild with her final preparations, whereas Aelfric waited patiently outside for her to be ready, so that he could escort her into the church in place of her father and pass her ceremoniously into Thurkill's care.

It had taken a long time for the two men to walk from the door, all the way up the nave to their position at the front of the church. Everyone had stopped Thurkill to shake his hand, clap him on the back or wish him well. The feeling of warmth towards him and Eahlmund was palpable. As they reached their allotted space, little Elspeth came forward and curtsied before presenting him with a tiny posy made up of snow drops that she had plucked especially from the woods that morning. Solemnly, and with great care, he inserted it behind the brooch which secured his cloak on his left shoulder. Bending down, he kissed her on the forehead. "Thank you, Elspeth. I was not prepared for this day until now. Your flowers have made me complete."

As they waited for Hild, Wulfric appeared from the side vestry where he had been putting on his robes. Shaking both Thurkill's and Eahlmund's hands, he asked "Are you ready, son? Soon there will be no turning back, you know."

"Aye. I'm as ready as I'll ever be." The nerves which he thought had been banished came flooding back. His face must have bled white as Wulfric leaned forward to whisper conspiratorially in his ear.

"Don't worry, lad. We'll get through this together and it will soon be over, you'll see. Can't be any worse than standing in the shieldwall, eh?"

Thurkill wasn't so sure; at least in battle there was safety in numbers whereas, here, he felt dreadfully exposed out front on his own with just Eahlmund for company. Before he could reply, however, there was a commotion behind him as many heads turned back towards the door. Standing there, framed in the door way, was his beloved Hild, clad against the cold in a deep green cloak that matched his own. Beneath it she wore a plain linen dress that was whiter than any snow he'd ever seen. Its lack of any ornate pattern was by design as it served to accentuate her beauty instead. Standing there with her hand looped through Aelfric's arm, her golden hair was framed by the brilliant sunlight which illuminated her from behind. She had never looked more angelic to Thurkill than now, the sun forming a golden halo encircling her head. Suddenly he felt a nudge in his ribs. "Close your mouth, Killi. You look more stupid than ever and she might not want to marry you if she sees."

"By God though, Eahlmund, is she not heavenly?"

It seemed that many others there shared his thoughts judging by the gasps that could be heard all around the church as she walked forward slowly, her eyes fixed all the time on Thurkill. Time seemed to stand still for all the while that Hild and Aelfric processed to the front of the church, until, finally, she stood in front of Wulfric. Then, Aelfric took her left hand and gently placed it in Thurkill's own outstretched palm, symbolising that he was willingly passing her over into his safekeeping. Turning to face him for the first time, Hild smiled. It was the same smile she had given him when he first met her several weeks before in her village of Brightling where he had recuperated after the battle at Senlac. It was as heart-stopping now as it was then.

"Welcome one and all, welcome." Wulfric's voice boomed around the stone walls. "It is my honour and my privilege to stand here today in the sight of God and this congregation to witness the joining together in marriage of Thurkill, Lord of Gudmundcestre, son of Scalpi, noble thegn of King Harold, of blessed memory, and Hild, daughter of Nothelm of the village of Brightling.

"But before I do, if there are any here present that know of any just reason or due cause why this man and this woman may not be joined together, let them declare it now or forever hold their peace." The pause Wulfric left seemed to stretch on forever to Thurkill's mind, but the silence thankfully remained undisturbed.

Nodding in satisfaction, the priest continued, "I repeat the same question to you both, Thurkill and Hild. If you know of any just reason or due cause why you may not be married here today, declare it now."

After another, seemingly interminable, Wulfric then said. "In which case, given there are no declared impediments, I must ask who stands here for this woman, Hild, daughter of Nothelm, so that she may be given to this man, Thurkill, son of Scalpi?"

"I do," Aelfric stepped forward, speaking with a voice that was used to giving commands on a battlefield. His duty done, he stepped back into the front row, grinning more broadly than anyone could have thought possible.

Satisfied, Wulfric turned back to the couple. "And, so, Hild, daughter of Nothelm, I must ask whether you consent to be taken as wife by this man, Thurkill, son of Scalpi?"

Hild turned again to fix her man with eyes which sparkled with half-formed tears of joy. "I do." Though quiet, it was as clear as a bell and resonated across the whole church so that none had difficulty in hearing her.

Wulfric smiled reassuringly at her, before turning that same smile on Thurkill. "And do you, Thurkill, son of Scalpi, consent to take Hild to be your wife, to protect her and put her before all others?"

Thurkill swallowed to try to force some saliva into his parched mouth. "I do." It sounded thin and reedy to his ears, but it was enough to satisfy the priest. God how he longed for this to be over so he could sink his first cup of ale. Never had he needed a drink more than that moment.

"Therefore, by the power vested in me by Almighty God, I do declare that you be man and wife. What God has joined together, let no man tear asunder."

Thurkill stared dumbly at the priest. Was that it? Was it really over? As if reading his mind, Wulfric grinned at him. "Well? What are you waiting for, man? Kiss your wife before someone else beats you to it!"

To the sound of raucous laughter, cheering and applause, Thurkill grabbed hold of Hild and enveloped her in his muscular arms. Having almost crushed the life out of her, he pulled back a few inches so he could see her face, as wet with tears as was his own. Then with great tenderness that grew into a surging torrent of passion, he kissed her full on the lips, pressing his mouth against hers until, eventually, they had to break for breath.

***

The wedding feast passed by in a blur. It was Aelfric's present to them both and the food was some of the best he had ever tasted. And the wine... It was rare for him to have wine, let alone the people of Gudmundcestre, and this was beyond doubt the finest he had tasted. Rich, dark and fruity, hailing from the southern lands of France, so Aelfric said. It must have been like the nectar that the legendary gods of ancient Greece used to drink, it was that good. Fortunately, Thurkill knew it was much stronger than ale and so he was careful to pace himself. After the first two or three cups, he ensured that the thralls brought it to him watered down. Sensibly, Hild followed his lead, but there were plenty who did not. There was a continual stream of revellers, many obviously the worse for wear, who staggered unevenly outside to vomit into the buckets that had been placed there for that purpose.

But Thurkill did not care. He was too happy to worry about anything. He laughed along as he watched the tumblers performing their tricks and turns; he sang along lustily with the bard as he went through the old songs, the favourites from his youth that were seemingly known the whole country over; and he listened in silence and with awe as the scop told his tales of great warriors performing daring deeds in far off lands from a dark and distant past. All the while he sat in his lord's chair, holding Hild's hand as she sat next to him, never wanting to ever let go of her again.

And it was not just him that was in good spirits. Away to his right his little band of hearth warriors were deep in their cups as well, singing along with the songs and laughing uproariously at every joke, pratfall or, indeed, at anything that they felt to be the least bit amusing. And chief amongst them was Eahlmund. But despite all his protestations, despite all his claims that he preferred his own company, there was no mistaking the fact that on his lap sat a slim, dark-haired girl, her arms draped around his friend's neck. She had her back to Thurkill meaning he could not recognise her, so he made a mental note to speak to Eahlmund the next day. It seemed that there was nothing like a wedding to bring out the romance in an otherwise cold fish.

Before he could bring Hild's attention to the strange spectacle, however, Aelfric chose that moment to come to sit next to Thurkill, slapping him hard on the back as he did so. "A grand day, my boy, a grand day. One of the best I can recall for many a year, without a doubt."

"Mostly thanks to you, Lord. Your generosity – as ever – knows no bounds. There's many who will recall this feast with fond memories for a good while, not to mention the wine with which they washed it down. Yet again, you have our gratitude."

Aelfric waved it away as if it were nothing. "Ach. It's no more than any lord would do for one of his most favoured sworn men, but I thank you for your words nonetheless. But, listen, I am sorry to bring this up on the day of your wedding but I have need of you."

"Name it, Lord. I am yours to command."

"I must be away back to my hall now but come to see me in Huntendune tomorrow or the day after. There are matters which we need to discuss, matters of great import which could affect us all." With that, Aelfric held out his hand once more for Thurkill to shake before rising to leave.

TWENTY

He woke to leaden grey skies. So dark was it that it was hard to tell whether the dawn had even happened. To make matters worse, rain poured down from the thick, forbidding clouds in stark contrast to the previous day's crisp blue sky. The rain was so heavy that it sounded as if an army of rats were running hither and thither across the thatched roof. Here and there, the water found its stubborn way through the tightly packed straw to form tiny little waterfalls that cascaded down to the floor. Fortunately, none of them was positioned over their bed, but Thurkill knew it was a job that could not be left for too long.

"Hild, while I'm gone, see if you can find a thatcher in the village and have them make repairs."

She pushed herself up on one elbow, curls tumbling across her face. "You're going out in this? Why not wait until tomorrow when the weather may have improved." Patting the covers where he had been lying, she added, "Come back to bed. It's warm and dry in here and we have unfinished business to attend to."

The look on her face left him in no doubt as to the business she had in mind and he had to admit he was sorely tempted. *What harm could it do to leave it a day?* He mused. But his lascivious thoughts were soon replaced with feelings of guilt. He owed everything to Aelfric and if he couldn't bring himself to do his lord's bidding for the sake of a bit of rain, then what sort of man was he? No, he would have to drag himself away to do the right thing, however hard it may be.

He sat on the edge of the bed to cuddle his new wife, kissing her on the forehead as he did so. "Forgive me, Hild. As much as I would like nothing more than to stay with you this foul day – or any other day for that matter – I must do my duty to my lord."

Rather than look disappointed, she broke into a warm smile. "I would have been surprised if you had said otherwise, husband. I am sorry to have tempted you so; it was more in jest than anything."

Kissing her once more, he rose to go, laughing as he did so. "Sore temptress, I shall think of nothing else now all day." Wrapping his cloak around his shoulders, he paused once more. "I shall take Eahlmund, the brothers and Eardwulf with me. I'll tell Copsig to look out for you. He's turning into a fine young warrior now. He'll soon have the beating of the others in sword-craft, if I'm not mistaken."

With that he pushed open the door and stepped out into the rain, pulling the cowl of his cloak down over his head as he went. Making his way to the nearby barn, which had now been given over to be a stable for their horses, he found the four other men already waiting for him, horses saddled and ready to go.

"We're definitely going then?" The look on Thurkill's face extinguished any spark of hope in Eahlmund's voice as if he had been doused with a full bucket of water.

"Indeed so, my friend. My duty is to our lord. I only wish the day were better for travelling. But take heart in the fact that it is but a short ride. We will be there within an hour or two."

"And you on the morning after your wedding night too. I am surprised you managed to drag yourself away. Or, more to the point, I'm surprised Hild let you go." Leofric nudged his brother in the ribs, causing the latter to let out an involuntary snigger.

"Believe me, I'd much rather be in bed with her than staring at your ugly faces, but beggars can't be choosers. Now, let's go and find out what our lord would have of us."

Although their destination was but a few miles distant, the persistence of the rain meant they were all soaked to the bone within a few hundred paces. There was nothing for it but to pull their cloaks tightly around them, put their heads down and plod on so that the journey might be over as quickly as possible. The track was already a quagmire in many places, making it hard for their mounts to keep a sure footing. Every step splashed mud up the horses' legs and – at times – as far as the men's knees. It was a truly miserable day that showed little sign of improving. Thinking to lighten the mood a little, Thurkill dropped into step alongside Eahlmund.

"Speaking of being in bed, my friend, would you care to share with us the name of that beauty I saw you with last night? The one who appeared to be chewing on your face."

Even with his face half hidden beneath his hood, Thurkill could see Eahlmund's cheeks flush with colour briefly before deciding to tough it out, ignoring the chuckles of the three other men. "Oh, you mean Hereswitha? She's the miller's daughter; you know, old Haegmund... What of her?"

"She seemed to be a friendly sort. But I thought you had no time for women. That you wanted to be your own man with no one to tell you what to do?"

"Did I say that? Well I must have been jesting. A man should think to his future and if a pretty woman wants to throw herself at you, who I am to refuse? And besides, her father could do with the help. He has no one to work the mill and to take over when he becomes too old, since he lost his son at Senlac."

Thurkill laughed. "Ah now we get to the truth of it. You're only using Hereswitha to get to the mill. You have an eye for a good deal my friend. Bed her and you get to keep the mill and all the coin it will make for you."

As the others roared in delight, Eahlmund took on a most affronted demeanour. "I'm shocked you would think me capable of such despicable scheming. Though, now you come to mention it, that would be a nice bonus should our relationship continue to flourish. I could see myself running a mill. It beats working in a field in the pissing rain like you sorry bunch of goats arses."

"I am sorry, Eahlmund," Thurkill struggled to speak, he was laughing so much. "I'm pleased that you seem to have found love, for I had feared you might grow old alone. I hope the two of you are very happy together. And, speaking as your lord to whom all must pay their dues, I'm also pleased at the prospect of the mill being handed down to such a hard and honest worker as you."

"Now I know you're having fun at my expense. Bastards, the lot of you." With that, Eahlmund kicked his heels into the flanks of his mount, forcing it into a bad-tempered trot leaving his companions in his wake, peals of laughter ringing in his ears.

***

They found Aelfric in his hall, warming his back by the hearth fire. He welcomed them all, summoning thralls to take their cloaks so that they might be dried by the heat, ready for their departure. Next, he invited Thurkill's four companions to help themselves to the steaming mutton broth that bubbled within a huge iron cauldron that was suspended over the flames. "A bowl of that will soon warm you through, lads. There's hot fresh bread to go with it as well."

With the men settled at a bench, happily spooning pieces of meat, turnip and carrot into their mouths, Aelfric pulled Thurkill to one side. "Thank you for coming so soon, my boy. I almost didn't expect to see you today. It's foul out there, is it not? Tell me, how is Hild? Enjoying life as Lady of Gudmundcestre?"

"As happy as I have ever known her, Lord, though we have been together but a few short weeks. She has all that she could wish for and you have my thanks for that."

"Good, good." Though the older man seemed genuinely pleased to hear those words, Thurkill could tell he was distracted, as if something else weighed heavily on his mind.

"I am sure, Lord Aelfric, that you did not bring me here just to enquire after my wife's health? What would you have of me?"

"Ah, indeed. To the point as ever, eh? Well, look, I hear that William plans to return to Normandy in the next few weeks. Word is that he feels he has been away for too long and that his presence is needed there lest there be trouble brewing."

"His rule there is not secure?" Thurkill was genuinely surprised by the thought.

"It very much is, never fear. But like with any field in spring time, if you don't take care of it, weeds quickly rise up to choke your crops. I suppose it is to be expected, though; now that he rules two great lands on either side of the narrow sea, he'll be forced to divide his time between the two."

"What of it? Why do we care what he does?"

Aelfric grinned. "A point with which I can find little fault, lad. But there are two factors that concern me, seeing as you ask. Firstly, William has decreed that many of the great English lords will accompany him. Whether it's because he favours us and wishes to lavish his hospitality on us or whether it's because he wants to keep us where he can see us, I know not – but I can guess."

"When you say, 'us', Lord?"

"Very astute of you to observe that, Thurkill. Along with Edgar and the Earls Morcar and Eadwine, I am to be a member of the Saxon party that goes with the king. And this is why I summoned you, to call on your support to take care of things in my absence. My Steward, Alwig, can look after my affairs quite admirably, I'm sure, but he is no warrior. I would have him be able to call upon someone of your ilk in case of need."

"You expect trouble, Lord?"

"Not necessarily, but it pays to be cautious, I always find. That said, there are rumours of large bands of lawless men roaming the countryside. If that's true, I don't doubt for a moment that they might try to attack a village should they become desperate for food or shelter."

"Whence come such men and why have they not been dealt with before?"

"They are the product of William's harsh treatment over the last several weeks. While he was waiting for Edgar to submit, he did what he could to encourage him by laying waste to large swathes of land between Warengeforte and Lundenburh. Several towns were burned to the ground and many of their people – those that were not killed – fled into the hills and forests as their homes were destroyed behind them and their livestock stolen or slaughtered. They've nothing left and no hope of rebuilding. Through no fault of their own they are now destitute and having to live off the land or from what they can steal. I do not blame them, they did not ask for this, but I have a duty of care to protect my own people. And now I lay that duty on your shoulders while I am in Normandy. You are my sword and my authority in this matter."

Thurkill knelt. "And you may trust that I will be steadfast and my sword true." Rising back to his feet, he continued. "But you said there were two matters?"

"Ah yes." The tone of his voice darkened noticeably. "I confess this other matter concerns me even more than the thought of marauding brigands."

"Speak, Lord. Whatever it is, you can rely on my sword and those of my men to put it to rights."

"I'm not sure you can, Thurkill. It is bigger and potentially more damaging than any of us can deal with. Since Edgar submitted to William at Beorhthanstaed, the new king has been true to his word and has proved to be fair to us Saxons. Harsh admittedly, but ultimately fair. Yes, there have been some arrests and some land dispossessions from those who refused to bend the knee, but nothing that couldn't be reasonably justified. Nothing that you might not expect any king to do when needs must. But what worries me now is that those who William leaves to rule in his place while he is in Normandy may not be so inclined."

"Surely they'll follow the orders they're given?"

"Who knows what orders they'll have let alone whether they choose to follow them? What if they decide to invent some charge or conspiracy as pretext to take what they want? Without William to keep them in check, I truly worry what may happen to the people."

Thurkill was doubtful. *Who would dare so openly defy the king's command*? "Who does William leave in his stead? Do we know?"

"His half-brother, Odo, Bishop of Bayeux and another called William FitzOsberne. Though I have met neither, they each come with a reputation. They appear to have less of William's wisdom and restraint and more of his aggression."

"What would you have me do?"

"I am not sure there is anything you can do, if I am honest, lad. Just keep an ear open for news. I am sure there will be word on the roads should things take a turn for the worse. Listen to what the merchants are saying as they travel north. There's not much that escapes them."

***

The journey back to Gudmundcestre was only slightly more pleasant. Mercifully, the incessant rain had finally stopped, though vast banks of thick cloud still shrouded the land like a smothering grey blanket. At least their clothes had mostly dried out and their cloaks were still warm from where they had been hung by the hearth. Nevertheless, it was not enough to lift Thurkill's mood for Aelfric's words weighed heavily on his mind.

Over recent days, he had begun to hope that things might just be bearable under the Normans; that they had, perhaps, simply swapped one king for another. One that spoke French rather than English but – to all other intents and purposes – the same. But now he found himself wondering if he had been fooling himself, allowing his own little piece of paradise to mask what might be going on elsewhere? If Aelfric was right – and he had no reason to doubt him – then who knew how long their happy existence might go on? Would Aelfric himself be in danger while he was in Normandy? What if the Normans decided to take action against all those that had stood with Harold at Senlac? God knew that they would not need much of an excuse. William had always been open in his claim that Harold was a usurper. It would be but a short step to declare any who had fought for Harold to be outlaws, their lands forfeit to the crown.

What's more, he knew one man who would take great pleasure in seizing his lands. There had been no sign of FitzGilbert since the coronation, but Thurkill did not doubt he was still in the country. The Norman was not the type of man to forgive and forget. Thurkill had managed to put him out of his mind for a few happy days but he could not pretend forever. Sooner or later he would have to deal with it. He would also have to tell Hild soon. He scolded himself for not having done so before, but he knew it was because he had been trying to protect her from the worry. Beyond everything else, he wanted her to be happy. She would have to know about the threat that hung over them both. Thurkill had little doubt that, should FitzGilbert get the better of him, things would not go well for his woman. The best she could hope for was a quick death.

He would have preferred to bring an end to it himself – to go seek out the Norman and deal with him – but he had responsibilities now. Not least of which was his duty to Aelfric and to the people of Gudmundcestre. What sort of lord would he be were he to abandon them to resolve his own personal feud? No. He would have to stay put and wait. Perhaps he would not be able to find him this far from Lundenburh? As his horse plodded along, hoof after muddy hoof, Thurkill set his face in an expression of grim determination. *Let him come. I will be ready for him, come what may.* He might just have need of the new palisade.

Turning in his saddle, Thurkill looked back to the four men who trudged along behind him. "Lads, it's time we readied the people of Gudmundcestre to look to their safety. You heard Lord Aelfric's words; with the threat of bandits around, it would not hurt to have the men train with spear and shield so that they may protect their hearths and homes."

"Aye, Lord. An hour spent practising with blade and shield is never an hour wasted."

Thurkill nodded, smiling at Leofric's enthusiasm. He chose not to mention Robert FitzGilbert, but he felt sure that the Norman whoreson could not be too far from their thoughts as well.

TWENTY - ONE

"What is it that you want, FitzGilbert? Are you still chasing shadows, looking for your brother's killer?" Odo, Bishop of Bayeux, yawned, as if to emphasise just how much the whole business bored him.

Robert FitzGilbert was not so easily put off, however. He had come to petition the king's half-brother for more troops with which to extend his search. "I will not rest, Lord, until I've had my revenge. I suspect I am not alone in my desire. Any brother worth his weight in salt would move heaven and earth to avenge his kin. Why, even you, the mighty Bishop of Bayeux, would want William to exact a price were you to be most foully murdered, I presume?"

"Yes, yes, of course. But with my brother back in Normandy, I do have rather more pressing matters to see to, governing this God-forsaken, rain-sodden, foul midden of a country, than worrying about your search for some low-born Saxon farm-hand with one ear."

"He's no farm-hand, Lord. Whilst he may not have elevated titles, vast lands or wealth, he is – nonetheless – a warrior of some renown. I've heard many tales of his feats of valour and martial skill. You'd do well not to underestimate him, as I do not."

"Such as?" Odo swung his booted legs idly back and forward where they hung over the thick oaken arm of the chair in which he lounged. He longed for the comfort and warmth of his castle back in Normandy. These Saxon halls – even this one that had belonged to the Saxon king in his greatest city and was, therefore, supposedly the grandest of all his dwellings – were little more than pigsties dressed up with rugs and a hearth. The sooner they could construct some proper buildings, more fitting to their station and wealth, the better. Work had already begun on a new stone tower down by the river, close to the bridge over to Suthweca, but it would take some months before it would be habitable, let alone completed. Till then, they would have to slum it in these draughty, wooden cess pits.

Oblivious to the bishop's concerns, FitzGilbert continued. "It's said that this man brought down a Viking warrior at Stamford who had, until then, held up the whole of King Harold's army and prevented them from crossing the bridge. He had killed over forty men single-handedly before this Saxon took him down with a spear by floating down the river until he was under the bridge."

"Seems a bit cowardly if you ask me. Killing a man without facing him in combat."

"Whatever the rights or wrongs of it, King Harold himself rewarded him personally for that particular act. Then there was the battle at Senlac itself, where this man stood alongside his father with the king until the end; Harold's last two defenders in fact."

"Well, that didn't turn out too well either, did it? I can't say that you are impressing me too much with these feats of valour as you call them."

"Though he could not prevent Harold's death, the fact that he stood when all was lost, killing six of our best knights in so doing, tells me he is a man of courage and no little skill. He's not a man to shrink from danger, nor will he shirk a fight. For this reason, I beg of you to afford me a conroi of forty knights with which to seek him out and kill him."

"And if I were to give you these men, what would you do with them? How, in God's name, would you find him? He could be anywhere in this foul country."

"I have men out in the market places and taverns, watching and listening. It's just a matter of time until someone hears something."

The bishop's face showed he was anything but convinced. "Look, FitzGilbert, I've no problem with you embarking on this quest, however foolhardy I might think it to be. If you want to get yourself killed then that is your business. If this Saxon is as fearsome as your stories suggest then I'm glad that it is you who plans to face him rather than me. But what I would have a problem with would be trying to explain to my brother how I allowed forty of his cherished knights to be slaughtered on some fool's errand."

FitzGilbert's face flushed with anger, but he held his peace. He had every ounce of his younger brother's fire in his belly, but where he differed was that he was not ruled by his emotions. Robert was far more calculating, weighing up the likely consequences of his actions before committing them. So, whilst he longed to retort to Odo's jibe, he knew that to do so would risk rejection. He could take a few insults as long as he got what he wanted.

His suspicions proved correct almost immediately when Odo – perhaps realising there was no sport to be had in goading him further – sighed and swivelled round in his chair so that he could take up the writing materials that lay on the table in front of him.

"Fine. On your head be it, FitzGilbert. Go see the Master of Horse and give him this note. It authorises you to assemble the men you want for your purpose."

FitzGilbert bowed briefly. "My thanks, Lord. I will not let you down."

As the younger man grasped the note, Odo held on to it, fixing FitzGilbert with a gaze that burned through his eyes and left no doubt as to the strength of the threat that followed. "See that you don't. Bring at least half of them back or don't bother coming back at all."

TWENTY - TWO

The training was finally starting to bear fruit. After the first few days, Thurkill had despaired, wondering whether the villagers would ever get the hang of standing in a shieldwall. It was not a natural thing for a man to do after all, standing placidly to face an onrushing enemy. Every bone, every muscle in your body told you to run; either away from the danger or headlong towards it depending on your disposition. But for the shieldwall to work, it relied on every man being steady; every man keeping his shield overlapped with that of the man to his right, protecting him from the thrust of spear or sword.

And a well-formed wall of shields backed by strong, disciplined warriors, did work. It had been proven time and time again over the centuries. It had nearly worked at Senlac. If only they had stayed put on top of the ridge, the Normans might never have broken them

Those lessons had not been lost on Thurkill and so he schooled the men tirelessly day after day until they finally began to show signs of skill and proficiency. Excluding him and his five companions, there were roughly thirty men of fighting age and strength, ranging from the youngest, a boy of sixteen winters – Thurkill would take none younger – up to the oldest, a grey-haired bear of a man who reckoned he was at least forty but could not be sure.

He had the strength of two men and a ferocity that was an inspiration to his fellows. Thurkill placed him on the far left of the shieldwall in the most exposed and, therefore, most dangerous, position of all. You needed your best and strongest man there as the strength of the shieldwall rested on his courage and steadfastness. In Urri the blacksmith, Thurkill had found the ideal man for the job.

But it had been a struggle all the same. It took most of the first day just to have the men hold their shields correctly. Most of them had little or no experience at all, having never been called up for the fyrd before. Those who had any battle experience had been lost at Senlac, leaving the village shorn of fighting men.

Once they had finally mastered how to link their shield with that of the man next to them, Thurkill had slowly begun to introduce spears as an added complication. He had the men form two ranks, with the one in front focussed on presenting an impenetrable barrier, while those behind looked for gaps through which they could thrust the seven-foot-long ash shafts, topped with the wickedly sharp leaf-shaped blade.

After a week of intense practice, Thurkill finally pronounced himself happy that they had mastered the basics. His words were greeted with much cheering and slapping of backs. He had learned, from building the palisade that the men were willing to follow his commands and responded well to encouragement. So, he made sure that, every now and then, he singled out a man here, another there, to compliment them by name. To be praised in front of their comrades gave a man a boost which, more often than not, saw him apply extra effort to the next activity, which in turn made his fellows work that bit harder so that they too might earn their lord's approval.

Even Toki came out to join the training, though Thurkill refused to allow him to stand in the wall with the others, despite his fervent protestations. Whilst his leg was healing well – Wulfric had, a few days earlier, announced that the bone had knitted together as well as he could have hoped – he was by no means strong enough to take the added pressure that being part of a shieldwall entailed. After all, he was still hobbling and walking with the aid of a stick that Leofric had fashioned for him, which fitted snugly beneath his armpit.

So, while the others toiled, Toki sat on a log by the side of the drilling yard, his damaged leg stretched out in front of him, and watched. Though he was not taking part, he could still listen and observe so that he could pick up the sense of it all. When the time came, he would be able to join the others without too much difficulty.

During the second week, Thurkill considered it was time to move up to the next level in their drills. Up to that point, his five hearth-warriors had positioned themselves amongst the villagers so that they could show them how it was done and give the shieldwall greater shape and strength. But now, with the core skills mastered, Thurkill removed them and had them charge the wall to try to break it instead. At first it had been an unmitigated disaster. Even with just six men against thirty arranged in two ranks, they had broken the line without difficulty. None of the defenders had expected their attack to be anything like as ferocious as it was, and they scattered in confusion at the first impact. One or two in the centre had even fallen backwards to the ground only to find themselves staring at the point of a sword held to their throat by a grinning attacker.

Though he had expected such an outcome – he had told his companions to go in hard to teach the lesson well – Thurkill was still disappointed that they had broken quite so easily. "This is no game, gentlemen," he'd roared. "The shieldwall is the only thing that stands between you and death; between the enemy and your women and children. Had that been for real, you would all now be dead and your wives would be screaming as soldiers forced themselves upon them."

He allowed the silence to grow, letting his words sink in. He was deliberately harsher than perhaps he needed to be, but it was important that they realised what was at stake. For them to have the image of a faceless enemy raping and killing their womenfolk was no bad thing if it gave them the resolve to stand firm. His outburst also told him that shame and guilt could be a strong motivational factor – just as much as praise – as, on the second attempt, the wall almost held. The look of determination on their faces, one or two of them even snarling in anger, told him that the message had hit home. They understood now what defeat meant and they were desperate to show their lord that they could do better. Though they had still broken, it was not the craven attempt he had seen before.

They broke again on the third charge, but only due to bad luck. The man in the centre had lost his footing as he turned his ankle treading on a small stone. Down he went, yelping in pain, and Thurkill lost no time in stepping into the gap and bashing the man in the second rank out of the way with his iron shield boss. On this occasion, however, he had not even opened his mouth before Urri was lambasting them from his position on the left.

Thurkill smiled, using his shield to hide his face so that his mirth would not detract from his tirade. He was pleased to see the blacksmith take on this responsibility; every wall needed a leader and if Urri wanted to assume that role and if the men were prepared to listen to him, then it suited him down to the ground.

Urri was already a well-known and well-liked figure in the village; his job as blacksmith brought him into contact with almost everyone, whether for making and repairing farming equipment, casting nails for house-building or shoeing horses. Everyone knew Urri and depended on him for their livelihoods. Added to that, his size and great strength made him stand out from the rest. His booming voice would carry far over any field of battle, making sure none could be in any doubt as to his orders.

"My thanks, Urri," Thurkill stepped back into the centre once the blacksmith had exhausted his vocabulary. "On this occasion – it was ill luck rather than poor skill that led to your downfall. Had it not been for that stone, I believe you would have held. Nonetheless, it teaches a valuable lesson. Always be sure of your footing. In a real battle there will be stones, there will be discarded weapons and – on top of that – the ground will be slippery with the blood and guts of fallen men, friends and foe alike. You must take care where you place your foot for once you go down, not only are you a dead man but, in all likelihood, you will also have the deaths of your comrades on your conscience – however briefly – as your trip could split the wall apart."

Thurkill's confidence grew over the course of the rest of the day. Though it buckled at times or took a step or two back, the shieldwall did not break again. What's more, encouraged by Urri's example, the men began to talk to each other: to warn where there was danger; to exhort each other to greater efforts; to cheer every little success as it came. A *few more days of this,* Thurkill thought, and *we'll have a shieldwall worthy of the name.*

But he was not to be afforded the luxury of time. The shieldwall would be put to the test far sooner than he would have hoped, as the peace of the last several weeks was to be shattered, like the ice covering the village pond breaks when children throw heavy rocks into its midst.

***

The first inkling that all was not well came two days later. Most of the men were out working their fields, preparing the ground for the spring when they would spend long, back-breaking hours driving their ox-drawn ploughs back and forth across before sowing seeds in the resulting furrows. As the training had been going so well, Thurkill had relented in the face of their impassioned entreaties, allowing them time to tend to their neglected farms.

Meanwhile, he was in the mill, helping Eahlmund service the cogs and gears under old Haegmund's close instruction and watchful eye. Though still active, the miller was not as strong or as fit as he had been in his youth and he was glad of the help that Eahlmund provided, so much so that he had overcome his distrust of any man who showed more than a passing interest in his daughter. Many was the tale told in the tavern by rueful young men who had tried to steal a kiss from Hereswitha only to find themselves boxed round the ears by her father and sent on their way.

But with Eahlmund, he at last seemed satisfied that he'd found a man worthy of his daughter. That he was close friends with the new lord of the village doubtless helped, which was why Thurkill was only too glad to support his friend if it made the path of true love run more smoothly.

Despite the brisk chill of the February day, they were sweating in their shirt sleeves as they laboured. Everything had to be checked to ensure that it remained in full working order. Stocks of grain would soon pile up if the mill broke down for more than a day or two. Parts had to be inspected and those that were broken, damaged or otherwise worn out had to be repaired or replaced. Then there was the rust, all of which had to be scraped away and re-greased to avoid seizures. All to make sure that, when the time came, the mill would be ready to grind the mountains of grain that would come in from the fields.

They were just resting with a refreshing cup of watered ale, when Unferth, the pig herder's youngest son, came running in.

"Lord…" He stood there panting, bent double with his hands on his knees, breathless from the exertion of having run to the mill. The lad was in obvious distress, his thin body wracked with heaving sobs, while tears flowed freely down his cheeks leaving pale channels across his dirt-streaked cheeks.

Placing his cup down on the bench beside him, Thurkill rose to comfort the boy. "Take your time, Unferth. Pause a while so that you may catch your breath."

The poor boy tried to take a few deep breaths but each time he did so they turned into sobs. It was several moments before he had recovered his composure sufficiently to enable him to blurt out his news. "It's my father, Lord. He's dead."

Eahlmund rose to his feet, ready to run out of the mill, but Thurkill held him in check with a raised hand and an ominous look. "What do you mean 'dead', lad? How has this come to pass?" A myriad of thoughts raced through his mind: had he simply dropped dead from a failed heart as many of his age seemed to do? Had some accident befallen him in the forest? Or, worse, had someone killed him?

Though still snivelling piteously, Unferth was calmer now under Thurkill's soothing presence. "I don't know, Lord. I went to take him his lunch in the forest where he tends the pigs, as I do every day, and I found him lying on the ground. I hoped he was but sleeping but, as I came closer, I could see that he was dead."

"How so? Could you tell what had happened?" Thurkill dearly wanted to shake the boy to get the facts he needed from him as quickly as possible, but he knew he needed to tread lightly. He didn't want to upset him any more than he had to.

"There was blood. Lots of it from a big gash in his stomach, like a sword or spear would make."

"Who would do such a thing to a harmless old man? We should find the bastard and make him pay."

"Without doubt, Eahlmund, but we need to know what we face before we commit ourselves to an irrevocable course of action."

He could see the frustration etched on his friend's face, but he could also see that Eahlmund knew he was right. To blunder into a situation without knowing what awaited them would be foolhardy in the extreme. While it was his duty to avenge Egferth, he could not put the lives of others unnecessarily at risk. Already his mind had taken him back to his meeting with Aelfric a few weeks back.

As he saw it, there were four possible causes of this death. Least likely was an attack by one of the other villagers. Egferth was well liked and had no enemies that he knew of, so why would anyone want to kill him? Second, it could have been a passing thief who had tried to steal a pig, only to be surprised in the act. The other two possibilities were the least appealing. Either a band of lawless men had gathered nearby – the sort of which Aelfric had warned. Such people would be starving and would want to take livestock to stay alive. Emboldened by their numbers, they might well stoop to the level of killing the herder if it meant stealing a good number of pigs. Most worrying of all, though, would be if it was FitzGilbert with a force of soldiers come to kill him. He considered it unlikely as they would surely not want to draw attention to themselves until they were ready to attack, but perhaps Egferth had surprised them in their lair? One question should clear it up one way or another.

"Were many of your father's pigs missing, lad?"

"I could not swear for certain, Lord, for I did not stay to count them all, but I would reckon at least half were gone, from what I could tell."

"And what of your brothers?" He wasn't sure how many brothers Unferth had, but thought it was at least two."

"Egfrith was at home with mother as he hurt his foot yesterday, but Agbert was with father and he is missing."

"You're sure he is not dead like your father?"

"I don't know, Lord. I only know that I only saw one body."

Thurkill frowned. It was clear to him now what had happened. But how to respond? Time was critical if they were to find those responsible and save Agbert, if he still lived.

"Your orders, Lord?"

Thurkill glanced over to where his friend stood, next to the miller, both eager to help. He could delay no longer. "Eahlmund, go prepare the men, we will have need of them.

Then wait for my orders. And send Leofric to meet me at the gate, I have need of his tracking skills."

"Aye, Lord." Eahlmund rushed off, glad to be put to use. Like him, Thurkill was burning inside. A villager had been killed. One of his villagers. It was the first time such an atrocity had happened under his lordship and he yearned to run into the woods to hunt down those responsible. But he knew he had a duty of care to the rest of his people. He had to find out who was out there rather than blunder in blindly to avenge Egferth. What if there were dozens of them hidden in the woods? He would be no use to anyone dead having stumbled into an ambush. No, he would have to be patient, keep his rage in check, until he found out what they were facing.

Leaving Unferth with the miller with orders to take him back to his mother, Thurkill made his way to the village gate, arriving shortly before his companion. Thurkill was glad to have Leofric with him. Not only was he probably the fittest of his men, his skills as a hunter were second to none, having been taught to him from an early age by his father back in Haslow.

As they walked into the woods, heading to where Egferth took his pigs to root amongst the mast every day, Thurkill filled Leofric in on what he knew. "I need you to find the trail back to wherever the attacker or attackers have gone. I would know if they are still nearby, how many they be and whether they be ready for battle."

Leofric nodded and set off at a trot to where Thurkill had indicated that the pig herder's body would be. On arrival, they found that it was as the herder's son had described; Egferth lay on his back, arms outstretched and mouth open as if mid-scream. The wound was actually in his chest, though, deep and ragged. Death must have been almost instantaneous.

"Looks like he put up a fight, though, Lord."

Following Leofric's gaze, Thurkill noted that, clasped in the old man's left hand was what looked like a clump of human hair, the ends of which were matted with blood. It must have been ripped out in the struggle, Thurkill surmised. The tresses was long and straggly, another sign that they were not dealing with Normans, but he still needed to be sure before he gave his orders. He didn't suppose a Norman soldier would have allowed old Egferth to get close enough to grab his hair and, besides, didn't they all keep their hair short? This was much more in keeping with the Saxon style.

Meanwhile, Leofric was down on all fours, inspecting the ground around the body, scrabbling in an ever-widening arc until he rose back to his feet, a look of grim satisfaction on his face. "They went west, Lord, away from the village."

"Can you tell how many?"

"It's hard to say, but I would hazard half a dozen at least. The ground is soft which has helped preserve the tracks of all those involved, but that also means that there is much confusion and criss-crossing. On top of which, there are hundreds of hoof prints intermingled with human where they have sought to drive the panicked animals before them. All the signs tell me it's a raid intended to steal the pigs. But I can't say how many men were involved."

"Nor how many may have waited further back in the trees."

Leofric shrugged.

"No matter, let's follow the tracks a while and see where they lead us."

In all honesty, the path was not hard to follow. As his friend had said, the ground made soft from the wet winter weather meant that even someone as unskilled as Thurkill could easily stay on the tracks. Leofric, meanwhile, ranged widely from side to side to see if other clues were to be found. It wasn't long before he called Thurkill over. "Look here, Lord, another set of tracks. It seems to be just one person, smaller and lighter than the others so his prints are less deep, but there is no doubt in my mind."

"Agbert?"

"Yes. The tracks seem to run parallel to the main group, as if he is himself tracking them. I hope he stayed out of sight. It wouldn't go well for him were he to be spotted."

"We should hurry, Leofric. I fear for the lad."

As quickly and as quietly as they could, the two men ran on, staying low and moving from trunk to trunk as much as possible. It was hard to remain silent, though, as the forest floor was carpeted in leaves which in turn concealed any number of twigs. It was fortunate that there had been a lot of rain recently; the moisture having helped to dampen the noise that they made, but it still sounded to Thurkill's ears like a herd of cattle stampeding through the trees. He just prayed they could find the attackers soon and Unferth's brother.

"Lord, down!" Leofric's hissed warning brought him to a complete and sudden halt. He dropped to his knees beside his companion and leaned in to listen to what he had to say. "Voices up ahead. See where the ground rises a little? It looks like there's a hollow on the other side and I'll wager that's where we'll find our quarry."

Urging his heart to calm itself so that he could at least hear over the sound of blood rushing through his head, Thurkill lifted his head a little and turned his one good ear towards the direction of the voices. Though he could not make out the words, it sounded like an argument was in progress. *Pray God they are not so numerous that we cannot best them.* "How many do you think?" he whispered back at Leofric.

"There's three or four that speak, though there's no telling from here how many others watch. We'll have to get closer."

Gently, the two men lowered themselves until they lay flat on the leaf-strewn ground. Thurkill shuddered involuntarily as the cold and damp began to seep through his clothes. "Slowly," cautioned Leofric. "Feel for sticks as you go and move them rather than risk them cracking under your weight."

It took an age to cover the twenty or so paces to where the ridge peaked. Each movement had to be carefully planned and executed lest any unforeseen noise betray them. Just before they reached the edge, they pulled their hoods forward over their heads; the dark material would hopefully disguise them from any who casually glanced in their direction. The last few paces were taken at a pace that a snail would have been able to match, such was their proximity to the gathering.

The argument was still in full swing, giving Thurkill hope that all attention would be focussed on the protagonists. Eventually, they reached a position where they could look down into the hollow and, when they did so, Thurkill's heart sank. It was not just that he could count upwards of thirty men arrayed below them, but also what he saw lying on the ground around which the majority of the bandits were clustered. Agbert.

He was too far away to tell whether the boy were alive or dead. His face was, however, turned towards them and Thurkill could see a dark stain that ran from his forehead down to his chin. The poor lad had clearly been bludgeoned but was hopefully just unconscious.

To his great joy, this was soon confirmed when it became apparent that Agbert was the cause of the argument. After listening for a few moments, Thurkill could tell that the leaders of the group seemed to be split between those that wished to kill the boy and be done with it, and those that urged restraint. *At least the boy lives!* Thurkill grinned to himself. But he knew they would have to act fast if they wanted that to remain the case.

"What does it matter? We've already killed his father, what difference would it make if we do for his boy too? Two dead bodies are much the same as one."

"And one is already too many. I told you not to use your seax, Beorhtric, but you wouldn't listen. We only wanted the pigs. We could have just knocked him out and been on our way."

"You're too soft, Lilla. Always have been. What if he'd woken up and raised the alarm before we'd escaped? We'd have the whole village down on us by now."

"And who's to say that won't still happen? How many sons does he have? What if this lad has a brother who has already raised the alarm? You saw the village. That wall and the ditch that surrounds it tell me that there are men there that know how to fight. We should have passed it by and sought a softer target."

"Too late for that now, Lilla. You know how hungry we are. You know how long we've been wandering the forests with nothing more to eat than what berries and mushrooms we can find. We needed meat now or else we'd soon starve. These people have plenty; more than enough in fact. What's a few pigs to them?

"It's his own fault that he got himself killed, anyway. If he'd just let us take them and be done with it, he might still be alive.

Bastard tore half the hair from my scalp too." The man named Beorhtric placed his hand gently to the side of his head where Thurkill could see there was a bloody patch where old Egferth had done his damage. *Good for you, old man. Rest assured we will finish the job for you.*

Meanwhile, Lilla still did not look convinced but chose to say nothing. With matters left hanging in the balance, Thurkill gently nudged Leofric in the ribs and indicated with the briefest of nods that they should retreat back from the ridge. Once they were a safe distance away, he grabbed his friend by the shoulder.

"Hurry back to Gudmundcestre and gather the men without delay. Eahlmund will have already roused them so they should be ready to go. Bring them back as quickly as you can. I'll keep watch here to see what they do. Hurry back, man, Agbert's life is in grave danger. I just pray that Beorhtric doesn't carry the day while you are gone."

Leofric turned and ran. It was not far back to the village – no more than a mile – but Thurkill still reckoned it would be a half hour or more before they returned. *Please God stay their hand for a while longer. The boy doesn't deserve to die.*

***

All thirty of the men from the village were armed with shield, spear and seax when they arrived. Leofgar held them back, well out of earshot while Leofric and Eahlmund went forward to where Thurkill waited to discuss their plans.

"Are they ready for a fight? They know what is expected of them?" Thurkill asked, anxious that this would be the first time they would have had to use their weapons in anger. Practice was all well and good but nothing could really prepare you for the stark reality of battle when the snarling, screaming man in front of you was intent on taking your life. He hoped their nerve would not desert them when the time came.

"As they'll ever be," Eahlmund growled. "They want the blood price for Egferth and to save his son. There could be no greater motivation. The boy lives still?"

"Aye. A truce appears to have settled upon them and they seem unsure what to do next. The fools believe themselves safe here; they've made no attempt to place sentries to watch for attack."

"Well, then let us teach them the error of their ways and what it means to kill one of our own."

"Let's not be hasty. I would offer them the chance to surrender and face justice, if they would take it."

"They deserve to die."

"That's as may be, but it is not our place to play God. There is a law in this land and we should offer them the choice to subject themselves to it. They may still be condemned to die for their crimes, or at least those that perpetrated the foul murder will, but if they refuse to submit and choose instead to fight, then so be it. May God have mercy on their souls for I will not."

Eahlmund grinned and shrugged. "That logic explains why you are lord and I'm but a hairy-arsed oik, I suppose. What would you have us do, then?"

"Leofric, take a dozen men and sweep around to the rear; we must cut off any possible escape. Hoot like an owl twice when you're in position. Eahlmund, you bring the rest of the men up behind me when I give the signal. Have them form a shieldwall in two ranks as they have learned. Go now – but quietly. I'll not have them forewarned of our presence."

While Leofric took his men on a wide circuit of the hollow, Thurkill armed himself, putting on the mailshirt and helmet that Eahlmund had brought from the village. He took his time to make sure everything was just so for he wanted his appearance to frighten the bandits. With luck they might submit without bloodshed. Lastly, he slipped his left arm into the leather straps at the back of his shield, feeling the familiar heft and weight of the round wooden board and taking comfort from it.

As he readied himself, he felt the familiar knotted sensation take hold of his stomach, as anxiety grew about what the next few moments would bring. If held no fear, though. If anything, he welcomed it, grateful for the sharpening of his senses that came with it.

An owl hooting in the distance brought him back to the moment. There it was again. It was the sign that Leofric was ready. It occurred to him, briefly, that the sound of an owl in day time might seem incongruous to anyone who took the time to consider it, but he hoped that the brigands were too otherwise preoccupied to worry about strange bird noises. Besides, the shadows were lengthening now as the short winter day approached its end, so perhaps it was not all that out of place.

"Here, Lord. Go with God." Thurkill nodded his thanks as Eahlmund handed him his two-handed war axe, the same one that King Harold had gifted him after his first battle at the bridge near Stamford. It felt good to be holding it once more, its wooden handle worn smooth by years of use by its Norse owner before it came to him. He hoped one day to hand it on to his son, with the story of how it was won, and that the boy might also hand it on to his own son in the fullness of time. He prayed he would not have to dip its blade in Saxon blood that day, though; that the sight of it alone might be enough to give them pause. But he would be ready, should it come to it, to plunge it once more into the flesh of another man.

"Thank you, friend. Watch for my signal and then bring the men forward. It's my hope that they surrender, but if God wills it then we must all be ready to fight."

Turning back to address the men, he could see that a several of them had turned white, their eyes wide and staring. He remembered back to his first time and knew only too well the feelings that filled their souls at that moment. Eahlmund had already positioned himself, Eardwulf and Copsig evenly amongst their number so that none was too far away from an experienced man, and then there was the dependable Urri in his usual place out on the left. As ever the huge blacksmith looked ready for anything. His teeth were bared and Thurkill could swear he could hear a low growl coming from him. The blood lust was beginning to descend. If it did not come to a fight, that one might need to be restrained, he mused grimly.

"Remember your training, lads. Keep your formation, protect the man to your right and all will be well. Though their numbers match ours, they have no armour and no shields. If they are foolish enough to stand against us, we will cut them down like wheat falling to the sickle. Keep your nerve, keep your footing and you will have nothing to fear, I swear it."

Satisfied that they were ready, he strode forward towards the edge of the ridge. He walked up behind the largest tree so that he might be hidden from sight until the very last moment. Then, when he was ready, he stepped out from behind its gnarled and knotted trunk that was the width of at least two men.

Such was the stealth of his approach that it took a while for his presence to be noted. He stood with his feet planted shoulder width apart, his right hand resting on the end of the axe handle, while its blade rested casually on the ground mid-way between his feet. The height of the ridge added to his already imposing stature, lending him an appearance that he hoped would strike awe into those below.

Eventually, one or two heads began to turn in his direction, a movement which soon spread across the whole group. A hush fell as they took in the sight of this fully armoured warrior. He had no idea what was going through their minds but he hoped his appearance would go some way to robbing them of any bellicose intentions they might have harboured.

Thurkill chose to let the silence fester for a while. It would do no harm to let their fear grow unchecked. He could see that Agbert was conscious now, but still groggy. He was lying on the ground curled up like a new-born foal. That was something that went in the outlaws' favour, at least, but there was still the small matter of the boy's father to avenge. When he felt they had waited long enough, he spoke.

"My name is Thurkill and I am Lord of Gudmundcestre, the village to the east of here. I believe you have some things that belongs to me." Every word, though delivered with calm assurance, dripped with menace, leaving them in no doubt that he was deadly serious. " You must send the boy back to me, return my pigs, and submit to my authority. If you do not, things will not go well for you."

There was no immediate reaction to his words. One or two of the men looked frightened, on the verge of panic almost, glancing wildly in every direction as if fearing they would be attacked at any moment. These men would be of little use in a fight, Thurkill thought to himself. Their first thought would be to run. Many others, however, were made of sterner stuff including Beorhtric, who appeared to have emerged from his leadership struggle with Lilla as the winner. He spat contemptuously on the ground and pulled his seax from his belt.

"My apologies, Lord," he bowed ostentatiously to add weight to the sarcasm that laced his voice. "I had not realised he was your own little plaything. Or perhaps it is the pigs you prefer in the bedroom? Either way, you shall have neither without a fight, and I don't rate your chances too highly as you are but one man and we are many."

Thurkill had not really expected them to give up easily, but he had a duty to his own people to avoid bloodshed if he could, so he ignored the crude taunt and offered them another chance, appealing to those who were less belligerent than this scar-faced bully.

"You must know that you all stand outside of the law right now. You are lordless men with no standing and you should think about your position carefully. A man has been killed and I have a responsibility to his family to see the blood price paid by those who committed this heinous crime. Now I don't doubt that not all of you were involved or even wanted this outcome, so if the killer or killers are handed over to me now for justice, I will see that the others are treated fairly at the next sitting of the lord's court.

"I urge you to think well on my offer for it will not be made again. Should you choose to reject it, I will have no mercy and you will only have yourselves to blame. I will give you time to consider your response."

Whether or not there were those who wished to accept his terms, Beorhtric gave them no choice. Doubtless he was one of those directly responsible for the death of the pig herder so, he had nothing to lose.

"Fuck you and your justice. You must be as stupid as you look to have come here alone."

With that, he began to run towards the slope, yelling at the others to follow. But before he could reach Thurkill, two things happened in quick succession. First, Thurkill shouted "Now!" as he raised his shield ready to receive the bandit's wild lunge. Second, almost twenty men sprang to their feet and stepped forward until they were level with their lord on the edge of the ridge. While Thurkill had been talking, they had slowly inched forward through the leaves until they were as close as they dared to be.

The effect was mesmerising. A look of utter shock and bewilderment spread across the faces of hapless brigands. But they were too far committed now to stop. With a roar of frustration, they pressed home their attack. But it was a futile enterprise, doomed to failure, like a storm blowing against a stone wall. Though they gave it their all, the shieldwall stood firm. It did not even bend.

Before they had a chance to gather themselves for a second surge, Thurkill gave the order. "Advance, slow walk."

Like the well drilled war-band they now were, the spearmen took a step forward, taking their lead from Urri on the left, keeping pace with him so that the impenetrable line of shields remained intact. Those in the second rank raised their spears to shoulder level and began thrusting through the gaps between the heads of those in front. Straightaway men began to fall, screaming, blood gushing from fatal wounds to the neck or shoulder. It was an uneven fight from the beginning and the brigands never stood a chance. It was just a matter of how many would die before they surrendered. Already at least half a dozen men were down and the rest were starting to give way before the villagers' inexorable march down the slope.

Thurkill knew he had to bring matters to a swift conclusion. Agbert was safe for the moment but there was no telling what Beorhtric or any of his henchmen might do in their madness or panic. It would take but a moment to stab the lad where he lay. He had to either force them to surrender or kill them all. He could not risk losing the boy as well as his father in the space of a day.

"Finish them!" He roared, swinging his deadly axe down hard on the head of the unfortunate man in front of him. The blade split the skull in two, splattering grey brain matter over all those nearby.

That single act proved to be the tipping point. Distraught with grief, half threw down their weapons and sank to their knees, imploring their assailants to spare their lives. The other half, including Beorhtric, turned and fled, running headlong into Leofric and his warriors who now emerged from the trees at their rear. Those that put up a fight were cut down almost before they knew what had hit them, while the rest saw sense and gave up.

There were too few villagers to block every route out of the hollow, however, and Thurkill saw two of the bandits were able to evade them and make good their escape to the south, running as if the very devil were on their heels. He resolved to let them go.

For the rest, however – a mere eight of the original thirty – they were soon rounded up and made to sit in a small circle surrounded by a dozen hard-faced spearmen who left them in no doubt that any attempt to run would be met with a blade in the gut. It had been a short but bloody encounter. Twenty brigands lay dead or dying on the forest floor. They would do what they could for the wounded but most would die a slow agonising death from their horrific wounds.

On the other side of the balance sheet, one of their own number had been killed, an older man who had been too slow to raise his shield in the face of Beorhtric's attack. It irked Thurkill that the ringleader had managed to account for a second man from the village but, when all was said and done, the shieldwall had acquitted itself well on its first proper engagement. There were a few cuts and bruises that would mend with time and, here and there, one or two of the younger men had been violently sick when the battle ended, but none had disgraced themselves during the conflict. They had all fought with valour for the honour of the village. The blood price demanded by the death of Egferth had been met in full.

TWENTY - THREE

Agbert's mother, Ella, was overjoyed to see her son safely
returned, none the worse the wear for his ordeal but for a narrow
gash to the head. Whilst she would mourn her husband's death
for some time to come, she at least could do so with her eldest
son by her side. Every single one of the pigs had also been
recovered and returned to their pens, though it had not been easy
as they had scattered far and wide when the fighting started and
had little inclination to be rounded up by those same men who
now smelled of blood and fear. But at least Agbert had his full
herd to care for now, as his father had done before him.

As for the captives, Thurkill had them locked away with two
armed guards stationed at the door. Within hours of their return
to Gudmundcestre, their number had reduced to five as three of
them succumbed to wounds inflicted during the fighting.
Wulfric had done what he could for them, but to no avail. He
had no difficulty overlooking the fact that they were thieves and
outlaws, proclaiming "We are all God's children. It is for Him
to judge them when the time comes, not me."

Of the five remaining prisoners, Beorhtric still lived, having
led his compatriots to their doom. Even now, he remained sullen
and lacking in any remorse and it pained Thurkill for he knew
what he must do, however distasteful he might find it. For the
others, however, he had some sympathy. They had been led to
this fate, rather than chosen it for themselves. Yes, they could
have found a different path, but what option did they really
have? It was the Normans who were the true architects of their
downfall, having destroyed their homes and taken away their
livelihoods. Who could honestly say they would have behaved
differently in the same circumstances? What would have
become of the people of Gudmundcestre had the Normans
destroyed their village?

With Aelfric still away in Normandy, it fell to him to decide
what to do. But, with no knowledge in matters of law, he wasn't
comfortable acting on his own so he sent Eardwulf north to

158

Huntendune to summon Alwig the Steward. With the older, more experienced man by his side, he knew he would feel more able to act with the authority invested in him by Aelfric. He had to be sure that everything that was to be done would be carried out in accordance with the laws of the land, and for this he needed Alwig's guidance.

The Steward arrived the next day, coming straight to lord's hall where he was welcomed by Thurkill and Hild. "I am glad you called for me, Lord. From what I hear, a most heinous crime has been committed and justice must be seen to be done and done swiftly, so that a clear message may be sent to all others who would seek to live outside of the law."

"I agree, Alwig, but there is a minor complication here. We have five captives, only one of whom – I believe – was directly involved in the killing of the pig herder, Egferth. The others had no part in it."

"How do you know this?"

"I have spoken to them. I have seen the fear in their eyes, they know what fate awaits them and I have no reason to believe them liars. They tell me that six men only went to steal the pigs, four of whom died in the subsequent fight. Another was one of the two men who escaped us, and the last is Beorhtric, their leader, who is also our captive. The tracks we found by Egferth's body bear witness to the truth of it."

"I see. And what of Egferth's widow? Have you spoken to her? Has she let it be known what price she would see exacted for her husband's murder?"

"I confess I have not. I've left her in peace to mourn her husband ahead of the funeral which takes place later today."

"Perhaps wise, Lord Thurkill. Once he's been laid to rest, then we can see to the business of justice. I suggest you summon the folkmoot for tomorrow. Let the landholders and best men of the village assemble to sit in judgement on these brigands. As lord of the village, you will preside over the hearing while I shall speak against the men on behalf of the widow, if she will have me. I will speak to her tonight."

Thurkill nodded in agreement, happy for Alwig to take charge of matters. With his help, he hoped to navigate a safe path through the thorny matter of dispensing justice for crimes committed.

***

Egferth's funeral was a sombre affair. The old man was well liked; as one of the elders of the village, he had been a member of the folkmoot as well. To help matters, Thurkill had paid for one of the recovered pigs to be slaughtered so that there would be meat aplenty for all to enjoy in the gathering that took place once the burial was over. He had paid well over the odds – perhaps ten times its value – to ensure that Ella had a little extra coin to tie her over while her sons took time to assume their father's duties.

As for Ella, herself, she did her best to present a brave face to her fellow villagers, but it was plain that she was in great pain. Her eyes were red rimmed from crying continually since the news was first broken to her. Although death was not uncommon, Thurkill mused, people could rationalise it, accept it even, when it happened as a result of age, sickness or childbirth. These things happened often and – though immeasurably sad of themselves – were not so rare that they warranted such an intensely emotional response. Egferth's death, however, was senseless and callous. It should not have happened and was wholly unnecessary. They could have taken the pigs without killing him.

They had been together for over twenty years and had grown to love and care for each other greatly. Everywhere they went, they were always seen holding hands and smiling, sharing a few words or even a kiss as they went. It was no wonder that her husband's murder had hit her so hard.

Thurkill had little doubt in his mind how she would react when he went to talk to her at the end of the wake. Hild accompanied him, breaking away on arrival to hug Ella tightly to her chest. With tears in her eyes, she pressed the older woman's head into her shoulder, telling her how sorry she was for her loss. The show of compassion brought forth a renewed bout of sobbing from the widow which she fought to bring under control. Thurkill was happy to stand back, waiting at a respectful distance for Ella to regain her composure; he had no wish to make matters worse if he could help it.

"Forgive me, Lord, for the wound still runs deep."

"Worry not, Ella, for you have nothing for which to apologise. I know the pain you must be suffering and I thank God that you still have your three boys to care for you at this time."

"Thanks be to God and to you, Lord, for seeing my eldest safely home. To have lost both in one day would have been truly unbearable."

Thurkill guided her to sit at her table, taking the stool next to her in turn. "It is on the question of your loss that I must talk to you, though. Forgive me for raising this with you now, but you will have heard that I've summoned the folkmoot tomorrow to stand in judgement over those brigands that survive and are in our custody. As painful as it may be, Ella, I must ask you what recompense you would seek from those that inflicted this misery upon you? As wife to the murdered man it is your right to have a say in such matters."

Ella was silent for a moment, while she pondered the question. Thurkill did his best to hide his surprise for he had expected her not to hesitate to call for them all to die for what they had done. But, when she answered, it was clear that he'd misjudged her. Despite her grief and sense of loss, she had not lost any of her compassion.

"I know that justice must be done, Lord, that an example must be made so that all might see that unprovoked murder has its consequences, but I would beg of you to show what mercy you can. From what I hear some of these men are young lads, not much older than my own boys, and I don't believe that they all chose this path of their own volition."

Thurkill nodded, his brow furrowed while he considered her words. "But what would you have me do, Ella? These men are responsible for your husband's death. They have blood on their hands."

"Not all of them, Lord. Would it not meet the requirements of the law, but also show mercy too, if you were to see to it so that those who had a hand in his murder pay the price the law demands, while those that didn't are spared? Did our Lord Jesus not beseech us to show mercy and to turn the other cheek?

Perhaps some of these poor wretches are deserving of a chance to redeem themselves here on earth."

Thurkill smiled. "I applaud you for your honesty and your wisdom, Ella. I must admit that this was not the answer I had expected and, for that, I have no doubt that God will reward you for your humility and foresight. For now, however, I will take your words with me into the folkmoot tomorrow and have them guide us in our deliberations."

**

The folkmoot assembled the next day on the open ground in front of the church in the place where the market usually met. As was traditional, they gathered in a semi-circle in front of the old stone cross that had been erected there many years earlier. No one knew exactly when but it was said to date back to when the first, wooden church had been built there well over three centuries before. It was the height of two men and heavily weathered in places, especially on the side that faced the worst of the wind and rain, so that some of the carved designs had long since worn smooth. But it was still an imposing sight, nonetheless, and a fitting place for the villagers to gather to hear proclamations from the king or for the business of justice to be done.

Usually, the folkmoot had little more important to debate other than disputes over land boundaries or whether deals struck between two men had been transacted fairly; so, a hearing relating to the murder of one of their own was certainly out of the ordinary. So much so that most of the villagers had abandoned their fields to watch the proceedings.

In addition to Thurkill, there were twelve members of the moot, meaning that he would have the casting vote should there be an even number of voices on either side. He prayed it would not come to that as he did not relish the thought of holding a man's life in his own hands. Killing a man in battle was one thing – that man had the chance to kill or be killed – but ordering a man to be put to death was quite different.

The twelve were the most prominent men of the village, those in positions of authority or who held sizeable tracts of land, well in excess of most others. Thurkill already knew a good number of them well, but others less so. There was Haegmund the miller, Urri the blacksmith and Wulfric the priest. Those three he knew the best. Then there was Agbert who had taken his father's place, and – as a consequence – stood out as being several years younger than the next oldest member. Though it was unusual for one so young to be called to the folkmoot, he was there on account of his now being the largest land owner in the village, save for Thurkill himself. Of the others, he knew them by sight and many of them by name, but he had not had occasion to speak at length to them before now.

As he walked into the centre of the circle, the twelve men rose to their feet in acknowledgement of his authority. Yet again he was conscious of his youth and inexperience in the company of these much older men, but he told himself to straighten his back and lift his chin. He could at least look the part even if he did not much feel it. Nodding his greeting to those assembled, he walked over to the lord's chair which had been carried from his hall and set in front of the stone cross. Taking his seat was the cue for the others to resume theirs on the twelve upturned tree stumps that had been provided for them. At the same time, Alwig strode forward from where he had been waiting to one side of the cross.

"Bring forward the prisoners."

The five men made for a sorry sight; their clothes little more than threadbare rags stained with blood and filth that spoke eloquently of their predicament. All bore the scars and bruises sustained in the fighting which, combined with the contemplation of their potential fate, had turned them into empty husks of men. All, that is, except for Beorhtric who continued to maintain his arrogant mien. Together, they shuffled forward in single file, their ankles roped together so that they could not make a run for it. Each man was also secured to the one in front by way of a loop around the waist which then extended to the next man. Finally, their wrists had also been tied in front of their bodies, completing their humiliation. They were led forward by Eahlmund, fully armoured and with sword drawn. Behind them walked Leofric and Leofgar, spears pointing at the backs of the captives. There was to be no risk of them escaping justice.

With much pushing and shoving, the five men were made to line up facing Thurkill, in the centre of the semi-circle and surrounded on all sides by jeering and yelling villagers. For the most part, their faces were white with fear; they could be in little doubt as to their fate that day. Though, whatever Beorhtric felt inside, his face bore a sneer that showed, outwardly at least, that he was not afraid. He seemed determined to meet whatever was to come his way with his head held high and a hearty measure of disdain.

Whatever his feelings towards the man, Thurkill had to admire his courage. He must have known the evidence against him was overwhelming – that he was, in all likelihood, going to die that day – but he would not beg for mercy. In other circumstances, Thurkill could imagine fighting alongside him in a shieldwall and being glad of his presence. He had no doubt that the man had fought at Senlac; the recently healed scars on his face and forearms bore witness to the fact.

Meanwhile, as the shouted abuse showed no sign of abating, Alwig had to hold up his hand to appeal for calm. It was a charged atmosphere and one which Thurkill hoped did not spill over into violence. It was important that they allowed the rule of law to run its course and not resort to becoming a lynch mob. Everything had to be done properly. He knew these people to be reasonable and fair-minded, but it was clear that those values had been sorely tested by recent events. He gestured at Alwig to begin; the sooner matters were brought to a conclusion the better.

"My Lord and honoured members of the folkmoot, these men stand before you today accused of the murder of Egferth, the pig herder. Let it be known that their guilt is not in doubt, none has denied it, none has come forward to say that the foul deed was not perpetrated by these men. What is in doubt, what does need to be decided, is the extent to which each of these men is culpable.

"Which of them held the blade that ended Egferth's life? Should only those who were directly involved in the killing be punished? Or does it not matter? Are they all guilty of the crime by association, by the nature of their common purpose, if you will? Do they all deserve to die for this crime?" There was much murmuring and nodding at this last point, accompanied by more angry shouts from a number of the villagers.

Alwig held up his hand once more for calm. "Lord, before I ask the members of the folkmoot to speak on this matter, is there anything you wish to say?"

Thurkill rose to his feet, trying hard to affect his most stern expression as the occasion warranted. He was very much aware that this was the first time he had been called upon to hold court in the village and that he, too, would be judged that day, on the fairness and wisdom of his ruling. Whatever decision the folkmoot came to, he could overrule it, though it would be unusual and he would need a very strong reason for doing so.

"My thanks, Alwig." He turned to face the half-circle. "Members of the folkmoot, all that I ask is that you do your duty before God. I know Egferth was well-liked, and his loss has hit the village hard, but I would urge that you do not allow emotion to cloud your judgement. And I would also ask those who have assembled here to observe proceedings – as is your right to do so, for we have no secrets – to maintain a respectful peace so that we may deliberate unhindered. Finally, you should all know that Egferth's widow, Ella, has called for us to show mercy where there is mercy to be found. Let us not take life for the sake of showing that we have the power to do so. Let us be sure in our hearts and our souls that the decisions we reach are both fair and just for all concerned."

The debate ranged back and forth for some time. From what Thurkill could see, of the two matters in question, there was a clear distinction. Of the matter of Beorhtric's guilt, there was no doubt. He had been heard to admit the deed by both Thurkill and Leofric. Once that had been established, early on in the proceedings, matters turned to the second point which was the extent to which the other four men who stood accused had been involved in the death. Thurkill remained aloof from the debate, as his role as lord and holder of the casting vote demanded, but from what he could see, the twelve men seemed evenly split; half calling for them all to be dealt with as one for they all acted as a group and none had tried to stop Beorhtric or rein him in; and the others claiming that the four deserved clemency for they had been powerless to prevent his actions.

Leofric was called to relay his recollection of the conversation he had overheard between Lilla and Beorhtric. He recounted how there had been a dispute between the two men with the former berating his fellow for killing the pig herder and seeking to spare his son. He was asked whether he could identify any of the four men as being staunchly in one camp or another, which he could not. But the fact there had been an argument amongst the outlaws carried some weight as it cast doubt on whether they had all acted with a single purpose.

At length, Wulfric – who had remained largely silent to this point – rose to speak. Thurkill leaned forward, eager to hear what the priest had to say. Though he thought he knew the man quite well, he realised that he had little idea which way he would cast his vote. Would he demand justice before God for the crime of which they were all accused, or would he call for mercy? The four prisoners had also noted Wulfric's priestly garb and were also listening intently, perhaps hoping that a man of God might be relied upon to have a more rational view than most. Those hopes were dashed as soon as he began to speak, though.

"Of all the people that live in this fine village of Gudmundcestre, Egferth stood above most others. He was a fine man, an honest man, always ready to lend a hand or an ear to any who was in need of either. Many is the jar of ale he and I sank together, talking long into the night for his was an opinion and a friendship that I valued above all others. It pains me beyond measure that I have had to bury in the grounds of my church, for I am older than he and it should have been me that went to meet our Maker first. I pray that I will be reunited with him there when the time comes, so that we can once again sink a cup of ale together. Until then, I shall miss him terribly and, until then, I shall hate those responsible for his death. I shall never forget what they have done and were it down to me alone, I would have them put to death without delay."

Wulfric paused to let his words sink in. There were those, Thurkill amongst them, that were aghast to hear the priest speak so vehemently whilst others among the assembled villagers roared their approval of his words. Once the tumult had finally subsided, the priest continued.

"But though I will not forget, Jesus teaches me to forgive; to love my fellow man as I would love myself. He would have me show understanding and compassion in all things. And let me tell you this, my friends, it shames me to hear Lord Thurkill convey to us the words of Egferth's wife. If she who, of all of us, has been most wronged by these men can learn to forgive, then who am I to say otherwise?

"She has taught me that my thoughts of revenge were base and she has reminded me of the duties of my faith, for which she has my gratitude. For this reason, I will follow her example. Let Beorhtric be put to death for he has condemned himself from his own mouth. Our laws demand it. But of these others, we cannot say that they held the blade that killed Egferth, we cannot say that they desired him to be killed. Indeed, I think it more likely that they abhorred this act as much as do we. I say that these men should be allowed to live. They should be punished for the crime of brigandage but no more than that."

As soon as Wulfric resumed his seat, the crowd erupted once more. So many voices were raised in anger that it was hard to tell for which side they shouted. Eventually, Thurkill lost patience and signalled to Alwig to bring the moot to order.

"We have heard the evidence and we have heard many opinions both for and against. There is little to be gained from extending this process further and so I call upon all members of the moot to cast their vote. Firstly, in the matter of Beorhtric. He stands accused of the murder of Egferth. What is your decision? Do you find him guilty of the crime?"

As one, all twelve men shouted "Aye."

Alwig nodded, signalling to the scribe he had brought from Huntendune for the purpose, to make a record of the decision. "I see there is no need to call for a count of the "noes", so the "ayes have it, the ayes have it."

Beorhtric showed no emotion at the decision; he must surely have expected it. He merely spat on the ground to show his contempt for the whole affair.

Thurkill found himself wondering how a man could be driven to such a position that he had no remorse for his actions and no care for whether he lived or died. His own grip on life was so strong that he could never contemplate going quietly to his death. He had seen too much and lost too many to not want to fight for his existence in any way he could.

"Moving on to the second matter. Of the four other men who also stand accused of the same crime, how do you find them?"

This time, however, a chorus of ayes and noes could be heard around the folkmoot circle. Alwig turned to converse with the scribe to check if their tally agreed before confirming. "My Lord, I must inform you that the vote is split: six for the Ayes and six for the Noes. The decision therefore rests with you. You have the casting vote."

Thurkill's worst fear had been realised. He now held the power of life and death over these four men. Each one of them stared at him, imploring him with their eyes to be lenient. In his heart he knew what the right thing to do was, but he also had to consider the mood of the villagers whom he knew to be ardent in their desire to have fitting retribution for the loss of Egferth. Would Beorhtric's execution satisfy that hunger sufficiently? If not, was that even a reason to condemn four other men, men whom he believed innocent of the murder, to death? Just to satisfy their blood lust?

He was aware that a deathly silence hung over the village square. All that could be heard was the birds chirruping in the branches of the huge oak tree that stood not far from where they sat, and the sound of the wind whistling through its leaves. It would be from one of those branches that Beorhtric would soon be hanging, but how many more bodies would there be alongside him, gently swinging in the breeze while crows pecked at their eyes? All eyes were now on him, awaiting his decision. Not for the first time he wished he did not carry the weight of responsibility for these matters. If only his father were here to shoulder that burden. He was also aware that Hild was now standing by his left shoulder. She had sensed his discomfort and had moved forward, as unobtrusively as possible, to lay a comforting hand on his shoulder. Thurkill took heart from the gesture, knowing that despite what he felt, he was not alone. Whatever decision he made; he knew that Hild would back him.

Slowly, deliberately, he rose to his feet. "Gentlemen of the folkmoot, I thank you for your diligence and your wise counsel on this matter. Your words have been fair and well-considered; rarely can a lord have been better served. Having heard opinions from both sides, I have reached a decision. Given the gravitas of the situation, you should know it is not one I take lightly. I would also remind you all that my decision is final and I will brook no dispute. The scribe will record the verdict and that will an end to the matter. I hope that is understood." Though he spoke to the twelve men before him, his eyes surveyed the crowd of villagers behind them, for it was they who most concerned him.

"I must be guided by the words of Ella, for it is she who has been most wronged here, as Wulfric so eloquently reminded us. As we heard no evidence that proves beyond doubt that these four men were involved in Egferth's murder, I decree that they will not pay for their crimes with their lives." A low, angry grumble greeted his pronouncement but he pressed on before it could develop further.

"However, that is not to say that these men are without blame. Though they may not have committed murder, they must still answer for the crime of brigandage. Stealing my pigs cannot go unanswered. It is my ruling, therefore, that these men be separated from their left hands so that they may learn that taking what it not theirs carries a consequence. All sentences will be carried out at dawn tomorrow."

TWENTY - FOUR

FitzGilbert's mailed fist smashed into the Saxon's face, spraying tiny drops of blood from his split lip and ruined nose in all directions. His head snapped back from the force of the blow and he slumped yet further between the grip of the two soldiers that struggled on either side to hold him upright. An evil sneer played across the Norman's mouth; he could not deny that he enjoyed the sense of power and control it gave him to inflict such violent punishment on a man as defenceless as this. In truth, he had no real reason to harm the man; they had found him wandering the woods along with another whom they had already killed when he tried to flee from them; the fool had believed he could outrun their horses. When would these people learn they were no match for their new rulers? But it was sport nonetheless, something on which he could unleash his pent up frustration.

His anger had been growing unchecked over the last several weeks spent fruitlessly searching for this damned Saxon dog who had killed his brother, Richard. Nowhere could they find any sign of him, nor had anyone heard tell of him or, perhaps more likely, had not been willing to tell him if they had. But now he had run out of patience. He was no longer prepared to enquire politely at every village or town he came to. Now he would do it his way and to hell with the consequences. William was still in Normandy and his half-brother, Odo, who had been left in charge seemed to be less inclined to tread warily around their new subjects. As long as he didn't get his conroi of forty knights killed, he felt he could do much as he liked.

"So, I'll ask again, you snivelling wretch, tell me your name."

The man had to spit to clear the blood and phlegm from his ruined mouth, taking care not to splatter his tormentor's boots. "Lilla, Lord."

"See, Lilla, that was not too difficult was it? You didn't really need to take all that punishment just for your name, did you? Now, if you would be so kind, please tell me what the two of you were doing in the woods on your own, covered in blood? And why did your friend run from us?"

Lilla's eyes filled with tears, though whether from the pain of his nose or despair at his situation was unclear. "We thought you were coming to kill us."

"And why would you think that?" A look of understanding slowly began to spread across FitzGilbert's face. "Wait. Are you telling me there were more of you before but that you had been attacked and many of your number killed? That would explain the blood, after all."

Lilla nodded miserably, but offered no further detail.

"Why on earth would anyone do that? I am aware of no other Norman soldiers in this area, so it must have been Saxons who did this, am I right?" Taking Lilla's continued silence as confirmation, he continued with his reasoning.

"I can only conclude that you and your friends have been living outside of the law in the forests, and you started to run out of food. There's only so many berries and mushrooms to be found, right? And after a while you become bored of such paltry fare; a man needs meat after all. And from there it was but a short step to stealing something that does not belong to you. And it sounds like you found out the hard way that such actions carry consequences. Where was all this happening eh, Lilla? Not far from here I'll wager."

The dazed Saxon made the mistake of hesitating too long before answering. His head was swimming with pain and his vision blurred as a result of the beating he had endured to that point, so it was no wonder that he struggled to stay focussed on what his interrogator was saying.

None of that mattered to FitzGilbert, though. He was not inclined to be kept waiting while this pathetic excuse for a man felt sorry for himself. Bunching his hand into a fist once more, he punched Lilla square in the mouth, loosening two teeth in the process which the bloodied wretch then spat onto the floor along with copious amounts of blood; no longer caring whether any found its way onto his captor's clothing.

Between sobs, Lilla managed to croak "Gudmundcestre."

"In the name of Christ our Saviour, your language is a garbled mess at the best of times. Where in the name of God's hairy ball sack is that?"

"A day's walk north of here, along the old Roman road."

"Hmmm. We had not ventured that far north as yet. Tell me about this Gudmundcestre. What sort of place is it and what sort of man is it that is called lord there?"

***

FitzGilbert removed his mailed gloves finger by finger before flinging them at one of the two nearby soldiers. "Have them cleaned up. I want all the blood and other bits of Saxon washed out before dawn. And see you don't leave them wet; I'll not have them back covered in rust, mark you."

As the man scurried away to do his master's bidding, the Norman turned to his second in command, the captain in charge of the small unit of horsemen. "What do you make of that, Hugh? Sounds like this Saxon lord at Gudmundcestre is quite a character. Taller than most men, young – not yet full bearded – a warrior of some renown. Could he be our man do you think?"

Hugh shrugged. FitzGilbert's petty feud was of no particular interest to him. As long as the men got paid, had the chance of a little booty on the side and had their pick of women every now and again – willing or otherwise – then all was fine with him. For the last few weeks, though, they had seen precious little of either coin or girls and he knew the men were becoming restless. Whether this Lord of Gudmundcestre was the man his master sought was immaterial; his men were itching for a fight and the promise of spoils that came with it.

"I think it worth a look, Lord. My men could do with the sport."

TWENTY - FIVE

Thurkill shuddered as he slipped out from beneath the furs under which he and Hild slept. The planks that formed the walls of their chamber were frosted white on the inside bearing witness to another frozen night. As he sat on the edge of the bed, pulling on his boots, his thoughts turned to the day ahead. Not for the first time, he found himself ruing his role as lord of the village, but it was a duty he knew could not be avoided, however unpleasant. Those who had been wronged had to know that their lord would enforce retribution and that compensation would be imposed upon those who were found guilty. The law had to be an effective deterrent so that those who chose to act outside of its constraints knew they would not escape the consequences when they were brought to justice.

Despite all that his rational mind told him, however, it did not make the job any easier, any less distasteful. He would be heartily glad when it was over. Thankfully, he would not have to wield the axe himself; Urri had already stepped forward to volunteer for that task. It pleased Thurkill that the blacksmith was once again showing such strong leadership, not least because he remained acutely aware that he was still a newcomer here. To have one of the villagers carry out the folkmoot's sentence could only help to increase its validity in the eyes of all those who witnessed it.

A rustling sound behind him told him that Hild was also now stirring. "Hurry up, my love. The sooner we get this over and done with the better."

When they were ready, Thurkill pushed open the door to find most of the villagers already assembled in the space in front of the church, ready to bear witness to the carrying out of the sentences. Although there were no clouds, the sun had only just begun to rise above the tree-line to the east and so the village was still shrouded in the dawn's drab grey hue.

Together, they walked hand in hand to take their position in the centre of the folkmoot, close by the stone cross that faced

173

the great oak. As they walked, their feet crunched over the hard frost that had formed overnight. He was glad he had worn his thickest cloak. Not only did it keep the worst of the chill air out, but it also helped mask the fact that beneath it, he was shivering like a petrified dog. It would not do to have folk think him in any way afraid of what was to follow.

Once greetings had been exchanged, Thurkill wasted no time in giving the order to begin.

"Eahlmund, bring forth the prisoners."

The crowd parted like the Red Sea once had for Moses, to allow the small group to come forward. The five men shuffled forward in single file, flanked by three spearmen on each side. They halted by the old oak tree in front of which five tree stumps had been lined up. Above the middle stump, there hung a rope which had been slung over one of the oak tree's thickest branches; at the end of which had been knotted a loop just larger than a man's head.

Urri stood behind the stumps next to a brazier that already burned fiercely. Thurkill reflected that the blacksmith must have been up for some time already to have achieved such a blaze. Protruding from the brazier were a number of irons, tools of the man's trade, which Urri rearranged from time to time to ensure that the heat was evenly distributed amongst them.

The five men stared at the scene in front of them. Four of them were white with fear, their eyes wide and staring in every direction as if hoping for some late reprieve that might spare them their fate. The fifth, Beorhtric, stood as impassive and as sullen as ever, as if bored by the whole affair. The man had been resigned to his fate as soon as he had been captured, if not before, and today was no different. He was not going to give anyone the satisfaction of seeing him beg for mercy.

With the men now assembled in a line, Thurkill saw no reason to delay matters further. "Beorhtric, you have been found guilty of the murder of Egferth of Gudmundcestre. The sentence is death. Proceed." His voice as cold as the bitter chill that burned at his fingertips.

Without hesitation, Leofric and Leofgar grabbed Beorhtric and manhandled him up onto the middle tree stump. Stepping up behind him, Leofric reached for the noose before pushing it down over the condemned man's head, adjusting the knot until the rope sat snugly under his chin. Jumping down, he then looked over for final confirmation. Thurkill nodded briefly, his face an emotionless mask. The two brothers then turned to face Beorhtric who, even now, scowled his defiance, and – raising their right legs in unison – kicked away the stump with the flats of their feet.

The brigand let out a sickening gasp as the rope snapped taut around his neck. The depth of the drop was not sufficient to break his neck and, instead, he was left to dangle, his legs kicking futilely as he struggled for breath. Within moments, his face began to turn purple, his eyes bulging in their sockets as the strain for air became unbearable, while his kicks became weaker and weaker. Then, his body gave one final jerk before convulsing no more and he was left swaying gently in the breeze. Rather than cheer or shout, the crowd were deathly silent, the only sound being the creaking of the rope as it swung back and forth, protesting at the weight it still bore.

Those closest to Beorhtric now covered their noses with their hands as they became aware that the dying man's bowels had voided at the point of his death, a fact which – Thurkill knew – did not reflect on the man's courage. His father, who had seen many such executions, had once told him many years ago that the victim often soiled himself through no fault of his own as the body let go of its tenuous grip on life. Unbidden, an image flashed into his mind of his aunt slapping his father's face for 'scaring the young lad with your horror stories'.

As the hanged man breathed his last, so Thurkill spoke once more. "You four others have been found guilty of the lesser crime of brigandage, for which the punishment is to have your hand removed so that you may be perpetually reminded of your misdeeds. Proceed."

Grabbing the nearest man – whose face was now streaked with tears as he realised the dreadful moment was upon him – Leofric forced him to his knees as his brother pulled the wretch's left arm out straight so that it was stretched across the flat surface of the next tree stump.

175

Without giving the man time to think, Urri stepped up with his woodsman's axe, its blade sharpened to a keen edge in readiness. In one smooth movement, he raised it above his head before delivering a single sweeping blow, the speed and strength of which cut through the bone and sinew of the wrist as cleanly as if it were a pat of butter.

Before the man even had time to scream in pain, Leofgar pulled him over to the brazier where Eahlmund took one of the irons – its end glowing red hot – and pressed the metal against the stump, cauterising the wound instantly. The whole thing happened so quickly that the wound had hardly even had time to bleed. But it was never going to be painless. Almost immediately, a gut-wrenching burst of pain set in, overcoming the brigand's initial shock and causing him to unleash an horrific scream which pierced the ears of all those assembled.

Looking away, Thurkill noted the incongruous sight of the man's severed hand lying upturned on the ground where it had fallen, its fingers curled up towards the sky. As he stared, he was horrified to see one of the village dogs seized its moment. Darting forward between the legs of those standing nearest to the stumps, it grabbed the hand in its powerful jaws before slinking off behind the hall to enjoy its prize.

The remaining three captives were dealt with in similar quick and efficient fashion. The trick to it was speed. From the point that the hand was severed to the hot iron being applied to the wound was no more than a few heartbeats. In that way, the men were spared the worst of the pain and given a decent chance of survival as the blood flow was stopped and the wound sealed from dirt or foul pestilence. Some might consider the punishment cruel, but Thurkill saw no reason to make its enactment any more so. It was not an uncommon punishment for the crime of thievery. In Lundenburh, he had seen any number of men so maimed as evidence of their past misdemeanours.

With the grisly task finally complete, Thurkill addressed the four outlaws, each of whom now cradled their injured arm, the stump of which had been wrapped tight with clean strips of linen cloth which Wulfric had treated with honey mixed with a herbal poultice to ward off the risk of infection.

"The sentence of the court has been carried out; justice has been served. You are now free to go, though you should know that if you are caught stealing again, the penalty will be death. You are welcome to stay here in the village as we can always find work for eager men, even those with but one hand. But should you choose to do so, we will watch you closely for as long as you stay. You will have to earn our trust and respect over many months. Give me your decision: stay, work hard and want for nothing, or leave now with just the clothes that you stand in."

The four men looked at each other uneasily, as if unsure what to make of the offer. It seemed plain that none of them had expected it. Eventually, after no little discussion between them, two of them stepped forward and knelt before Thurkill, accepting his offer, swearing fealty to him and promising to work hard. Thurkill was not surprised, if he was honest; being a lordless man was no life for anyone. Without a lord, you were a man with no protection. Anyone could accuse you of a crime and you would have no defence, no one to speak for you, to vouch for your character. If anything, he was surprised to see two of the men turn and leave. Still, it was their choice and he wished them luck, for they would need it.

TWENTY - SIX

"I'm glad to have put it behind me, Hild. I take no enjoyment from inflicting punishment on defenceless men." Stooping down, Thurkill grabbed a flat sided stone which he then launched into the water, grunting with satisfaction as the projectile bounced off the surface four, five, six times before clattering onto the pebbled bank on the far side of the river.

Hild smiled, amused and bemused in equal measure by her husband's fascination with such things. That must have been at least the twelfth such stone he'd thrown since they'd set off walking south from the village to clear their minds after the morning's troubling scenes. Each one had, to a greater or lesser extent, performed its little trick, seemingly defying the water's embrace at least for a short while. But even though the stone might skip across the water several times, she knew that Thurkill was not truly happy unless it made it all the way to the other side, as if claiming victory in its escape from its cold dark doom. She knew better than to ridicule him for his games, though, accepting that it helped to take his mind off his problems at least for a while.

She linked her arm through his as they strolled further along the bank, Thurkill's eyes cast continually on the ground as he searched for the perfect missile.

"You had no choice in the matter, husband. Every lord has to be seen to be strong and to uphold the law. Were you to have not done so, the people would soon lose faith in you. Despite the punishments inflicted, there are still those who believe you to have been too lenient, that they all deserved death for their actions."

Thurkill stopped, pulling Hild round to face him. "But most agree with me? Most think the outcome fair?" The anxiety in his voice could not be hidden. Hild knew he worried whether he could live up to the trust placed in him by Aelfric. Even though he was doing perfectly well, she knew that he set his own standards in line with what he saw as his father's example. Was any boy ever any different, she mused, always seeking to prove themselves worthy of their father's pride?

"Yes, Killi. They saw a lord who did his duty, a lord who wasn't afraid to make a tough decision and one who did not shrink from following through on his words. I suspect that few of them would wish to carry that same burden on their shoulders."

Just then, Elspeth came running up to them carrying a posy of freshly picked flowers – bluebells and snowdrops mostly – taken from where they grew thickest around the base of the tree trunks in the dense woods, a hundred or so paces off to their left. Giggling infectiously, she gave her best approximation of a curtsey before presenting the posy. "For you, Lady Hild."

Hild smiled warmly, making great show of sniffing deeply of their scent. "Why, Elspeth, they are beautiful. They shall brighten up my bed chamber and make a nice change from all the axes, swords and shields that my husband keeps in there, cluttering up the place. But look," she turned towards Thurkill, "My Lord is bereft, for he has no flowers of his own. Quickly, go find some more so that he may be sad no longer, and then, when we return to the village, will you help me arrange them in vases?"

Laughing gaily, Elspeth sprinted back towards the trees. Hild called after her. "Don't go too far, my dear, stay where we can see you for there may still be outlaws in these parts."

When she had gone, Thurkill launched another stone, though this time it failed to bounce even once. He had been too hasty in his selection, a fault which he then compounded by failing to execute a proper flick of the wrist as he loosed it. "Bugger."

They walked on in silence for a while until Thurkill continued. "I hope Aelfric returns soon. I miss his guiding hand on my shoulder."

"As do we all, husband, but do not think for one moment that you've not done well in his absence. He could not have wanted for a better deputy."

"With Alwig's help."

"True but do you not suppose that the Steward helps Aelfric too? Of course he does, for that's his job. No one man can manage all things by himself. To believe so would be arrogant or foolhardy at best."

Thurkill nodded. She smiled to herself, pleased that she was able to provide him with the comfort he needed at times of doubt. That he relied on her wisdom and advice to keep him steady in his resolve was a source of joy for her. She'd heard of many ladies who were little more than adornments on the arms of their husbands, no more than any of the gold arm rings or brooches they wore. A thing of beauty to be admired. Not so her Killi; he respected her and trusted her judgement in all matters. Though he might not always do as she suggested, he did at least ask her opinion.

***

Thurkill walked on in silence for a while, turning Hild's words over in his mind. Just then, though, the peace was shattered by a terrifying, ear-piercing scream, the kind that only a young girl could make.

"Elspeth!" He turned to the woods where they had last seen her.

"By Almighty God, you told her to stay in sight. Why could she not do as she's told?"

His anger did little to mask his fear. Had she run into the two brigands who'd left the village earlier that day? Was it a wild boar? All manner of dark thoughts flooded his brain as he desperately searched the tree line for a glimpse of the girl.

"There." He followed the line of Hild's pointing finger and saw a flash of colour flitting between the trees, the same shade of blue as Elspeth's dress. Just then she broke free from the woods and began to run as hard as her little legs could carry her towards them, her face frozen in a rictus of fear. Thurkill ran forward to meet her, dropping to his knees to wrap her in his arms as she crashed into him, barely slowing her pace in her dread.

"Soldiers." She gasped, her little shoulders heaving in an effort to suck more air into her lungs. "In the woods."

"How many? Were they Saxon?" Thurkill's heart began to race as if he too had been running. He fought to keep the anxiety from his voice so he did not add to Elspeth's terror.

"I don't know, I saw two but they did not speak. They were moving slowly, from tree to tree, as if looking for something or trying to stay hidden."

"Was their hair long or short? Did they see you? Did they see which way you went?"

Elspeth stopped to think. Thurkill marvelled at her resilience. Already her calm had returned as she thought back to what she had seen. "I think their hair was short, at least it was not long and nor did they have beards. I'm sorry but I am sure they saw me. I was so scared I didn't know what to do, so I just screamed and ran."

"Don't worry, Elspeth, you did the right thing and you have done well." Already his mind was racing ahead. It sounded like Normans, but what were they doing here? Could there really be only two of them? It would be surprising were it to be so. He had to assume there were more of the bastards in amongst the woods. In the back of his mind, an image of Robert FitzGilbert was forming. He didn't want to think it, but was there really any other logical explanation for the presence of Norman soldiers near his village? Had they finally found him?

By now, Hild had caught up with him and was soothing the girl, wiping the tears from her face. "What is it?"

"Normans in the woods. Two of them that she saw, but I don't doubt there are more." Yet again, he cursed himself for not having told Hild about FitzGilbert before. He'd never really been able to find the right moment, and now it might be too late; it had been forced upon him. "Listen, Hild. You remember I told you about the man I killed back at Haslow? The one who murdered my sister and aunt? Well, it turns out he has a brother. I saw him in Warengeforte with King William and then again at Beorhthanstaed. I'm told he has sworn vengeance on the man who killed his brother and I fear he may be here now to do just that."

"Why in God's name have you not mentioned this before? Did you not think it was something I might want to know?"

"At first, I didn't want to alarm you as you were so happy here, and then I could never find the right time. I'm sorry, Hild, but nothing can change my mistake now. We have to consider what to do for the best. First, however, I want you to take Elspeth back to the village and raise the alarm."

"And in the meantime, what are you planning to do? Bugger that, you arrogant fool, I'm staying with you. I have my bow with me and you know more than most that I use it well."

Despite her anger, Thurkill grinned. He remembered how she had first tried her luck with a bow when the Norman raiding party had come to Brightling on the day Eahlmund's father was killed. Since then she had been studiously practising with it against targets hung from trees and also by going out with the hunters to bring down deer and even rabbits at times. Old Hafdan the head huntsman had told him many a time how impressed he was with her skill. "She shoots as if she were a man, Lord." Thurkill had laughed long and hard and told him not to let Hild hear him say that.

"Fine, I can see that this is an argument I won't win even if we had time to debate further. But Elspeth must go. Placing his hands on her shoulders and fixing her with his most serious expression to ensure she was in no doubt as to the gravity of the situation, he explained what she must do.

"Run back to the village as fast as you can. Stop for nothing or no one, whatever you might see or hear. Do you understand? Can you be brave and do that, do you think?"

The girl nodded, her face still pale with fear. Thurkill knew her to be a sensible girl, old beyond her years having had to take her mother's place in the household long before her time. He had no doubt that she would do as she was told.

"When you get there, find Eahlmund or any of the others in my war-band – I suggest you try the tavern or the mill first of all. Tell them that there are Normans in the woods and that they must close the gate and assemble the spearmen and archers. Tell them to man the walls and to let no one in or out, other than Hild and me. Now, repeat that back to me."

Elspeth needed only one attempt, confirming Thurkill's opinion of just how bright she was. Rising to his feet he kissed her on the forehead and bade her to run as if the devil were on her heels. She needed no second bidding and was away, almost flying over the ground. Turning back to face the trees, he half expected to find hordes of Normans streaming into the meadow, but there was nothing to be seen.

"I suggest we head back towards the village, Hild. Slowly and steadily that we might keep a close eye on things. Be ready with your bow, though. String it now for I fear we'll have need of it before long."

While Hild bent the wooden stave against her instep in order to slip the twine loop over its other end, Thurkill cursed himself for having left his war-axe back at the hall, even though he'd had no reason to believe he'd have need of it that day. All he had was his seax, which in itself was no mean weapon. Its blade was as sharp as any and, though not as long as a sword, it still extended almost to the length of his forearm. But, if the Normans had swords or, worse still, spears, he would be at a serious disadvantage. It would be the devil's own job to get close enough to use the damned thing. He would have to place his trust in Hild's bow to even the odds a little if it came to it.

They'd not gone more than a hundred paces towards the village when Hild grabbed his sleeve and pointed towards the woods. "There. Three of them. On horseback too."

Thurkill's heart sank. That was why they'd taken so long to appear; they'd gone to retrieve their mounts. No doubt they thought it would be easier to ride down their prey rather than chase after them on foot. It made a lot of sense for they were only about two hundred paces away. It would take no time at all for a galloping horse to cover that distance. What was worse was that he could see each man carried a long spear in his right hand. They were tucked under their armpits, already levelled at the two of them. His seax would be next to useless against them.

"You should run, Hild. The odds are against us."

"Why do you have trouble understanding me when I say I'm going nowhere? You don't have the sole right to die with honour. I choose to stand here beside you and fight. Even were you to order me gone as my lord or as my husband, I would defy you."

Thurkill knew that to argue further was futile, her mind was made up and she would not budge for anything or anyone. Smiling grimly, he hugged her close and kissed her fiercely. "In which case, I will see you in the afterlife, wife. I wish we could have had longer on this earth, for I would've dearly loved to have honoured you with the gift of children."

"Well, you'd best figure out a way to keep us alive then, because you have already done just that."

Thurkill's jaw dropped. "What do you mean, Hild? Speak plainly."

"I did not bleed last month. I think I'm pregnant."

Thurkill did not know what to say, or even think. To be met with the news that Hild was with child should have been one of the happiest moments of his life and yet all he could think about was the fact that death was staring them in the face. It was a cruel irony to find out he was to be a father moments before being stuck by a spear like a wild boar in the hunt. He roared with frustration, sensing the familiar red mist beginning to cloud his mind. He would make these Norman whoresons pay before he died. He only hoped that one of the three that now bore down on them was FitzGilbert, so he could have the pleasure of killing the bastard and sending him to meet his brother in hell.

He hugged Hild close to his body and then, with no further thought as to his own safety, he began to run towards the advancing horsemen. There was no sense waiting for death to come to him, he would rather meet its cold embrace on his own terms. Even at this distance he could see the look of surprise on the knights' faces. Doubtless, they believed it would be a simple matter to ride down and kill their quarry. What was this mad man doing charging at them with nothing but a knife?

Thurkill could hear nothing as he ran, but the sound of his feet pounding across the turf and the wind rustling in his hair. He had no thought other than to kill them all; he had to stop them from reaching Hild at any cost. She was carrying his child; she must survive to have their baby. He cared nothing for his own life now, but he prayed to God as he ran to see Hild safely home.

Noticing something out of the corner of his eye, he crouched to scoop it up, barely slackening his pace as he did so. As he regained his stride, something whizzed past his head with a high-pitched swish. Alarmed, he looked up to see the Norman on his left clutch at this throat, an arrow shaft protruding from between his fingers. Within another two paces he had fallen from his saddle to the ground, the horse continuing its mad charge without him.

By Christ, Hafdan was right, he grinned to himself. What an incredible shot. He made a mental note to ask her later whether she had meant it and then laughed demonically at the foolhardy notion of him still being alive to do so.

Seizing on the initiative Hild had temporarily won for him, Thurkill let fly with the stone he had grabbed. It wasn't the biggest, but it fit snugly in the palm of his hand and had a decent weight to it. Combined with the power he could put into his throw, it would do some damage but would be unlikely to kill or even disable. It might be enough, however, to distract. The projectile flew straight and true. From a range of only twenty yards, there was little danger that he would miss, it was just a question of where it would land and what impact it would have.

As it was, he could not have hoped for a better outcome as he watched it strike the right-hand of the two knights just to the left of his nose guard. In shock the horseman dropped his spear as he instinctively reached up to his damaged face, whilst keeping his left hand on his mount's bridle to avoid falling.

Thurkill roared in triumph. Now the odds were a little more to his liking. There was still the third man to deal with, though, and he was almost on top of him now, hurling hatred and insults at him. The blade of his spear seemed to fill Thurkill's vision to the exclusion of all else.

With an effort of will, he slowed his pace a little to allow himself more time and space to react. He would have but one chance to get this right or else he would find himself stuck like a wild pig on the end of a sharpened spear point. He needed to judge it just right or he would be done for. An image of Hild came into his mind as it often did in times of need, but this time not only was it her but, balanced on her hip, she held a baby, gurgling and grinning as she bounced it up and down as she sang. There was no way he could allow anything to happen to her.

As they closed within range of each other, the Norman raised himself up in his stirrups ready to stab down at Thurkill with his spear, but the Saxon was ready for it. He'd seen the same move back at Senlac and had rightly assumed that this Norman would act no differently. It was part of their training and worked well against a standing unit of foot soldiers, but against a sole, elite warrior such as he, it was a different matter.

Just when it seemed that the point would strike home, Thurkill darted to his right, narrowly missing the horse's pounding hooves as he passed in front of them, before reappearing on the horseman's other, unguarded side. The look of surprise on the man's face quickly turned into one of horror as realisation dawned.

Howling like a wolf, Thurkill plunged his knife into the Norman's thigh, just above the knee where it was not protected by his mailshirt. Holding on tightly, he simply allowed the horse's momentum to carry its rider past him, ripping open a huge gash up his leg all the way to the hip. The knight screamed in agony as blood arced from the severed vessels.

Thurkill had seen such things before and knew that the man was done for. There would be no stopping the flow as it pumped in time with his rapidly failing heart. He would be dead within minutes, literally drained of blood.

No longer concerned about the doomed man, Thurkill spun round to take stock of the situation. The first solider, whom Hild had struck with her arrow, was lying on the ground a few yards away. He was not yet dead, but by the way his limbs jerked feebly, Thurkill could tell his end was near too. That left the third man, the one he had hit with the stone. Where was he? For one horrible moment, he feared that he had ridden on to attack Hild but, no, she was where he had left her, a second arrow notched and ready, watching events unfold. Finally, he spotted the man. He'd seen what had befallen his two comrades and decided that he did not wish to share their fate. Even now, he was galloping hard back whence he came. In moments, he reached the safety of the trees and was gone from sight.

Thurkill grunted with satisfaction and began to trot back to where his wife stood. He was disappointed that the last man had escaped as he would carry news to the others. But when he considered he'd fully expected to die, he reasoned that the exchange was fair.

Hild ran the last few steps to greet him. From the ferocity of the hug she gave him he could sense that she too knew how close they had come to death.

"Never have I been more grateful for your bow, wife, and your skill in its use. Without that arrow flying true to its target, I fear we would have both been lost."

Hild glanced down at her feet, shame-faced. "My thanks, husband, but I cannot claim to have aimed at his throat. I was hoping to bring down the horse, but I snatched at it a little in my haste and it flew a little higher than I had intended. I actually feared it would pass over his head by some margin."

Thurkill laughed. "Well, I thank God then, for it must have been He who guided your hand. Now, let us return to Gudmundcestre with all haste. We must organise the defence before the rest of the bastards reveal themselves. I pray Elspeth made it safely, though I doubt any could catch her, the pace she was going."

TWENTY - SEVEN

Thurkill needn't have worried. By the time they arrived back at the village, the gates were shut and men lined the palisade on either side, weapons at the ready and alert for any movement. As the two of them approached, the gates were thrown open and closed quickly again behind them. He was pleased to see they were taking no chances. Elspeth had done her duty well.

Once inside, the villagers flocked around him, their faces betraying the worry they all felt. They were eager to hear what he had to say, how he would defend them from this new threat coming so soon after the brigands that had killed Egferth. Why had they come?

They were frightened; he could see it in their eyes, in their faces. The news had spread like wildfire; the same warriors that had defeated and killed Harold not four months ago were here. This was no rag-tag bunch of outlaws at their gate.

As he looked at them, Thurkill felt a pang of guilt. If FitzGilbert had come to claim the blood price for his brother's death, then these peoples' lives were now at risk for no other reason than his own actions in the past. It was nothing to do with them and none of them deserved to die on his account. He was at a loss for what to do. In his heart, he knew he should spare them the coming fight, but could he just leave and abandon them? They looked to him for justice and protection. Whatever the events of his past, he had a responsibility to the people of Gudmundcestre; that was not something he could easily renounce.

Wulfric stepped forward, electing himself spokesperson for the rest. "Lord, why have the Normans come here? What have we done to so offend God that He sends this scourge against us?"

What could he say? He wanted to tell them the truth but he needed to consult with his companions first, the men who had been with him since Haslow. He owed it to them to talk through their options before making a decision that could affect their future as well as his own.

"The answers to these questions are not clear to me at this time, Wulfric. It is true that Hild and I were attacked by three Norman soldiers just now, but I know not how many more there be, nor on whose orders they act. May be they are renegades, deserters from King William's army and little more than outlaws.

"Until we know more, I suggest we keep our gates closed and a careful watch on the walls. Perhaps they will pass us by when they see how stoutly defended our village is. There must be easier targets elsewhere if booty is what they want, eh?"

His calm words had the soothing effect he'd hoped they would. Slowly but surely people began to disperse, to go about their business. Still wary but no longer at the mercy of unfettered panic. As for Thurkill, he felt disgusted with himself. Though he had not lied, he felt he had not been truthful either. Whilst he did not know for certain, was there honestly any other likelihood than it being the past catching up with him? Still, there was no more he could do about that now. Spying Eahlmund up on the wall, he beckoned him down to join him.

"Friend, go find the brothers, Copsig, and Eardwulf and bring them to my hall. We need to talk."

While they waited, Hild pressed him about FitzGilbert. "So how do you know that he has sworn to kill you?"

"Wouldn't you if you were in his position? The Normans have a similar honour code to us; they demand a price to be paid for a wrong done to the family."

"But that man murdered your sister and aunt. He deserved to die."

"I will not argue with you, Hild. Presented with the same opportunity, I would do the same again. My only regret is that I did not make him suffer more or for longer and I care not who knows that. Richard was scum and I did the world a service by ending his life. But none of that matters to Robert. All he knows is that his brother is dead and that I killed him. He was always going to try to even the tally."

"So, what can we do?"

"That is what I intend to discuss with you and the others when they arrive for it affects all of us, especially you."

"How so?"

"What if you are pregnant? You were already the most important thing in my life before, but now you are doubly so. I cannot risk anything happening to you."

Hild placed her hand delicately on his cheek and fixed him with her gaze. "I may not be, you know?"

"Are you sure? My aunt always used to say that a woman knows these things; that she somehow feels different. Do you feel... different?"

Hild paused. "Well, I have been a little out of sorts, I suppose. My breasts for one, feel heavier, as if they have somehow grown. Have you noticed, husband?"

Thurkill stared at his feet, feeling his cheeks flush red as he did so. "I..."

Hild laughed. "I'll take that as a 'yes'. I've caught you staring at me when you think I'm not looking. I'm not a fool."

"Well, you can hardly blame a man blessed with a wife as pretty as you, can you?"

He thought it was a valiant attempt to recover some of his lost dignity but Hild was having none of it. "You men are all the same and don't try and dress it up otherwise," she sighed. "Always thinking with the contents of your trews."

***

Thurkill stood facing his companions, seeking some sign of their mood from their expressions. They were sat at a single bench close to the blazing hearth, their faces inscrutable masks leaving him with no clue as to their innermost thoughts. Briefly, he filled them in on what had happened by the river and how he suspected the knights they had encountered belonged to Richard's brother.

"I have called you here so that we may talk about what should now be done. If we accept my assumption to be the truth, you can be sure there will be many more than three of them out there."

Eahlmund, so often the spokesman for the group, wasted no time in speaking his mind. "I would hope you would not need to ask me, Lord, but in case there's any doubt, I say we kill the bastard and any that ride with him."

It was as if it were a signal to the others as, one by one, they voiced their support.

Thurkill smiled. "I knew in my heart there would be no doubt, my friends, but things have changed. I'm now lord of this village and have a hundred or so souls in my care as well as yours. Their lives are not mine to squander in some personal feud."

"I wouldn't be so sure, Lord. My father always taught me that my lord's fight was my fight, no matter the cause. It is our duty to do your bidding, even if that means to fight and – if necessary – to die for you. In return we benefit from your protection in times of conflict and also from the prosperity that comes in times of peace. I think if you were to put it to them, most would not hesitate to stand by you."

Thurkill flopped down in his chair, his head between his hands. "I don't know, Leofric. I hear the sense in what you say, but my conscience rebels against it. How could I live with myself if these people were to die because of me? It's not as if the Normans have come here to take the village is it? It's me they want, just me."

"We may not have been here long, Lord, but we are a part of the village for sure. We have built the defences up from the sorry state they were in, we have trained the men to fight so that they can defend themselves. We helped them defeat the bandits just a few days ago. On top of that, some of us are putting down roots here." He looked sideways at Eahlmund with a grin and a nudge.

"I can't help it if I'm irresistible to women. Anyway, you're one to talk. Don't think we haven't noticed you and your brother making eyes at Urri's daughters, or is it the blacksmith's trade that interests you now?"

Leofric laughed, holding his hands up in surrender. "Well, yes, but does this not also prove my point? We're part of the family now, we have been accepted into their lives and I'll wager they'll want to stand and fight for their lord."

Hild sat down next to her husband, taking his hand in hers. "Let's not look too far ahead, husband. We don't know yet what awaits us outside the walls. We have seen nothing more than three lone horsemen, two of whom now lie dead for their troubles. Perhaps there are no more of them?"

"I hope it is so, Hild, but I fear your thinking is wishful. I can think of no reason for Normans to be here other than it being somehow related to FitzGilbert. But one thing you say is true; we don't know how many are out there and that is my biggest fear. What if there are more than we can resist? I'll not commit these people to a fight they cannot win. I will not have my last act in this world to be leading these people to their deaths."

The silence that followed his impassioned words was broken moments later when one of the wall guards came running into the hall, shouting for him to come forth. "Lord, there are men outside the gates. They would speak with the lord of the village."

Thurkill nodded. "My thanks, Wigmund. Please inform them that I shall be there presently." Turning back to his men, he continued. "Prepare yourself for war, my friends. We will meet whatever awaits with dignity and honour. Show them no fear. Show them what it means to be Saxon warriors. We can strike fear into their hearts if they believe the same fate that met their fellows also awaits them should they not leave this place."

***

Together, they made their way to the palisade, picking their way through the lines of silent villagers, fear and worry etched on their faces. Climbing the five shallow steps that had been cut into the steep earthen bank, they reached the line of timber posts and looked out over the meadow that stretched away to the distant treeline. There they stood, proud and unflinching, resplendent in helmets that shone in the weak winter sunlight. Each man carried their shield along with a stout ash spear, the burnished blade of which stood a foot higher than their helms.

Thurkill was reminded of the moments before the battle at Senlac when he had stood shoulder to shoulder with Scalpi and the other huscarls facing the Norman horde. The pride he felt to have these five men alongside him, each one ready to die for him, was beyond reckoning. *This is how my father must have felt too,* he thought as he blinked away the moisture that had come to his eyes. He allowed himself a moment to survey the scene before him, hoping he would regain his composure sufficiently so that his voice, when he spoke, would not fail him.

Ranged across the path that led to their gate were what looked to be three dozen or so Norman knights, the same as he had encountered at Senlac and at Suthweca. His heart wavered for a moment. It was a greater horde than he had hoped. And whatever they might think of the Saxons facing them, they were no less imposing themselves. Each was arrayed in familiar knee-length mailshirt that was split up the thigh to allow them to move with comfort on horseback, and each was equipped with the long shield that was rounded at the top and which then tapered to a point at the bottom, effectively covering most of the body.

As he watched, Thurkill could not help wondering if their design was better than their own. It certainly looked as if it would provide greater protection for a man, but would it be as strong in a shieldwall?

By the looks of things, he had roughly the same number of men available to him, but his villagers were not fighters by trade, unlike these knights. The men of Gudmundcestre could hold their own against thieves and brigands but trained soldiers were another matter. Still, if they held their ground within the walls, what could the Normans do? They had no siege engines and they would lose men to his archers if they tried to batter the gate down by hand. All in all, he felt secure, though he prayed they had no more men hidden in the woods to their rear.

He cleared his throat. "My name is Thurkill, son of Scalpi, Lord of this village of Gudmundcestre. State your name and your business here or begone." He hoped his voice sounded authoritative, and that his height and stature would offset his obvious youthfulness.

In response, a knight from the middle of the pack, jabbed his heels into his mount's flanks, urging it forward a few steps before pulling back on the reins to bring it to a halt. Removing his helmet, he grinned up at Thurkill, though there was no warmth in it.

Straightaway, Thurkill recognised FitzGilbert. He had the

same mop of dark hair, the same hooked nose and heavy forehead that overshadowed his narrow, dark eyes. The only difference was that this brother had no scar to disfigure his features. So be it then, this man was here to kill him, to take vengeance for Richard's death. However this played out, Thurkill knew that one, or perhaps both of them would be dead by the end of it.

"Go and get your father, boy, I have business with the lord of this shit hole. Tell him Robert FitzGilbert, eldest son of Count Gilbert of Clare wishes to speak with him."

Thurkill knew the barb was meant to rile him. If FitzGilbert knew who he was then he would know this father was dead. It was a cheap trick to try to undermine him in front of the others or to goad him into some rash response. "I am lord here, Norman. You may speak with me here or take your business elsewhere."

FitzGilbert pretended to look surprised, still intent on mocking him. "Your pardon, Lord. I had not expected one so young to have command over others. I see no beard on your chin; is this the new Saxon fashion or could it be that you not yet old enough to grow one?"

"There are many who could tell you that my sword speaks for me more than my age. At least they could, were they still alive."

"Ah, yes. That would include the two men of mine whom you killed earlier today. Or at least, I understand you did for one of them. You had to rely on your woman to take the other, so I am told. Do not fear, though, they have been added to the tally sheet for which I now seek a reckoning."

"What ill have I done you, Lord? Your men attacked my wife and me as we went about our business. There was no provocation on our part."

"An unfortunate business, I'll admit. They had orders not to attack, but they saw an opportunity to earn my thanks by ending your life. Misplaced ambition is all it was. Still, no matter, I have more than enough men here, as you can see, and the promise of more if needed, to conclude matters satisfactorily."

"I'll ask one final time. To what matters do you refer?"

"It surprises me to see you act so coy, Thurkill, son of Scalpi.

But if it pleases you then I shall spell it out in words so simple that even a child such as you can understand. You killed my brother. I have come here to seek payment. You are the boy of whom they speak that has but one ear, are you not? I am told that this is what marks out the man I seek. Do you deny it?"

Thurkill didn't hesitate; he knew there was no point as the villagers would find out the truth soon enough. "I do not deny it. Your brother was murderous scum who deserved to die for what he did to my family. If you hail from the same litter, then I do not doubt that you also deserve that same fate. Stay here on my land and it will find you before too long."

"These are fine words for a pup like you. I had imagined some mighty Saxon warrior had been the architect of my brother's doom and yet I find a beardless girl in his place. Are you sure it is not your father that I seek?"

"My father died with King Harold, defending him from you Norman whoresons. He was twice the man you'll ever be."

"And yet he failed to save his lord and was killed in the process. At least there is honour in that, I suppose. But you stand here in his stead, cowardly killer of my kin and now hiding behind these pathetic walls like a craven dog."

Thurkill could feel his ire rising but knew he had to keep control. The knuckles on his right hand were showing white through the skin where he gripped the shaft of his war axe with a furious intensity. He knew the others would be experiencing similar thoughts and willed them to maintain their calm demeanour too.

"I do not go seeking a fight where none is warranted, Norman. Accept the truth that your brother was evil and merely reaped the crop that he had sown. The slate's been wiped clean and the scales of justice are balanced once more. Go now, or I shall not be held responsible for what comes to pass."

Thurkill could see that Robert was beginning to lose patience with their exchange. No matter, he was not in the least bit concerned about that. What worried him more was what would happen next. He knew FitzGilbert would not simply ride away. He had his own honour to consider and could not back down in front of his own men.

"I can see I'm wasting my time exchanging words with you, Saxon. It would appear that the only language you have mastered is violence. I call on you therefore to be the warrior you claim to be and come out here to fight me. This is the only way to spare your people from annihilation. Stay behind your feeble defences and all will die, whether spearman, old man, woman or child. It matters not to me. Refuse me and I'll kill everyone."

Robert had raised his voice for this last challenge, to ensure that all within the village could hear and would be in no doubt as to the fate that awaited them if their lord did not meet his demands. "I give you until dawn to decide. Choose wisely."

With that, the Norman pulled on his horse's bridle to turn it away from the village. Kicking his heels into its flanks once more, he trotted away towards the trees, his knights following suit behind in ranks of two. Thurkill watched them until they were gone from sight, his mind working over the ramifications of the options open to him. Eventually he stood down from the parapet, calling Eahlmund to his side. "Assemble the folkmoot at sundown. I would address them on this matter."

TWENTY - EIGHT

The atmosphere inside the hall was tense and not at all helped by the smoke that billowed from the hearth fire. It was rare for so many to be gathered in one place, though it seemed to be happening with increasing regularity, what with the trial of Egferth's killers and now this, altogether more worrying, threat. But Thurkill had thought it important that all should have a chance to hear his words. Then, when the heavens had opened a short while ago, he'd given the order to assemble inside.

The members of the folkmoot were positioned at the far end near the lord's chair, while the remainder of the hall was given over to the rest of the villagers. Thurkill sat on his chair next to Hild, waiting for the last few stragglers to settle down. Although his companions remained confident of their support, Thurkill himself was less certain. To chance your life on the throw of a loaded dice was not a matter for any man to take lightly.

Not willing to wait any longer, Thurkill stood, raising both hands to call for quiet. "Members of the folkmoot and people of Gudmundcestre, I welcome you to my hall. I only wish I could do so in happier times but, as you know, a grave threat now faces the village, the likes of which has not been seen since the days of the Viking great army almost two hundred years ago. To help decide our response, I have summoned the folkmoot to seek its counsel."

A hush fell over the room as everyone absorbed Thurkill's words. Then, as the most senior man in the village, Father Wulfric rose to speak. "Lord, I think it would help if you were to share all that you know about the position in which we now find ourselves. You have knowledge that is not yet apparent to us all."

Thurkill nodded his thanks. Wulfric knew the truth of the matter as he had confessed his sins to the priest on the day before his wedding. Thurkill had wanted to enter into his marriage with a clear conscience before God and so he had told Wulfric about the cold-blooded killing of Richard FitzGilbert.

Though the priest had admonished him for the murder, he had absolved him of his sins before later, over a cup of ale, confiding that he too would have done the same thing had he been in Thurkill's position, God or no God. He knew he had an ally in Wulfric that night, a powerful one at that as the priest's word carried much weight amongst the villagers.

So Thurkill told his story, from the time of the battle against the Vikings up to the present day. He left out no detail. He described his father's death in battle, how he'd watched, powerless, as King Harold was cut to pieces in front of his eyes, how Eahlmund had then found him close to death and had taken him back to his village to recover.

The villagers listened in awe, for few if any had ever experienced anything even remotely close to what they heard in the hall that night. By the time he came to relate how he had come home to find FitzGilbert in his father's hall and how the Norman had slit the throats of his aunt and sister without the merest hint of mercy, there were growls and shouts of outrage on all sides.

"So, as you see, this man's brother, the man I killed to avenge my kin, has now come for the blood price. But in doing so, he threatens you; he brings the fight to Gudmundcestre and, for this reason, I would hear your mind on this matter."

There was a moment's silence before everyone erupted at once. Voices on all sides clamoured to be heard, each one increasing in volume in a bid to stand out above the furore. To Thurkill's ears, such was the cacophony that he could not tell who spoke for or against him. Eventually the tumult became so out of hand that Wulfric had to stand on his chair to appeal for calm.

"Gentlemen, Ladies, I urge you to stay calm. As our lord has stated, we find ourselves in the midst of a crisis and we will not find the answer by having everyone shout at the same time. The folkmoot is appointed to represent the interests of all, so please allow them to speak freely so that we may proceed."

Grudgingly, the people quietened – save for the odd indignant shout – but, with peace finally restored, Haegmund the miller rose to speak. "I say to hell with the Normans. I for one stand with Lord Thurkill. Though he may have only been our lord for a short while, I have seen nothing in that time that tells me he does not have our best interests at heart. I say we fight to protect what's ours and that's an end to it." With that, the barrel-chested man sat down heavily and folded his arms, his fierce expression daring any to take issue with him.

Urri was next. "I stand with Haegmund. If it were not for Thurkill and his folk, these Normans would have already overrun the village for we had no wall until a few short weeks ago. What's more, he has taught us how to defend ourselves with spear and shield. If a lord's first duty is to protect his people, then who can say that he has not done so? In return, our duty is to serve our lord in whatever way he asks."

Just as Thurkill began to think he would carry the day, Eadwig the farmer rose. He had not had occasion to speak with Eadwig much before now but he knew him to be a prickly character whose outlook on life was often as dark as a rain-swept November sky. As soon as he began to speak, he realised his reputation was well earned.

"I hear the words of my fellow brothers, but I for one wonder whether we should be so quick to risk life and limb in this escapade. We all heard what this Norman said; he only wants one thing. He has no interest in us and will surely leave us in peace once he gets it. This disagreement between him and Lord Thurkill took place several weeks before he came here to Gudmundcestre. It is not our fight. Why should we risk our lives in this conflict?" He paused, looking round at the other members of the folkmoot for support, before continuing.

"We are not warriors. Yes, we may have learned how to hold a spear and shield and stand in a straight line – and we should be rightly grateful to our lord for that – but we are no match for these Normans. They had the battle-skill to kill our king and his best warriors, so what hope would we have?"

Some murmurs of assent greeted the farmer's speech, but Thurkill noted they were muted and few in number. Before they could spread any further, however, Wulfric was on his feet once more, nostrils flared and cheeks reddened in anger. "There is merit in Eadwig's words." His measured tone did little to hide the strength of his feelings.

"It is true that we are not warriors, but farmers, millers and blacksmiths. But more than that, we are Saxons. Men of honour with traditions that stretch back hundreds of years to the time when our people first came to these shores after the Romans left. Those traditions dictate that if a lord fulfils his duty to his people, then those people are bound to him in return. Who here can say, with hand on heart and before God, that Lord Thurkill has in any way failed us? Well?"

Silence filled the packed hall. None would willingly speak against Wulfric's tirade, not even Eadwig who sat staring at his feet, as if conscious of the many eyes that fell upon him, as if daring him to rise to the bait.

Seeing his challenge go unanswered, the priest continued. "I for one will not be the first to abandon my honour. I will not anger our forefathers by refusing to do my duty. Though my vows forbid me to take a man's life, I will stand by our lord to lend him whatever support I can and I cry shame on any who refuses to do likewise. We may have lost our king in battle but we can yet hold our village and our pride."

The priest's intervention brought matters to an end. There were none who chose to speak after that, not that they could amidst the cheers and shouts of defiance that ensued.

As the people began to file out of the hall, Thurkill summoned his five warriors to give orders for a watch to be established on the walls.

The thirty or so men who had been trained to stand in the shieldwall were divided into three groups of ten. At any one time, one group was to patrol the wall while the other two rested. Thurkill would have liked to have more men on the wall as the gaps between them were larger than he would have wanted, but it was more important that as many men as possible were rested and fresh for a fight should it come to that.

To Hild he gave instructions to ensure that food and water was kept in plentiful supply. They would have no problem with either if it came to a siege as a small stream broke off from the nearby river and flowed through the village ensuring a constant supply and their granary was still more than half full from the previous harvest and supplemented with good stocks of apples and cheese. He had no fear of their running short of supplies for a good while yet, not that he thought FitzGilbert would have the patience to starve them out.

Over the next few hours, Thurkill noted the mood began to lighten in the village. Though the anxiety was not far below the surface, the priest's stirring words, combined with decisive action on his part to organise the defences, seemed to have rallied the people behind the common cause. Everywhere he went, people smiled and called out words of support and encouragement. Even Eadwig nodded and offered a grim half smile when Thurkill came to stand by him to look out over the wall in the direction of the woods where they believed the Normans to be lurking. In truth, Thurkill's purpose for going to that part of the wall was two-fold as he felt he owed the farmer some words of apology.

"I respect your views, Eadwig, so I thank you for standing with me. I'm truly sorry this has come to pass. If I could change things, rest assured that I would."

The farmer grunted. "You know if it were down to me, I wouldn't be here. Better yet, you wouldn't be. This trouble has come to pass only because you're here. None of us invited it upon ourselves."

Thurkill felt his anger rising and fought hard to keep it under control. "So why fight then? Why risk your life for me?"

"Do you know nothing of honour and brotherhood? Did your father teach you nothing?" He didn't pause for a response. "I fight because my fellow villagers voted to fight. Whether I agree with the decision or not, I will not stand by while they put their lives at risk instead of me. What would be said of me were I to stay at home out of harm's way? That I were a coward who stood aside while his friends died? I will not have that shame on my name, I will not allow my children to grow up in that shadow. I would rather die with a spear in my hand next to Urri or Haegmund, than skulk in fear in my home."

"I understand that, Eadwig. It is why I stood with King Harold at the end, even after my father had been killed in front of my eyes and after many others had already fled. There are few who understand honour better than me and few have lost more because of it. I did not ask for this Norman bastard to come here, but I accept that I brought it on myself by killing his brother. But can you honestly say that you would've done differently to me were you in my shoes? Would you have stood by and done nothing having seen the throats of your womenfolk slit for no reason?"

Eadwig stared at the ground and said nothing. Thurkill needed no further confirmation than that and felt no need to push his point further. He did not wish to challenge the man's courage; it was enough that he was here on the walls.

"Let us at least part as comrades in this endeavour, even if not friends. Will you take my hand, Eadwig?"

Thurkill proffered his right hand as a gesture of reconciliation. For a moment he feared that the farmer might not take it, but then the older man shrugged and grasped it firmly, applying pressure as if to tell Thurkill that his commitment should not be doubted.

Thurkill bade him goodnight. "'Til tomorrow, then, when we shall see what FitzGilbert has in store for us."

TWENTY - NINE

Thurkill was awoken by the sound of retching. It was still dark outside, the only light coming from a small candle by the bed. Bleary-eyed, he padded over to where Hild knelt in the corner, her face hovering over a small wooden pail. "What ails you, my love? Was the fish not properly cooked? I'll have a word with Aebbe, tell her to be more careful."

Wiping her mouth with the back of her hand, Hild sat back on her haunches smiling benignly at him as if talking to a child. "It is not the fish, or anything else I consumed last night, husband."

Chuckling at Thurkill's quizzical expression she continued. "I think this is the proof of my condition, my love. There is little doubt now I am with child, for this must be the sickness comes in the early stages. It is nothing to worry about, so the other women tell me. It passes in time."

Gently, Thurkill raised Hild to her feet, wiping the corner of her mouth with the linen cloth she had draped around her shoulders against the chill. "You have made me happy beyond measure, wife. I cannot wait for the moment to come when I shall be a father. Will it be a boy or a girl do you think?"

"I have no idea, and in truth I care more that when it comes it is healthy. So many die so young or even before they come into this world. To have a child that survives to adulthood will be a blessing indeed."

Thurkill nodded. "And before that, we must see to FitzGilbert or none of us will live to see the birth of our child. Will you be alright if I leave you for a while? I should go to the wall to check on the watch, now I am awake."

Thurkill climbed up to the palisade where he was greeted by Eahlmund who had overseen the change from the night watch to the first of the two day-shifts. The weary men had just trudged off to the hall where fresh bread and a hot broth awaited them before they would go to find their beds. Thurkill hoped they would be able to sleep but he feared they would soon be back on the wall if FitzGilbert was the kind of man he took him to be.

Idly thumbing the blade of his war axe, he stared out across the meadow that stretched from the gate to the treeline, a hundred or so paces distant. The early glow of the dawn was now colouring the tops of the trees, where the first buds of spring had already started to appear. Listening to the chirruping of the birds, Thurkill wondered what the day would bring. What would they do when he refused to accede to their demands? In all likelihood it would be violent and, in his heart, he knew that men would die on both sides. He just prayed that not too many of them would be Saxon. His mind filled with images of Hild, a new born babe suckling at her breast. Inwardly, he cursed the fates that had conspired to bring such happiness into a time of such despair.

As if reflecting the state of his mind, a low mist had formed overnight clinging to the meadow. It was growing thicker by the moment, so much so that he felt sure it would soon be enough to disguise the sight and sound of any Norman manoeuvres. Leaning out over the top of the wall, cupping his hand around his one good ear did not help. He could hear nothing but the birds singing in the tops of the trees that were, themselves, now obscured from view.

"Who knows what goes on out there?" Urri had come to stand by him, having recently arrived to take up his guard duty. "I've rarely seen a fog as low and as dense as this. I doubt we can see more than thirty paces, if that."

"Aye. Can't hear or see a thing under it. But I'm sure the bastards are out there. I doubt we'll have long to wait now."

It was as if his words were prophetic. No sooner had he finished speaking than the blacksmith grabbed his arm, nodding towards the path. Squinting in the direction indicated, Thurkill could still see nothing, but he could definitely hear something now. Horses. And the sound of clinking metal. The Normans had returned.

"Go rouse the others, Urri. Bring them to the wall. We must make a show of our strength. We must let them know we're ready for a fight and don't fear them. Hurry back, mind, for you're the scariest of them all."

Urri grinned. "Aye, Lord." With that, he loped off towards the hall, his great lumbering strides making short work of the distance.

Turning back, Thurkill peered out once more, trying to make out the first signs of movement. Moments later he saw them, just six of them but all on horseback and all fully armed. They walked their mounts to a point about ten paces from the gate and then halted, the horses shaking their heads up and down, blowing steam through their nostrils. After a short while, FitzGilbert removed his helmet to reveal his shock of unruly dark curls perched on top of his otherwise clean shaven head. Thurkill never could get used to the way the Normans wore their hair. Short hair with no beard or moustache was a look that spoke of childhood to him.

"Saxon!" Thurkill's pushed such idle thoughts to one side. "Have you made your decision? Will you come forth to answer for your crime or will you continue to hide behind this puny wall?"

Hefting his great war axe in both hands – an unmistakable threat – Thurkill drew himself up to his full height before replying. "Go home, Norman. You'll get nothing here but pain and death."

"Those are brave words for one that skulks in the shadows. I doubt you'd be so brave were you to stand face to face with me."

"Do not doubt my courage, Norman. Those that do rarely live long enough to realise their error."

"Well, I have only your word for that, boy. You should come out here to show me so that I might see for myself."

Thurkill chose to say nothing. He knew FitzGilbert was hoping to prick him into a reaction, but he was not even remotely interested in rising to the bait. Instead, he stood staring down at the small group of horsemen, a look of complete disdain etched on his face.

Eventually, FitzGilbert lost patience. "Yet again, I find myself at a loss to understand how one as womanly as you managed to best my brother. Nevertheless, you've made your choice and must now take the consequences." With that, he replaced his helmet and raised his right arm, before letting it fall in a sharp cutting motion. Almost immediately, another – much larger – group surged into view from the fog where they had been concealed until now. It took Thurkill a moment to realise what was happening, but once it dawned on him, he yelled. "Archers! To the walls!"

Below him, the six knights peeled off to each side, allowing the new arrivals through. A group of men, a long, thick tree trunk between them, ran forward. Its branches had been removed and one end sharpened to a blunt point. Ropes had been lashed along its length from which the six men now carried the whole contraption, three on either side. Next to them, a further group trotted along holding their long shields above them so as to protect themselves and those that held the log.

In no time at all, the Normans reached the gate, where they readied themselves to begin. The first blow caused the wooden planks to shudder but no more. It was a solid construction backed by a heavy wooden cross-piece that rested snugly within a pair of iron braces on either side. Thurkill knew it was well made and would stand up to no small amount of punishment, but he also knew it would not hold forever. Impatiently, he looked behind him towards the centre of the village to see where the archers were. Sure enough, they were coming. Half a dozen of them, led – he noted with a mix of worry and pride – by Hild. Hot on their heels came another group, with Eahlmund in front, pushing a couple of carts filled with rocks. *Excellent. The more missiles we have the better.*

By the time the archers reached the wall, the battering ram had already landed another four blows. They were aiming for the join where the two halves of the gate met, correctly identifying that to be the weakest point.

"Come on, come on. Hurry," he yelled. "Who knows how long the gate will stand?"

Without pausing to aim well, the archers quickly loosed off a volley. At that range, though, they could not miss. But not one shaft found its mark. Rather they all either embedded themselves in the protective shields or bounced harmlessly off. One even stuck in the log where its goose feathers stood quivering.

"Again!"

Time after time, the six archers let fly. Each one was an expert with their weapon, trained from an early age to bring down animals on the hoof, but none could find a target, so well covered were the soldiers. Meanwhile the gate was weakening all the time. Great splinters were now being shorn off the solid oak planks, while a worrying crack was beginning to form on the cross-bar. There was no telling how long it might be until the whole thing split asunder and then it would all be over. Once the Normans were within the walls of the village, it would be a massacre. They had to keep them out at all costs.

"Rocks!" Thurkill roared. The three men nearest to him raced down to grab the biggest stones they could find from the carts before lugging them back up to the wall. Just as the first man raised his missile above his head, ready to launch it at the men below, he gave out a blood-curdling shriek. Spinning round to see what had happened, Thurkill saw him lying on the ground, a bolt protruding from his eye socket. "Ware, Ware! Crossbows. Hild, have half your men target them. The rest can carry on as before."

Three of the Saxon bowmen trotted along the wall to where they were closer to the crossbowmen. There, they bent their bows back aiming at the new group of Normans who had come into view. With their weaker bows, designed for hunting rather than warfare, there was little likelihood of them being able to kill a man, especially one equipped with a mailshirt. But they did enough, nonetheless, to disrupt the flow of bolts.

The stone throwers needed no second invitation to take advantage of the much-needed respite. The first volley met with immediate success. A heavy, jagged rock struck a shield bearer's exposed elbow, making him drop his shield in pain and shock, the bone broken by the impact. The second missile was timed and directed to perfection, bouncing off the now-exposed head of the lead man on the battering ram. Though not enough to knock him out, he went down on one knee, letting go of the rope as he raised his hands to protect his skull from further damage.

The log dropped to the ground with a thud as the remaining five men failed to cope with the sudden shift in balance. The defenders gave a great shout of triumph, as if their enemy were already defeated. The bowmen wasted no time taking advantage of the confusion. All six of them nocked a new arrow and sent them in one deadly salvo down on to the flustered men below. Half of them failed to find a target but the others flew true. The range could hardly be any closer and so the impact was fatal. The man who had dropped the log was struck where neck meets shoulder, the arrow biting deep into the flesh, penetrating straight down into the heart. He dropped dead so suddenly that he had no time to scream. The second arrow took a man on the other side who had been left unprotected by his companion who had moved his wooden board so that it covered him more. The iron tip punched a hole through his mailshirt and on into his gut. He fell sideways, hands clutched to his belly in pain as the barbed arrow ripped into his vital organs.

Without hesitation, though, two more soldiers rushed forward to take the place of the casualties, dragging the bodies to one side. At the same time, FitzGilbert roared at the shield bearers to keep their boards in place or suffer his wrath should any more of the log carriers be killed. Moments later, the pounding resumed. Nervously, Thurkill glanced down at the rear of the gate. It was holding for now but he could not say for how much longer. Even from his elevated position he could see the crack on the cross-piece had grown in size. Not for the first time, he offered up a prayer of thanks that Urri had insisted on it being at least as thick as a man's arm.

"Will it take it?" Hild's face betrayed her fear.

"Not for much longer."

"We need to prepare for that moment, husband. If they get in, we will all die unless we can hold them at bay with our shieldwall."

Her words cut through to his brain, shaking him from his torpor. Hugging her tightly to his chest, he thanked her for being a better war-captain than him and then turned to run down towards the hall. As he ran, he yelled back at his wife. "Keep your archers trained on the men holding the log. Aim for

208

anything that is not covered by a shield. Even an arrow in the foot will be enough to stop a man in his tracks."

Running into the hall, he found Urri and a good number of other men waiting patiently as they had been instructed. Thurkill kicked himself for his stupidity. In his concerns for the gate, he had completely forgotten his own plan. Hild's timely words may well have just averted a disaster.

"Urri, gather the men, we need you up by the gate before the Normans break through. Form a shieldwall, eight men wide and two ranks deep." Then to those within earshot he continued. "Remember your training. You must hold firm. If the gate goes, you're all that stands between the Normans and your families." He could think of no better words of encouragement; if that did not give them the strength to stand, nothing would.

Without waiting to see their reaction, he rushed off back to the wall. It pained him that he really needed to be everywhere at once. He wanted to stand next to each man, to give them courage to resist, courage to strike a blow even. He would have loved for Scalpi to be there to guide him. He was still not much more than a boy, in truth, forced by circumstance to take the role of one much older and more experienced than he. Yet despite that, he believed in his heart that his father would be proud of him, would approve of what he had become and what he had achieved. He swore to himself that now was not going to be the time that he started to let him down. Setting his jaw in a defiant expression, he launched himself up the small incline that led to the wooden parapet, coming to a halt next to his wife as she loosed yet another arrow. "How goes it?"

Breathlessly she turned to him, revealing a long gash that ran diagonally from her elbow towards the shoulder. "In Jesus' name, what happened, wife?"

Despite the pain she must have felt, Hild grinned. "A lucky shot from one of their crossbowmen. He caught me just as I was drawing back my bowstring." Seeing the look on her husband's face, she sought to assuage his fears. "Don't fret so, it looks worse than it is. It's not stopping me from using the bow properly anyway."

Trying to seem less worried than he felt, Thurkill laughed.

"Well, I hope you killed the bastard for his impudence. Or have you left that job for me? I would dearly love the chance to discuss this insult with him further."

"He's all yours, husband. I've been a dutiful wife, following your orders to attack only those who would try to break the gate. We've managed to injure two more, but they keep replacing them. I fear they have too many men for us to stop them."

"Either they break or we do. There is no third option." Risking a glance over the wall, Thurkill's heart sank. The fog had lifted now, allowing him to see all the way to the trees. But it was not the improved visibility that upset him, rather what it revealed. There, about fifty paces away and ranged across the width of the path, FitzGilbert sat a-horse along with roughly a dozen other knights. They were formed up in a wedge, Robert himself at the point, just waiting. Thurkill knew that as soon as the gate broke, they would charge forward into the village and cut down, indiscriminately, all who they found within. Spinning round, he looked back towards his hall. *Where is the shieldwall? What is taking them so long?*

If the gate gave way in the next few moments, then nothing could save them. There would be no defence against the marauding horsemen. Finally, the spearmen came into view, trotting forward in two well-disciplined rows under Urri's watchful eye from his usual position on the left of the front rank.

"Got the bastard." Behind him, Hild let out an excited yelp as another of the log carriers limped away, a shaft buried deep in his thigh. As before, however, the triumph was short-lived as another man immediately rushed forward to take his place.

Her small victory did, however, give time for the shieldwall to form up behind the gate. They stood about five paces back from the wooden posts so that they would not be hurt if and when it eventually broke. And they were not a moment too soon for, almost as soon as they'd taken up their position, an ear-splitting crack filled the air as the cross-piece finally gave up the uneven struggle, breaking into two and falling to the ground with a heavy thump. For a brief moment, silence descended as everyone, Norman and Saxon alike, stopped to watch as the two gate panels – still largely intact despite the heavy pummelling to which they had been subjected all morning – slowly swung inwards on their hinges.

"Forward!" FitzGilbert broke the spell, urging his knights forward. Viciously raking his heels along his horse's flanks, he threw the beast into a canter as he closed the distance to the now yawning gap in the wall. Behind him, his knights followed suit, pushing hard to catch up with their leader, knowing that the impact of their charge would be all the greater were they were to crash through at the same time.

Almost simultaneously, Thurkill yelled down at Urri and the rest of the men. "Close up. Fill the gap with your shields. Do not let them pass; the fate of the village, your wives and your children, rests in your hands."

"Ut, ut, ut!" The men chanted as they stomped forward in unison, smashing their spear hafts against the backs of their shields to add to the noise. The courage they gained from the noise would be a big factor in deciding whether they stood or ran. He couldn't fault their discipline, but he knew that could change in an instant when the Normans hit them.

Stand, you bastards, stand! He willed them to hold fast, wishing he was there alongside them. He had to trust them, though, had to hope that the training he had given them was enough. It had worked well enough against the brigands a few days ago, but what about against warriors such as these? Fear would be twisting their stomachs into knots, loosening their bowels. More than one would likely soil themselves before the fight was over. It happened to the best of them and there would be no shame in it, as long as they held.

"Brace!" Urri's voice carried clearly above the clamour of battle; a growl more than a shout.

And then the knights were upon them. The impact when it came was terrifying, causing Thurkill to think they surely could not withstand the onslaught. But by some miracle they did. The man in the middle of the rear rank – Haegmund it was – lost his footing, thrown back by the force of the knight clattering into the man to his front, who fell back against the miller's shield. Before Haegmund could react, the rim of his board smashed into his face, dumping him, dazed, on his arse, his mouth blooded and short of at least two teeth.

To his credit, though, the miller was straight back on his feet, forcing himself back into position. Thurkill doubted the poor wretch knew what day it was but the benefit of the training was plain to see. Haegmund was more worried about letting his comrades down than he was of his teeth. Doubtless, he was also fearful of the bollocking he knew that Urri would give him if he did not get straight back into line.

Thurkill smiled grimly, perhaps they might survive the attack after all. They had been fortunate, though. The narrowness of the gateway meant that the Norman wedge had been forced in on itself as their horses scrambled for space. The resulting crush had reduced the impact of their charge, not by much, but enough to mean that the full force of their beasts could not be brought to bear. Now the four men who formed the front row were trying to urge their mounts on whilst, at the same time, stabbing their spears forward, hoping to find a fleshy target. In both endeavours they were thwarted. The shieldwall, with Urri haranguing and cajoling, was not to be budged. They had taken a couple of steps back to absorb the force of the attack but now they had steadied and were holding firm.

Satisfied they were not in any immediate danger, Thurkill risked another look over the parapet, careful not to present an easy target to any opportunistic crossbowman. At least half the horsemen were fully engaged with the shieldwall; the rest were standing uselessly, unable to bring their spears to bear against any available target. But that might not last. At any moment the shieldwall might break. It certainly could not defeat the Normans on its own; all it could realistically do was stand and take the punishment. Something else was needed to help turn the tide. It was time to put his plan into action so he hailed his warband to join him.

"Ready?" Thurkill looked behind him to where Leofric and Leofgar now stood.

"Aye, Lord." They were crouched down behind the wall, out of sight of the attackers. Both men were ready with shield and sword in hand, the blades sharpened to the keenest edge possible. Their faces betrayed no fear, ready to do their lord's bidding come what may.

Thurkill then looked over to the other side of the gate, over the heads of the melee that was being fought out below. There he caught the eye of Eahlmund who stood with Copsig and Eardwulf, all three of whom nodded back to show their readiness. Grinning maniacally, Thurkill slung his shield across his back and gripped his huge war axe in both hands. Sucking a huge breath of air deep into his lungs, he stood up and yelled at the top of his voice. "Now!"

As one, the six men stepped up onto wooden benches to gain extra height before vaulting over the wall to land on the fresh piles of straw that had been placed at the foot for the palisade in readiness this very purpose. The height of the drop was a risk, but an acceptable one to Thurkill's mind and offset by the soft landing that had been prepared for them.

Nevertheless, a bolt of pain shot up his leg as his ankle gave way beneath him as he landed heavily. He went into a sideways roll to take the weight off it as quickly as he could. He didn't think it was broken – the pain seemed bearable, after all – but he prayed it would hold for what was to come. Then he was back on his feet, half hobbling, half running as fast as he could towards the knights' unprotected flank.

The surprise was total. The Normans could not have foreseen such a drastic turn of events. All their attention was focussed on the gate, but now they suddenly found themselves assailed on both sides by screaming, snarling Saxons intent on their destruction. At such close range, they did not even have time to wheel their horses to face the new threat.

Taking full advantage, Thurkill launched himself at the first man in his path. Leaping up as high as his armour would allow him, he brought the blade of his axe down in one great arc onto the man's head. The knight was dead almost before he knew what had hit him, his skull cleaved in two with bone and grey matter spraying to all sides. The blow toppled the man's body off his horse, causing the poor beast to panic. Rearing up, its front legs thrashed the air before hammering down on the hind quarters of the horse in front. Within moments, fear had spread to the rest of the knights. Those closest to Thurkill and his men were desperate to escape from the death-bringing fiends that had appeared from nowhere, while those in front, attacking the shieldwall, turned their heads to see what was happening to their rear.

Chaos now reigned as the knights fought to escape the danger. Those closest to the shieldwall were not willing to wait for those behind to get out of the way which just added to the confused mass of men and beasts. All the while, they presented easy targets to the defenders on the walls and to Thurkill's men on the ground. Four men lay dead before the rest were able to scramble away from the killing zone.

The outcome far exceeded Thurkill's expectations. It was a more stunning success than he could have imagined. He had been afraid that the whole thing could end in disaster, but when he had proposed it the night before, Eahlmund and the others had enthusiastically agreed. It was not in their nature to be couped up behind walls. They preferred their fighting to be done in the open.

Using the handle of his war axe as a crutch to favour his throbbing ankle, Thurkill surveyed the scene. In total, eight Normans lay dead or dying around the gate where the fighting had been fiercest. The more lightly wounded who had been able to move had managed to get away by either being pulled up to sit behind their comrades as they rode off, or by clinging on to their bridles and allowing the momentum of the horses to pull them along.

It was not a bad return for the first encounter, he surmised. But it came with a cost. The gate had been breached and would need urgent repair, and at least two of the villagers had been killed, both by crossbowmen. But overall, he knew that the reckoning scales had tilted in his favour. Nevertheless, there was much work to do, and fast, before the Normans rallied and came back. For return they surely would.

THIRTY

Thurkill limped over towards the church, knowing that was where the wounded had been taken for Wulfric and his wife to tend to. On the way, he gave orders to Urri to gather men to repair the gate and to do so as if the devil were coming for them. He knew they had a spare cross-piece, but they would have to assess the whole structure to ascertain the full extent of the damage. Only then would they know how long it would take to make the repairs.

"Hurry now, Urri. There's no telling how soon FitzGilbert will come back. The sooner you have it fixed the better."

"Aye, Lord. Rest assured I'll work the bastards until they drop if need be."

Thurkill was still smiling when he entered the church, but the sight which greeted him there instantly wiped it from his face. Several makeshift cots had been laid out on the floor, around half of which were occupied by villagers with a variety of injuries. Set apart from them, just to the right of the door, three shapes lay covered from head to foot by blankets. *Three dead! Forgive me, God, for what I have done.* He sank to his knees and bowed his head in prayer, waves of grief and guilt washing over him. These people had died as a direct result of his deeds in another place, at another time. He prayed for forgiveness and for the strength to face up to his responsibilities.

Moments later, he felt a hand on his shoulder. Opening his eyes, he found himself staring up into his wife's face, her beauty transcending the grime of the day and the concern that was etched into every line of her face. Rising to his feet, he embraced her, careful to avoid her newly bandaged arm. He hugged her tight to his chest before easing off as he remembered her condition. "I'm sorry, Hild."

"For what? It was not you who killed them."

"It was my actions at Haslow that caused their deaths, though. May God forgive me for the sin of pride that led me to take a stand against this Norman and risk the lives of my people

215

against his knights."

"You did what you had to do for your honour and that of our people, and I love you the more for it. I would not stand by a man who gave up so easily. Now, stop feeling sorry for yourself and speak to the injured. Give them succour, give them hope. Let them know they have done their duty before God."

Wiping the tears from his eyes, Thurkill nodded, knowing Hild was right. Whatever his own personal feelings, he had to continue to lead by example. He made his way slowly from cot to cot, asking after each person, complimenting them on their courage and stout resistance. In truth, he had seen very little of the fighting by the gate but the wounded souls did not know that or, if they did, they did not care. For them, the words of encouragement and praise from their lord were enough to bring a smile to their faces. More than one tried to rise to their feet to offer the respect due to him, but each time Thurkill held out a hand to stop them and begged them to lie still and rest. Mercifully, most seemed to have relatively minor wounds and looked to his – admittedly unskilled – eye as if they would make a full recovery in time.

The last pallet he came to, however, told a different story. The smell of death hung heavy in the air around him. With a start Thurkill realised it was Eadwig, his erstwhile critic who had spoken so vociferously against fighting the Normans. He lay on his back, unmoving, his eyes closed. It was hard to tell, in fact, whether he still lived. His face was drained of almost all its colour as if his life blood had already deserted his body. As he came closer, however, the sole of his boot scuffed the straw-covered, earthen floor, the sound of which caused the farmer's eyes to flicker open. Seeing Thurkill standing over him, a smile – or was it a grimace of pain – played across his lips.

"It's my own fault really," he croaked. "Forgot the first rule of the shieldwall; keep your shield up at all times. Norman goat-shagger speared me in the guts."

Thurkill looked down. Despite the gloom within the small church, he could now see that the grey blanket that lay over Eadwig had a huge dark stain where the wound must be. No wonder he's so pale, he thought. It's amazing that he is still

216

amongst the living. Surely, he wouldn't hold on much longer, though? With a wound like that, there would be little or nothing that Wulfric could do other than give him what medicines he could to dull the pain.

"Your bravery does you credit, Eadwig. Your honour and that of your family stands as an example to all."

Eadwig coughed, the effort of speaking clearly marked on his features. He was growing weaker by the moment, his life literally ebbing away through the hole that had been ripped in his stomach. He closed his eyes, as if summoning what little strength he had left to say a few last words. "I thank you, Lord, though little good it will do me, I fear. There is none that follows me; none to carry on my name."

"I will see it remembered in these parts for generations to come." Thurkill saw no point in making any pretence. The farmer knew he was close to death and to suggest otherwise would be to insult him. It was bad enough that the man was dying in spite of the fact that he had not wanted to commit the village to the fight. It was a cruel irony that was not lost on Thurkill. Before he could say any more, however, Wulfric came and knelt by the farmer's side.

"Are you ready to confess your sins, my son? I must prepare you to meet your Maker before it's too late."

"I am ready, Father. That I depart this life in God's house is a comfort to me and I thank you for your prayers."

Thurkill reached down to clasp the farmer's hand in gratitude. "Go with God, friend Eadwig. I wish this had not come to pass, but I will be forever in your debt for what you've done here today." With that, he released the man's hand and stepped back to allow Wulfric to say the last rites over him.

***

As the sun began to slip down towards the western horizon, Thurkill gathered his men into the hall once more, along with Urri and those shield warriors who were not on watch duty. All around them, men and women slept, wrapped in their cloaks, taking advantage of the calm that had descended after the storm. There had been no sign of the Normans since the battle at the gate but Thurkill did not, for one moment, believe that they had gone. He knew they would be back; it was a question of when rather than if.

The mood amongst the men, however, was buoyant, as though still drunk on their victory. They, a bunch of farmers, blacksmiths, tanners and millers - had seen off a small army of trained soldiers. It was the stuff of legend as far as they were concerned. The stuff that scops should write songs about. But Thurkill knew their joy would be short-lived; the Normans would return and when they did, they would not be taken by surprise again. They would be ruthless in their attack and, if they got in, they would spare no one. His twisted ankle still ached, the nagging pain adding to his foul temper.

As if sensing his mood, which was in stark contrast to most of the others there present, Urri came over to his side, standing as tall as him, but almost twice as broad. "Are you not pleased with the day's work, Lord?"

Thurkill broke out of his reverie and smiled. "More than you could know, Urri. To see the result of those long hours of practice with spear and shield brings me great joy. And then there is the leadership you have shown. Without your strength and example, I doubt the shieldwall would have stood today. When that gate broke, you and your comrades saved the lives of everyone within the walls."

The blacksmith was not used to such lavish praise and knew not how to react, choosing to stare at his feet to deflect the embarrassment he felt. "Well," he coughed, "I hear the gate has been repaired now, so we are safe once more."

"Indeed, it has. But I cannot claim we are safe, though, Urri. The Normans will come again and they will redouble their efforts."

"We'll stop them again. They won't breach our defences."

"God willing. But despite those we killed today, they are still many and I doubt they will make the same mistakes again."

Thurkill's sour mood began to affect Urri. "What hope do we have then, Lord? Are we doomed to defeat and death? Why did we even start this fight if we did not believe we could win it?"

Thurkill realised he had let his emotions get the better of him, and not for the first time. Urri was right. All was not yet lost.

Perhaps FitzGilbert would skulk off, not willing to risk further bloodshed. Surely, he could not have expected such fierce resistance? He must have assumed that as soon as the battering ram had done its work, his knights would simply ride down any that stood in his way. A wall of shields held by staunch, unmoving villagers holding them at bay must have come as a huge surprise to him and would have certainly given him pause for thought. That said, he knew it was just as likely that the Norman would merely send for reinforcements. If that happened, they truly would be dead. That thought, though, stuck in his mind.

"Reinforcements, that's what we need. If we had as many men again, we could deal with the Norman bastard... By God, I wish Aelfric were here." He had not realised he had said this last out loud until Haegmund spoke up from the back of the hall.

"I hear he has returned from Normandy, Lord."

Thurkill stopped dead in his tracks, unsure if he had heard correctly. "He's back, you say? Since when?"

"Two days since, I believe. He arrived in Huntendune at about midday, the day before yesterday."

"How do you know this? Come on, man, speak."

Haegmund looked unsure of himself, aware that every set of eyes in the hall had turned toward him. There was no sound other than that of the flames crackling in the hearth, the gentle snoring of the sleeping forms and the growling of two dogs as they squabbled over a bone left over from the previous night's meal.

"Well, I have not seen him with my own eyes, but Alwig's man, Sochi – he who drives the cart to collect grain for the mills in Huntendune – he was here just after dawn yesterday and he told me."

"This news changes everything."

"How so, Lord?" Urri's brow was furrowed in thought. "We're stuck here behind our walls, Aelfric's a two-hour march away. He doesn't know our plight, how could he?"

"If we could get a messenger to him then all that could change."

Eahlmund then voiced the concern that was also in Thurkill's own mind. "We have no idea where the Normans are. They could be anywhere in the woods around us. Who would be willing to risk their life by leaving the village? Not I for one. They're sure to be watching the gate anyway."

The hall lapsed into silence as each man pondered these words. Thurkill was willing to go himself but he knew that his place was here in Gudmundcestre, leading the people in their defence against the Normans. He could not leave them. On top of which, he doubted his ankle would be strong enough to take the punishment of a forced march to Huntendune. Just then, a small voice spoke.

"I'll do it, Lord."

"Who speaks? Step forward so that I may see you."

The men in front of Thurkill parted, allowing young Agbert to step into the space in front of Thurkill's chair. He looked frightened out of his wits but his voice was steady as he spoke.

"I have never thanked you properly for saving me after my father was killed by the brigands. Perhaps by doing this I may repay that debt?"

"My thanks, Agbert, but you have no need to prove yourself. You are young yet and there are others here who may be better placed than you for such a task."

"I want to do it, Lord. Moreover, I am small and quick; I'm sure I can pass unnoticed."

Thurkill thought for a while. It was true that someone small and light on their feet would have a better chance of success, but he was still only a boy with no hairs on his face yet. His mother, Ella, had not long since lost her husband and had come close to losing her eldest son too when he had been taken by the same bandits. And now the boy wanted to risk his life all over again?

"You realise the dangers? If they catch you, they will kill you without a second thought."

"I know, but we need to get word to Lord Aelfric to send help and someone has to do it. So why not me? I am not big enough or strong enough to stand in the shieldwall, so why not this? In this way at least I can be useful."

Thurkill held up his hands in surrender. He could see the boy was fiercely adamant and he could not help but admire his courage.

"If there is no one else that would go in your place, then I will not stand in your way, Agbert. But know that you do this not to repay me but because you have courage of your own and you know that with this action, you might yet save the village. If you succeed, we will all be indebted to you. As a sign of my own gratitude, I give you this ring." With that, Thurkill removed the small gold ring that he wore on the little finger of his left hand and passed it to the boy who received it with a mix of awe and reverence. It was doubtful he had ever held, let alone owned, a piece of gold jewellery, nor would he have ever believed he would be able to. Closing his small fist around it tightly, he knelt before Thurkill and swore to do his bidding.

***

Night had fallen when Thurkill stood with Agbert, Eahlmund and a few others by the north wall, at the point where the narrow stream flowed under the wooden posts. They had been careful, when building the wall, to make sure that there was little or no room for an enemy to enter the village through the gap but, nevertheless, they had taken care to post a sentry nearby to guard against just such an eventuality. The gap was so small that it was doubtful whether a fully-grown man – with or without armour – would be able to negotiate its passage, but a skinny lad such as Agbert should have no such problems.

Thurkill placed his hand on the boy's shoulder to offer a few last words of encouragement. "Stay low and go slowly at first, until you are sure you are well beyond the Norman lines. Follow the course of the stream as the sloping banks will give you cover from any that may happen to look in your direction. Do both of these things and there is little chance that you will be seen. Understood?"

Agbert nodded, his face, illuminated by torchlight, a picture of focussed determination. Thurkill could see the fear in his eyes; he knew that luck would play a big part in whether the boy lived or died in the next hour, but he also knew that the lad's odds would improve if he stayed calm and moved with care. The boy stood there shivering, despite the dark hooded cloak he wore. It was one of Hild's; she had gladly given it to Agbert along with a kiss on his cheek for luck. It would help mask the shape of his form in the darkness and even, if he stayed still long enough, make him look like a boulder or a lump in the ground if he needed to hide. Thick clouds were scudding across the sky, blown by a stiff breeze from the east, meaning that he would need to be careful not to move when the crescent moon was uncovered. Its light might be weak but it could be enough to reveal his presence to the enemy.

"When you know you are clear – after three hundred paces or so, I'd say – then run. Run as quickly as you can and rouse Lord Aelfric. Explain our situation, using the words I've told you, and have him bring his warriors here just as quickly as he can. Our survival depends on it."

Thurkill held the lad by his shoulders and fixed his eyes directly on to Agbert's. "Are you ready, boy? Then, go with God and may the angels guide you to Huntendune like an arrow flies swiftly to its target."

"Yes, Lord. Look for me at dawn. I will not fail you." With that, Agbert stepped into the stream. Though the water only came up to just below his knees, he could not prevent an involuntary gasp escaping his lips as the shocking cold sensation shot up his legs. He gathered himself for a moment, summoning the courage to take the next step. Thurkill was about to urge him to proceed, when the boy suddenly knelt and then lowered himself flat, face first into the water. It was the only way he would be able to pass under the wall, so narrow was the gap. Pulling himself forward, Agbert's head, followed by the rest of his body, slowly disappeared through the gap until he was gone.

Thurkill clambered up the palisade's slope so that he could follow the boy's progress. In the dark, it was hard to make him out, even at this close range, giving Thurkill hope that he might pass undetected. But then he spotted him. He was out of the water and crouching by the edge of the stream, taking a moment to gather his wits about him. Thurkill nodded and smiled to himself. The lad had a strong temperament and good control over his fear. His heart must be pounding in his chest, like a woodpecker building a nest in a beech tree, but still he crouched, not moving, making sure that all was quiet and still around him.

Then he was off, staying low as he had been told, and moving in slow, measured steps. He knew that sudden, jerky movements might attract the eyes of any watchers so the more cautiously he went the better, though every instinct must have been telling him to run.

Thurkill watched Agbert until he was lost to sight and then waited some more, listening with his good ear directed towards the north. As he waited, he prayed to God that the boy would be steered through the Norman lines like a ghost that casts no shadow and makes no sound. Their lives now depended on this young boy being able to pass, unmolested, through the Norman lines.

Eventually, Thurkill could stay and listen no more. There had been no sound, no shouts of alarm, no screams in the dark. He did not know for certain but he could dare to hope that the lad had made it through safely. With luck, the morning would come and with it the sight of hardy Saxon warriors under Aelfric's banner. It would be good to see the old goat once again, Thurkill mused, but even better if he comes at the head of a hundred spearmen.

THIRTY-ONE

No sooner had Thurkill lain down for some much-needed sleep, than it seemed he was being shaken awake once more. Was it dawn? Had Aelfric come already? He had left instructions with the leader of the watch to keep an eye to the north and to wake him as soon as the men of Huntendune were sighted. Perhaps their salvation was now at hand? Whatever hopes had been springing in his heart, though, were immediately dashed when he saw the look on the watchman's face. "The Normans are attacking aren't they?"

"Aye, Lord. They're trying to climb the walls and I fear we're too few to stop them."

Thurkill's shoulders slumped as he sat there. Exhaustion clawed at his eyes, urging him to succumb to sleep's warm embrace once more. He was sorely tempted to give in, what more could he do after all? There were just too many of them and all he had at his disposal was a handful of well-meaning villagers. Startled at just how sorry for himself he was feeling, Thurkill physically slapped himself hard on his face. *Bollocks, man! Remember your duty to these people.*

His cheek still stinging from the blow, he swung his legs off the bed, wincing as he tried to stand. He'd forgotten his damned ankle. It was sore and felt as if it might give way under his weight, but he had no choice but to force it to work for him. He could only it would ease with time. "Quick, man. Go rouse the rest of the spearmen and have them go to the walls. I'll be with you presently."

The man disappeared like a wraith, his cloak billowing behind him in his haste. Turning to Hild, he shook her awake as gently as he could. "Wife, the Normans are attacking the walls. I need you to bind my ankle so that it can support me in the fight to come. Do it as quickly and as tightly as you can. Then gather the rest of the women and children and be ready to flee to the north."

Hild rose quietly and began to rip an old tunic into strips,

224

using them to bind his ankle. Even in the half light, Thurkill could see that it was swollen to almost twice the size of its twin. The pain was still there, though not as bad as it had been, thankfully. With her small nimble hands, his wife made short work of the job, starting with his foot and then working the cloth round his ankle and up until it reached half way along his lower leg. After each wind, she pulled the ends of the cloth tight, scoffing at his grunts of pain as she did so. "Well, you said you wanted it tight, husband."

"Aye, the tighter the better, Hild. Don't worry about hurting me, it needs to be good enough to let me fight without hindrance."

As soon as she was done, Thurkill tested her work by pushing himself up to a standing position, using her shoulder for support at first. There wasn't a lot of movement, but at least he could cope with the discomfort now it was strapped. Taking Hild in his arms, Thurkill hugged her close before kissing her forehead.

"Now go and ready the women and children. I'll not have you fall into the hands of the Normans, so you must be ready to run if it looks like we're done for. Understand? And…" he paused, tears threatening to flood his eyes, "Don't take any risks; you are to be the mother of our child."

He could see the conflict on her face. He knew she wanted more than anything to stand and fight by his side, but she also understood her responsibility to the people of Gudmundcestre, to say nothing of the unborn babe she carried. As the lord's wife she had look after the other women and help them to stay safe in the fighting to come. "Yes, husband. I will play my part, but see you find your way back to us or I will come find your body and kill you all over again."

They laughed together, both aware of – but refusing to acknowledge – the fear that the other felt. There was nothing to be done about it, so there was little point dwelling on what might or might not be. With one final kiss, Thurkill was gone.

Outside, chaos reigned. Men ran in all directions, unsure where they were needed, unsure where the threat was coming from. Thurkill knew he had to get a grip of the situation quickly. He did not think that the Normans had enough men to invest them from all sides, so the point of their attack must be coming from one, or perhaps two, places. But where? Moments later, he caught sight of Eahlmund, and it was a sight that gladdened his heart. He could see his friend up on the wall, directing those around him, gesturing over the wall into the blackness beyond. Thurkill made his way over to his friend as fast as his ankle would allow. He hobbled with sword and shield, having left his axe behind. If the Normans managed to breach the walls then he would need the greater agility and speed that the sword provided.

"What news, friend?"

"The whoresons are attacking in force. It's too dark to see exactly what they're doing but we can hear them all right. Must be at least a dozen of them out there. A few have tried to climb the wall but we put a stop to it."

Thurkill grabbed the man nearest to them. "Fetch torches. We need light. We have to see what's happening." The man scurried off, grabbing a couple of others as he went.

Turning back to Eahlmund, he gave voice to the concern that was eating away at his gut. "Are they just here or do they try to hit us at any other point?"

"I know not, Lord. I have heard no other alarms raised. But they have more men than this, I'd swear, so who knows what they're up to."

Thurkill peered out carefully but could see nothing. The cloud had thickened since they had sent Agbert on his way, so that now no moonlight could be seen at all. But he could definitely hear movement and it was getting louder. Another body of men was approaching the wall. *What is keeping them with those torches?* Impatiently, he twisted his head to one side, staring off to the east. He looked in hope for the first glimmer of dawn, the first sign that the sky might be brightening where it met the tree line, but there was nothing. It would be some hours yet before they saw daybreak.

But wait, was there a faint orange glow after all? Had he misjudged the hour? Was it closer to dawn than he'd thought? It took just a few moments for his hopes to be cruelly and disastrously dashed. Before he could even speak, a half dozen arrows - each one aflame - arced high over the wall from the far side of the village. They hung in the air before beginning their downward descent, spiralling their way inexorably towards the thatched rooves of the many wooden buildings. *Bastards,* Thurkill cursed. Once again, he had been taken by surprise by the cunning of the FitzGilbert brothers.

"Fire!" He roared. "Fetch buckets. Anyone who does not carry spear or shield must form a line from the stream. Put those fires out before they catch and spread."

Even before the first villagers began to move, a second volley of arrows had followed the first. Six more firebrands seeking out their targets. The Saxons had been lucky with the first salvo. All but one had landed on the ground between buildings where they could do no damage. The sixth had buried itself amongst the roof straws of Urri's smithy, which were constantly kept damp to guard against wayward sparks jumping from the forge. The fire had thus failed to take hold and had soon fizzled out to just a thin stream of smoke. They were not so fortunate, however, with the next. Four of these arrows found thatched rooves and immediately ignited the dry straw. Within moments, flames were leaping high into the air, fanned by the breeze that blew from behind the archers' position.

Thurkill's heart sank. Despite the villagers' best efforts, he knew there would be no way they could put out all the fires. Even now, more arrows were in flight. He could see Hild in the middle of the village, outside the hall, directing and cajoling all those around her. Already she had a line organised, equipped with as many pails and other containers as could be found, running from the stream to the worst affected houses. Bucket after bucket of water was thrown over the flames, but no sooner had one fire been extinguished than another two had sprung up in its place. It was useless. They also had to contend with the risk of injury from those arrows that missed the rooves. Thurkill could already see one woman who was being helped, screaming, towards the church, a smoking arrow protruding from her thigh.

For the moment, however, Thurkill was caught in a moment of indecision. Should he stay where he was, where he expected an assault on the wall? But then what was the purpose of these fire arrows if not to presage the start of a second assault elsewhere? Turning his back on the chaotic scenes behind him, Thurkill once again leaned out over the wall, listening, looking for signs of the Normans. Silence. Where had they gone? He was certain he'd heard a body of men moving towards the wall shortly before the arrows began to fly. What was going on? He needed to know. The answer came almost immediately.

"The Normans are in the village. Run!"

Turning to face the sound of the voice, Thurkill scanned the scene, his eyes already beginning to smart from the acrid smoke that billowed from the burgeoning conflagration. The voice had come from the other side of the village, away from where the majority of the buildings were now burning. Of course. Setting the buildings alight on one side had been a diversion; a ruse to draw as many people away from the far side where the Normans appeared to have now launched their attack. But how had they got in? And how many were there?

He had no time to debate the answers to these questions. The fate of Gudmundcestre hung in the balance.

"Eahlmund, Leofric. Grab what spearmen you can find and follow me to the hall." His two trusted companions ran off in opposite directions to follow his orders. They met up with Thurkill a few moments later; a dozen men including all of Thurkill's war band and several other of the staunchest warriors. There was no time for long speeches; the Normans could be upon them at any moment.

"It's time to trust in God and the man next to you. If the Normans are truly within the walls, then now is the hour in which we shall be judged by our actions. Now is when we stand and fight for what is ours. If we lose, then you must know that our women and children will be put to the sword or worse. If you would spare them that fate, follow me and let's make them pay dearly for every one of us that they kill."

The roar that met his words was terrifying in its intensity. Anguish and hatred masked their fears so that they had no goal but to kill the intruders. Without waiting to see if they followed, Thurkill set off towards where he believed the enemy to be, knowing by instinct alone that they were with him.

Rounding the side of the church, he came face to face with the enemy. At least a dozen men – each armed with shield and sword – were inside the walls and already starting to move methodically from home to home looking for people to kill. He could already see two or three bodies on the ground where they'd been dragged from their homes and murdered in cold blood. Innocent, defenceless villagers who had committed no crime other than to live under his lordship.

Behind them, yet more men were climbing over the wall and dropping down to join their comrades. He could only assume they had used the time since the failed attack to fashion ladders in the woods and then waited until dark to put their plan into action.

What had been a burning anger before, now threatened to engulf his emotions. His people were dying and all because of him. The guilt he had felt ever since FitzGilbert had arrived was replaced by a visceral rage, a primordial urge to wreak carnage on each and every one of the Norman bastards. In the dark and with their helmets on, it was impossible to tell which one was FitzGilbert; hell, he might not even be there among them at all. No matter, the enemy was in front of him and he knew no other way than to attack them. Howling hysterically, ignoring the pain from his ankle, he threw himself forward into the midst of the enemy.

The sight of this huge Saxon warrior charging towards them was enough to give the Normans pause, but only for a moment. It was long enough, however, for Thurkill to reach them. He crashed into them like a stampeding bull, shoving his shield boss squarely into the face of the first man, the impact sending him sprawling to the ground. With him out of the way, he then swung his sword with all the strength he could muster, taking the next man at the base of his neck. The man's scream died on his lips as his head was all but severed from his shoulders, such was the power Thurkill had unleashed.

By now, however, the Normans had recovered from their initial shock. A series of short, sharp orders had been barked into the night and already those that remained were forming up into a solid mass. Men who had been ransacking houses ran back to join their comrades, adding depth and bulk to their formation. While those who were still making their way over the wall began to reinforce them from behind. None of this bothered Thurkill, though, he was lost in a rage the likes of which he had not experienced before, not even at Senlac when they came for Harold.

He no longer cared for himself, his sole purpose was to inflict pain and destruction on those who would hurt his people. Though he had not been their lord for long, he felt an overwhelming sense of responsibility for their safety, a duty in which he had already failed as the cruelly maimed and broken bodies on the ground reminded him.

Standing over the dead body of the almost decapitated soldier, Thurkill spread his arms wide, lifted his face and yelled up at the night sky. "Come on, you sheep-shagging whoresons. It's me you've come for. Come and take me if you can!"

Emboldened by their increased numbers, the Normans advanced to meet him. He immediately found himself facing two attackers and pressed on all sides. Offering his shield to block the thrust of the man on his left, he parried the cutting stroke of the man on his right. He felt a surge of energy flowing through his limbs, easing his muscles and dulling the pain in his ankle. Wild-eyed and grinning inanely, he feinted to strike to his right and, when the Norman moved his own sword wide to block the anticipated move, he reversed his thrust catching the man deep in his groin. He laughed mercilessly as the man doubled over, clutching at his ruined manhood, the blood pouring through the gaps between his fingers.

His joy was short-lived, however, as the man's place was immediately taken by two more. At this rate, it would not be long before he was overwhelmed. Sure enough, the numbers began to tell, and Thurkill felt himself being pushed back, step by step. Blow after blow landed on his shield causing him to turn his face away in case any splinters should find his eyes.

Just when he thought he could stand no more, he became aware of men appearing at his shoulder on either side of him. From his left, a shield pushed forward to overlap with his and, without thinking, he immediately did the same for the one to his right. Just in time, the rest of his men had arrived, joining with him in his hour of need.

He laughed to hear the familiar and comforting sound of Urri, over in his usual place on the left, shouting at the others, threatening them with all manner of foul deeds should they not stand firm. It was brave but it was also foolhardy. Deep down, he had been hoping that they would have used his crazed attack as the opportunity to escape from the village with their families before it was too late but, at the same time, he had also known that they would never do that. They would not abandon him to his fate. As suicidal as it was, Thurkill felt a surge of pride to have these men alongside him. Despite their lack of experience, to him each one was worth two of the scum they now faced. At least he could now die in the company of men he was proud to call his friends.

It was not long, however, before they began to give ground once more as the ever increasing number of Normans pressed hard against their little shieldwall. They had twice as many men as the Saxons, so it was only a matter of time before the inevitable happened. As they retreated, Thurkill could also begin to feel a growing heat at his back. Despite the villagers' best efforts, the flames had well and truly taken hold now with more than half the buildings ablaze. Although the archers had stopped their deadly volleys, it brought no relief as the fires raged so fiercely that the wind was able to help them leap the short distance from roof to roof. Whatever the result of the fight, Thurkill knew there would be little or nothing left of Gudmundcestre come the dawn.

Then, without warning, the man to his left crumpled to the ground. The spear point that took him in the neck was so sudden and so well-aimed that he did not even manage to utter a sound before he fell. The fighting was so intense that Thurkill, to his shame, had not even known who it was who stood next to him. He did not have time to check, though, as the Norman who had dealt the blow yelped in triumph and stepped forward into the hole left by the dying man. The danger was immediate; he had to close the gap before the enemy could exploit it. If he failed, it would mean the end of their valiant defence, for they had no second rank behind them. Risking everything, Thurkill turned slightly to his left, leaving his right side exposed, and lashed out with the point of his sword. He caught the Norman in the armpit as he raised his arm to strike another blow, forcing him to drop his sword and recoil in agony.

"Close up! Close up!"

But it was too late. Before the man to his right could react, he too was impaled on a spear point. His cry of pain cut the air, lancing Thurkill's heart as he saw another of his villagers fall. It was all over now. The shieldwall had broken in two and it was only a matter of time before they were overrun and cut down. Yet still he would not run. He would not leave these people to the mercy of FitzGilbert and his thugs. It was him they wanted and it was him they would have to take.

Turning to those around him, he yelled. "Get out. Get your families and go while you still can. There is nothing more we can do here."

A few of the remaining men looked at each other nervously, unsure what to do, none of them willing to make the first move. Eventually, Urri spoke, his words galvanising the others into action.

"I have no wife to mourn me; my children are full grown. I will stay and fight with Lord Thurkill. You others, go and save your kin. Do not let our sacrifice be in vain. Go!"

He roared this last word at the same time as he thrust his shield boss into the face of the Norman nearest to him, sending him careening back into the man behind him. In the few moments respite this gave, the other three surviving villagers turned and ran, rushing off through the narrow gap where the church and tavern stood on opposite sides of the main path through the village.

The sight of them going gave Thurkill an idea. Turning to those that remained he ordered. "Quick, to the church. We'll make our last stand there. We should be able to hold them long enough to let the others escape."

It made for the ideal location. Not only was the gap between church and hall narrow enough for just the seven of them to stand side by side, they were two of the only buildings that were, as yet, untouched by the flames. As quickly as they could, they disengaged from the Normans and ran backwards, never once taking their eyes off the enemy. Thurkill was surprised to see that the enemy let them go unmolested; he could only assume that they, too, welcomed the break in the fighting. If it had been him, however, he would have pressed home the attack to finish them. They were beaten, so why not end it now?

He had no time to dwell on it, though, as the Normans had now reformed and were advancing menacingly on their position. Glancing either side of him, Thurkill could see all his friends were there, as they had always been. Loyal and courageous to the end: the brothers, Leofric and Leofgar; young Copsig who had grown up far quicker than he should have had to; staunch Eardwulf who said little, preferring to speak with actions; and his first companion, Eahlmund, who hadn't left his side since finding him at Senlac, wounded and close to death. They, together with Urri the blacksmith, were now all that stood between the Normans and the rest of the villagers. They had to hold them long enough for the others to flee to the woods. Miraculously, none of them seemed to have been injured so far, but he knew their luck could not last.

"Die with honour, lads. Let's show these scum what it means to be a proud Saxon."

The Normans were now but ten paces away. Three times their number, they came on with malice in their expressions, determined to bring an end to the fight. But when they had covered no more than half the distance between them, they halted. *What now?* Thurkill thought. *Come on, have you lost your courage?*

Then, the figure in the middle of the front rank, lifted his helmet; it was FitzGilbert, grinning widely safe in the knowledge that the fight was won. "You should have surrendered yourself to me when you had the chance, boy. Several of your precious people lie dead already and now these last few who foolishly stand with you will die as well. And all for what? For your stupid pride and no more. Will you, even now, save them by giving up your sword? No more need die."

Thurkill burned with shame and anger in equal measure. "My sword is here if you are man enough to take it from me, Norman pig. I will not speak for my men – they have voices of their own – but I would rather die here fighting you than go meekly to my doom." The roar that greeted his words from those who stood with him, told him all he needed to know. Their fate was sealed; they would stand together and die together.

"So be it, then. You're all fools and deserve your fate." FitzGilbert raised his sword, bringing it down in a chopping motion in the direction of the little band of men that barred his way. "Forward!"

As they came on, Thurkill found himself staring dumbly into space, completely detached from reality. He knew his time had come, but he felt no fear, no regret. Thoughts of Hild, babe in arms, flooded his brain causing huge feelings of loss for what might have been to wash over him. He hoped he'd done enough to give her and the others time to escape. Now, his last wish was to die well – with Norman blood on his blade. Soon he would see his father once again, he hoped he would be proud of him for all that he had done.

Looking up at the sky, to where he supposed Scalpi might be looking down on him, he offered up a prayer. "Lord, watch over me and my brothers. Let us die with honour and speed our passage to Heaven that we may be reunited with our loved ones. See Hild and the others delivered from here to a place where they may be safe."

As he prayed, it occurred to him that the sky was no longer as black as it had been. At first, he presumed it was but the light from the fires that still raged around them, but no, this was a different, softer kind of light. Dawn had finally come. With luck, they would die with the sun on their face, a sword in their hand and joy in their heart.

The impact, when it came, was as bad as anything he'd felt in battle before. The weight of two dozen or so knights slammed into them with an irresistible force. Their tiny shieldwall never stood a chance, disintegrating on impact. To his right he saw Leofgar go down screaming, clutching at the stump where his left hand had been but moments before. Looking down, Thurkill was greeted with the incongruous sight of the severed appendage lying on the floor still holding onto his shield. Further along, Urri, too, collapsed under a flurry of blows, though it took three or four Normans to bring him down. As for the rest of them, they were forced back into the centre of the village, desperately defending themselves in any way they could with shield and sword, parrying every spear and sword thrust that was aimed at them.

Thurkill knew that it was only a matter of time now until either they were overwhelmed or their strength gave out. But he would not give in; he would not yield. As long as he had the strength to wield his sword, he would go on. He may yet be able to kill another of his attackers, the thought of which inspired him to keep fighting. He would have dearly loved the chance to face and kill FitzGilbert but, in the fierce melee around him, he could not make him out. No matter, he thought, any one of these bastards will serve just as well.

He shuddered as yet another blow landed on his shield, the impact reverberating all the way up his arm until it caused his teeth to chatter. Feigning injury, he dropped to one knee, looking up as he did so to make sure his attacker took the bait. Sure enough, he saw a look of triumph on the man's face as he raised his arm to deliver the killing blow. Timing his move to perfection, Thurkill used the strength in his thighs to push himself up. As he did so, he thrust his sword deep into the man's groin. As the Norman fell, Thurkill felt his sword being pulled from his grasp as the flesh clung to the blade as if unwilling to give it up. With a sharp jerk, he managed to retrieve it, the sucking sound as it freed itself from its fleshy embrace almost turning his stomach. It was not a moment too soon, however, as already two more men were closing in on him. Sparks flew as he managed to block a sword cut that would otherwise have taken his head clean off, but he was off balance and under unrelenting pressure.

All around him the sound of fighting continued, giving him hope that not all his comrades had yet been killed. The song of metal striking metal or metal against wood was deafening and his ears were ringing with the constant onslaught to his senses.

He pushed another blow aside with his shield, before quickly raising his sword once more to turn aside a spear that had been aimed at his face. How much longer could he go on? He could feel the strength draining from his limbs; his legs quivered as the muscles began to spasm.

A sudden bolt of agony shot up his thigh. Glancing down he saw an angry red weal from which the blood was already starting to flow. In his fatigue, he had lost concentration momentarily but long enough for a Norman to dart forward with his spear which he managed to force under the rim of his round shield to score a wound the length of his hand. On its own it was not life threatening, but Thurkill knew it would sap what remained of his strength even more quickly.

There was nothing for it now. He could stand back, defend and wait for death to take him or he could seek it out, meeting it on his own terms. Mouthing a silent apology to Hild for his failure to defend her and the village, he summoned up his last reserves of energy. Yelling incoherently, he threw himself forward, crashing into the first man before he had a chance to react. The next man in the way went down, transfixed by his sword. Lacking the strength to retrieve the blade, he let it drop and pulled his seax from his belt. As he did so, he flung his heavy linden-board shield at a third man who was rushing him with his spear aimed directly at his belly. As the man recoiled, his nose shattered by the metal rim, Thurkill finally saw FitzGilbert. He was pummelling Eahlmund's shield repeatedly while his friend just about remained standing, his face as white as the winter snow.

Screaming with hatred, Thurkill ran at him, all pain in his body forgotten. His target was but ten paces away, side on and, so far, seemingly unaware of his approach. Thurkill's heart surged; now was his chance. He cared not whether he lived or died as long as he could send this Norman sheep's turd to hell first.

He was so close now; exhilaration flooded through his body, washing away the throbbing aches that had dulled his muscles. One last effort and he would have him, and then he could die happy. He raised his seax above his head and emitted a blood curdling screech as he launched himself headlong at FitzGilbert.

He never made it. Just as his feet left the ground, he felt a sharp pain on his shins followed by the sight of the ground advancing to meet his face. One of FitzGilbert's thugs had managed to trip him with his spear shaft as he was in full flight. The nose guard saved his face from the worst of the impact but he still felt blood fill his mouth as his teeth were crushed against his lips. His eyes watered with the shock and pain of the collision and he was momentarily dazed.

FitzGilbert, meanwhile, had ceased his assault on Eahlmund and had turned instead to stand over his fallen foe. Even through his tears of pain, Thurkill could see the look of excited malice on the Norman's face. Frustration coursed through his veins; he had been so close only to now find himself helpless, prostrate at his enemy's feet.

The sound of FitzGilbert's mocking laughter did nothing to help, adding to his sense of abject failure. It was cruel fate if this was to be the last sound he would hear before death took him. He closed his eyes, resigned to his fate. He just prayed that when the blow came it would be clean and quick.

But death never came. Instead, he became aware of a new sound. The sound of many feet running. He felt the ground shaking as the sound came closer and closer. Accompanying the sound of heavy boots pounding the earth, he could now also hear many voices shouting and singing in unison. Then a voice called out above the uproar, a voice that he recognised.

"Men of Huntendune, clear this filth from this village. Spare no one!"

***

Thurkill took the cup of ale that was offered him by Aelfric. He used his first mouthful to swill out the blood, snot and dirt from his mouth, spitting the mess on the ground. At least two teeth appeared to have been loosened when he smashed his face into the ground. He then gulped the rest of the cup's contents down, feeling it soothing his parched throat as well as if it had been Wulfric's best honeyed wine. He sat on an upturned tree stump, every inch of his body aching but otherwise uninjured save for the spear cut on his leg. The priest had already seen to that, applying a herbal poultice packed with some of his fabled honey and herbs before binding it tightly with strips of clean white linen.

"I'd say we reached you just in time, lad."

"Too late for some, I fear, but I have no doubt you have saved many lives here today, Lord. But what of FitzGilbert? Does he lie dead with the others?"

Aelfric grunted. "I fear not. As soon as he heard us coming, he was away over the wall, like a rabbit down its bolt hole when the fox is on its tail. Like the coward he is, I doubt he'll stop running until he reaches Lundenburh."

"Shit." Thurkill was despondent. All that for nought. So many dead with little or nothing to show for it. "What of the dead? How many have fallen?"

Aelfric's jaw set firm. "A lot fewer than could have been the case but for your staunch defence, but still more than was warranted. Eight men lie dead with several more wounded, though the priest assures me they will all recover."

"What of Urri and Leofgar? Do they yet live?"

"Aye, they are made of strong English oak those two. Urri has a few broken bones but is otherwise alright, but your man may never carry a shield again. He's in a lot of pain but the wound will heal well enough now that the stump has been cleansed and seared.

"But Eardwulf did not make it, I'm sorry to say. He was killed as the Normans fled. By all accounts he fought well enough but was too exhausted to defend himself at the last. He will be buried with honour in the church here.

"All the women and children, I'm pleased to say, have survived. That wife of yours is a marvel, Thurkill. She marshalled them out of the gate better than any captain of war I have ever seen. Not one was lost."

Thurkill grunted. Pride in his wife's achievement only partially off-setting the pang of loss he felt for Eardwulf's death.

"We met them on the north road as we were marching down with Agbert, so we knew what we were heading into. We even ran the last half mile or so once we understood how grave the situation was."

"I thank God that you did, Lord. Those few moments were all that separated us from death."

Aelfric grinned, clapping him on the shoulder. "Anyway, for now we must focus on rebuilding Gudmundcestre. Once you are rested and we have buried the dead, then we can make a start with replacing those buildings that have burned down. It will take more than a few Norman thugs to stop us, eh?"

PAUL BERNARDI

EPILOGUE

A week later, Thurkill rode into Huntendune with Hild, and the surviving members of his warband. The repair work at Gudmundcestre was already well under way under the watchful eyes of Urri, Haegmund and the other members of the folkmoot. In fact, progress was so good that Thurkill had decided that he and his men could be spared for the day while he came to see Aelfric. There were things he needed to talk through with his lord, things he had been mulling over every day since the battle. There had been no sign of FitzGilbert in the last few days, though Thurkill knew that this could not be the end of the story. A man like him would not give up so easily, especially not now he had been humiliated in battle. It was for this reason that he had come to Huntendune to seek the older man's counsel.

They found Aelfric in his hall, deep in conversation with Alwig the Steward. Having not long since returned from Normandy, there was much for him to catch up on in respect of the affairs of his estates. Nevertheless, he lost no time in jumping up from the table as soon as he saw Thurkill. Striding over to him, he wrapped his arms around him in a warm embrace before then turning to Hild, placing a gentle kiss on her forehead.

"How's the leg, my lad? Not much of a limp there from what I can tell."

"It heals well, Lord. Wulfric's wife's skills are beyond compare."

"Excellent. And what of you, Hild? All's well with the child, I trust? And Gudmundcestre? The building works proceed well?"

"I am well thank you, Lord. The sickness fades with each new day, though there is much to distract me from it. I'm glad to say the works proceed faster than we would have thought possible."

Thurkill nodded, holding out his hand to take Hild's. "They are a resilient people who take tragedy in their stride. I am proud to have been their lord these last few months."

240

Aelfric raised an eyebrow as if something in the way Thurkill spoke had set him on edge. Before he could enquire further, however, they were disturbed by a loud commotion outside. As the shouting grew in volume, Aelfric's quizzical expression was replaced with one of irritation. "What in God's name is going on?"

Together, the two men went outside to find a conroi of ten Norman knights had ridden into the town, coming to a halt just outside the hall. Seeing Aelfric emerge, the leader amongst them jabbed his heels into his horse's flanks, nudging the beast forward towards him.

"You are Aelfric, Lord of Huntendune." It was a statement more than a question.

Thurkill was immediately wary; there was something about the manner of this man that did not augur well. All Normans were arrogant and self-assured, but this was something more. Had they come to seize him having had news of the fight at Gudmundcestre? He wouldn't have put it past FitzGilbert running home to tell tales if it meant he could arrest him. His hand strayed down to his sword hilt, taking comfort for the familiar feel of the wound-leather grip. All his senses now on edge.

"My name is Ralph Taillebois, newly appointed by King William as reeve of this shire of Grantabridge."

Aelfric's tone was polite but there was, nevertheless, steel in his words. "What business do you have here in my town, Taillebois?"

"It is fitting that you come straight to the point; I shall do you the same courtesy. My business here is to inform you that this is no longer your town and you are no longer its lord."

"By whose order?" The old man had just about kept his temper but Thurkill could tell that it had taken all his restraint to do so.

"By order of King William. It has been decreed that the lands of those who stood with Harold at Senlac against the rightful king shall be forfeit to the crown."

"He has no right to do this," Aelfric shouted. "These lands have been in my family since the days of King Alfred's son,

Edward. They were granted as payment for services rendered against the Danes. They are mine in perpetuity. I have the charters to prove it."

"He has every right. Your pieces of parchment mean nothing now. Need I remind you that William took this land by right of conquest? It is his to do with as he pleases and no amount of charters can stop him. If you wish to appeal, you may go to Lundenburh and petition the king, though I doubt there would be much point. In the meantime, you have until sundown to clear your possessions and begone, or face the consequences."

"Why you, lickspittle bastard." Aelfric leapt forward, reaching for his sword as he did so. He made it no further, however, as the knight to Taillebois' left kicked his horse forward, lowered his spear and drove it clean through the old Saxon's chest as he ran on to it. It happened so quickly that no one moved or spoke for several moments. Thurkill stood rooted to the spot, shocked into paralysis, unable to believe the evidence of his eyes.

Taillebois, meanwhile, turned his horse back towards the rest of his men, apparently bored by the whole affair. "See that this mess is cleared away and make sure any other members of his household are gone before nightfall. Burn his hall and kill any that resist."

Thurkill shook his head, as if trying to clear the fug that had descended. He had come to Huntendune to discuss his future with Aelfric, to ask permission to move on so that the people of Gudmundcestre could be free of the risk his presence presented to them. But none of that mattered any more. Aelfric was dead, cruelly murdered in front of his eyes not moments after he had been stripped of his lands and titles. He felt bitter bile rising in his throat, forcing him to swallow hard.

Tears flooded his eyes as he stared helplessly at the body of his friend and mentor lying in the dirt, an ever-expanding pool of blood forming around his body. In a daze, Thurkill turned to Hild, taking hold of her hands in his. He knew what he must do but he would not act without her permission; he loved her too much for that. His wife looked deep into his eyes as she had done on many occasions, both happy and sad. He saw in them a love and understanding that gave him the strength and courage to act. Then, almost imperceptibly, she nodded.

Thurkill then turned to his men; men he knew would follow him to the gates of hell if he but commanded it. They already knew what he had in mind; each one grim-faced and ready to play their part. He knew that what he was about to do would put them all outside of the law. It was a step that he did not take lightly but, even so, he could not allow Aelfric's murder to go unanswered.

His worst fears about their new masters were beginning to be realised, their true colours had been exposed. They cared nothing for his people, that much was evident. Thurkill could not stand aside and allow these whoresons from Normandy free rein to behave as they pleased. Smiling at Eahlmund and the others, he drew his sword and flung himself at Taillebois, slashing the newly sharpened blade deep into his neck.

"Kill them. Kill them all!"

Historical Note

This, the second novel in the Huscarl Chronicles, focusses on the period shortly after the Battle of Hastings up until spring 1066.

If you were to ask them, many people might state that William the Conqueror became King of England after the battle but that does not tell the whole story of these turbulent times. In fact, all that happened on 14 October 1066 was that the Norman Duke won a battle. It was undoubtedly a significant battle as he managed to kill the reigning King of England together with a significant proportion of his army, but it did not automatically mean he became king the same day. In fact, the battle had been a very close-run affair which – for much of the day – could have gone either way. There are also those who think – me included – that if Harold had but waited another week in London before marching south to face William, the additional soldiers he could have mustered might well have swung things in his favour.

In fact, it was to be a further ten weeks until, on Christmas Day 1066, William was finally crowned in Westminster Abbey, marking the official start of his reign. So, what happened during the intervening period? Far from giving up, the surviving Saxon nobles assembled in London to elect a new king, choosing Edgar Aetheling, last descendant of the House of Wessex.

Although he was king to all intents and purposes, Edgar is never listed as such in history books. This is partly due to the fact that history is always written by the victors and the Normans did not recognise Edgar's title. The other reason was that the Normans saw coronation as the rite that conferred kingship whereas for the Saxons, election – or acclamation – was enough.

Very little is known of Edgar compared to other notable figures of the time. He was the grandson of King Edmund Ironside (whose father had been Aethelraed Unraed - or Unready, more familiarly). Edmund was only on the throne for six months during which time he fought and ultimately lost against the Danish King Cnut. As a result of this defeat, Edmund's son – Edward the Exile – was sent abroad by Cnut, ostensibly to be killed. He actually ended up in Hungary where he married into the royal family and produced a number of children, the eldest surviving male being Edgar.

In the 1050s, when it looked like the current King, Edward the Confessor, was going to die childless, envoys left England to seek Edward the Exile's return so he could take the throne from his cousin. Edward arrived back on these shores in 1057 but was dead within days (no one knows why or how). That left Edgar – no more than a toddler at that time – as the likely heir.

However, when Edward the Confessor finally died in January 1066, the nobles faced a stark choice. The country was threatened by invasion from the south by Duke William and from the north by the Vikings. Could they really place their trust and hope in an unproven teenager? Perhaps understandably, they chose to elect Harold, middle-aged and a proven war-leader. Harold had no blood link to the 'royal family' of Wessex, thereby demonstrating how Anglo-Saxon kingship worked by election rather than by birth-right. He was nothing more than the brother-in-law of the previous king, but he was also the wealthiest and most powerful noble in England and in the right place at the right time. But when Harold met his end fighting in the midst of the shieldwall on Senlac ridge, there was little choice other than to finally elect Edgar to be the new king.

This story forms the backdrop of the first half of the book. Thurkill has made his way to London with his warband, eager to continue the fight against the foreign invader and having heard that the Saxon lords have rallied there around the new king. The Normans, meanwhile, had been making their slow progress from Hastings along the coast to Dover, which was burned to the ground despite having submitted to the Duke. From there, William marched on London, launching the attack at Suthweca (Southwark) that features in the first chapter. Suthweca stood at the southern end of the one bridge across the Thames and thus was the only way to enter the fortified city of London (known as Lundenburh at this time). The chronicles tell us that the Saxon defenders launched a sortie across the bridge and – though it was a defeat – they did succeed in preventing the Normans from crossing.

Unable to take London from the south, Duke William rode west to find a place where his army could cross the river. All the way, his soldiers ravaged the land, partly because they needed huge amounts of food for the army and horses, and partly to spread terror as a means of convincing the English to surrender. Though his precise route is not known for certain, it is a matter of record that he did cross at Wallingford (Warengeforte) and that, while he camped there, Archbishop Stigand of Canterbury did submit to him. This really marked the beginning of the end for Edgar. His support gradually melted away, most notably when the two most senior surviving Earls of Mercia and Northumbria (the brothers Eadwine and Morcar) left London to return to their lands to the north, despite having promised to fight for Edgar. Their motivation for doing so is unknown and many have branded them cowards (a line I follow in the book). What is certain, however, is that that without their warriors, Edgar could not hope to resist.

Accepting the inevitable, Edgar – along with many notables, including Archbishop Ealdred of York – met Duke William at Berkhamsted where the young man swore fealty to the new king.

The coronation took place soon after in Westminster Abbey on Christmas Day. The burning of houses around the Abbey is true but to suggest that it was the result of cheering during the ceremony that was mistaken for rioting is facile at best. Rather, this seems a poor attempt by the Norman chroniclers to excuse the violent looting of their soldiers.

One of the reasons why the English were prepared to accept William as king was that they hoped it would bring an end to the deprivations of the previous weeks. It is true that William – outwardly at least – promised to rule in a fair and just way and it could well be said that it was also in his interests to establish a new, peaceful norm as quickly as possible. His coronation did, indeed, include the promissio regis (a feature of Anglo-Saxon coronations since the tenth century), in which the new king would make a three-fold promise to provide peace, to forbid robbery and offer justice and mercy in all judgements. You can see why such words would appeal to the Saxons who were eager to put an end to the violence.

But words and deeds do not always match. William had many followers who expected to be rewarded for their part in his victory and – to achieve this – it was expedient to rule that the lands of any who had fought against the Duke at Senlac were forfeit. Thus was created perhaps the greatest grievance that the Saxons held in the months and years immediately following the Conquest; the wholesale transfer of land to the new Norman overlords. Taking the lands of those who had died might not seem unduly harsh on the face of it, but it created a class of disinherited heirs who, until then, had expected to succeed their fathers. No wonder that many of them chose to rise up against the Normans. But more of that in book three.

Printed in Great Britain
by Amazon

17771357R00150